HEIR OF FIRE

THE HEIRS SERIES
BOOK 2

LEJLA MURIC

Copyediting & Proofreading by Gabby D'Aloia of GCD Editorial
Cover Design by Georgia Stove of Pixel and Quill Studio

ISBN 979-8-9926679-3-6 (paperback)
ISBN 979-8-9926679-2-9 (ebook)

TRIGGER WARNINGS

Mentions of Grief, Mentions of Death, Violence, Blood, Explicit Sexual Content, Mentions of Child Abuse, Mentions of Rough Family Relationships, Mentions of Breakdowns, Mental Health, Mature Language, Mentions of Domestic Abuse, Light Exploration of Kinks.

To anyone who wants love to consume them like an inferno.

ONE

FINN

THE STENCH of sweat and liquor clung to the walls of the rundown dive bar, creating a foul odor. After spending the past five months hitting up random bars around the country with just his bike and a backpack, Finn had grown used to the smell.

He was somewhere in Pennsylvania now. The border fifty miles back. The bar was small, but it had liquor and that was exactly what he needed. He didn't come to socialize; he came to run from his issues like a fucking coward.

An older couple occupied one of the ripped-up leather booth seats that sat against the wall, and a couple biker dudes played pool in the center of the room. Everyone minded their own business, which was perfect.

He wasn't there to give them any trouble. These days, he kept his head down, sat at the counter closest to the bartender and ordered whiskey to get the buzz going as quick as he could.

There was something tranquil about driving all day, watching the sunset, and then drinking all night. It was a freedom he had never been afforded in his life. Ever.

Maybe he should have considered himself lucky now, but instead the thought made him nauseous. Thinking about the circumstances that brought on his freedom only pushed him to drink more.

He finished his whiskey and motioned for another one.

The bartender, an older woman with streaks of graying hair, slid another over. Ever since Finn came in, she'd been eyeing him suspiciously, most likely wondering if he had the money to pay for all the alcohol he'd been drinking. Honestly, he couldn't blame her. He looked terrible. His hair was past the point of being simply grown out, his stubble was now a beard, and the T-shirt he wore under his leather jacket was full of rips.

Keeping the same clean look from before hadn't been on his mind when he packed his backpack and left before anyone could stop him.

But he owned an empire now, even if he didn't fucking want it. The money flowed into his account like a waterfall, and he knew his sister and new asshole brother-in-law were to thank for it. He had never given them his bank information, but somehow, they'd found it.

They could keep it all. He didn't want any part of the Kingsley businesses or money.

As a matter of fact, they could cut him off completely. Finn wasn't planning on coming home. Ever. He had nothing left for him there. Sure, Luna was back home, but he could always stop by once a year for the holidays. Her calls and texts were still never ending, but even she would eventually get the hint he wasn't returning.

Augustus managed to come to terms with it easily enough. He called Finn a dumbass, told him he was a weak asshole, and then wished him the best before extending an invitation to his future wedding to Cecilia that would never happen. But he and Luna both had things for them there; they had families they were going to be starting and creating for themselves.

Finn had nothing.

He slammed down the next drink, not noticing the new presence sitting beside him.

"One scotch and another of whatever he's having."

Finn turned his head, finding the urge to slam it against the bar. "Are you fucking kidding me?"

He wished it was a cruel drunk hallucination, but life was just cruel and—unfortunately—real. Valerio fucking Vitali sat beside him completely out of place with a haughty look and his fancy suit.

"Wish I was. Believe me, there are a million places I'd rather be than chasing you down through the middle of nowhere, sitting at a sticky bar, and suffocating on the smells coming off your body." Valerio grabbed his drink, taking a sip and grimacing when it didn't match his standards. "I knew you had fallen low, but I didn't know you were beyond the depths of Hell."

"Fuck you. You know where the door is," Finn growled, grabbing the new drink the bartender had handed him. This had to be his fifth.

"See, that's the problem. My wife can't stop thinking about if you're in danger or not, and despite me telling her you're fine—even though I could care less about what happens to you—you being gone is putting a real damper on our marital bliss," Valerio said, shrugging.

"Tell her you checked in on me and that I'm fine. Then get the hell out of here. I'm not going anywhere."

Valerio let out a bitter laugh, shaking his head. He reached into his suit jacket, pulling out a gun and setting it on the bar. "I don't think you've realized that you don't have a choice."

Finn couldn't help but roll his eyes at the intimidation tactics. "You're not going to kill me."

"Easy for me to put a bullet in you, tell Luna they found your body on the side of the road in a motorcycle accident, let her mourn and then move on with our lives," he said. "But you're right, I won't kill you. I don't need to kill you to bring you home, though."

Finn narrowed his eyes, confused at the words. It didn't matter when a single pinch went through his neck, followed by a burning sensation. He tried to fight, to stand, but his entire body felt like jello, forcing him to fall against the bar.

He fought against the drowsiness long enough to see Allister Moretti set a briefcase of cash on the bar to pay off the bartender from saying anything. Valerio stood, pulling out his phone before walking out the door.

To make matters worse, Dante Vitali entered his eyesight. He stared down at him with narrowed eyes. "Huh, I thought I gave you enough to knock you out. My bad."

And then he slammed the butt of the gun against Finn's head, knocking him out cold.

TWO

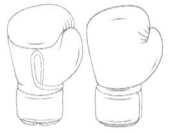

FINN

FINN'S HEAD hurt like a motherfucker. Truly and honestly, he was going to kill Dante.

He didn't even need to open his eyes to know that he was back in New York. The plush of the couch under him gave it away. That, and the different sets of eyes he could feel staring into him from all angles of the room made his skin crawl.

Luna was the first person he saw when he finally decided to come to life. She looked the same way she did when he left, maybe a little older and more mature. Her eyes still had that same kindness toward him that they always did. The only difference was the big ass diamond ring on her lefthand ring finger that glimmered and likely gave her wrist problems from holding it up. She gave him a warm smile, sitting on the couch across from him, but her guard dog of a husband still didn't leave her side.

"Welcome home," she said. "I was wondering when you were going to wake up."

"That rabid asshole didn't have to knock me out," Finn said, motioning to Dante who sat on one of the decorative chairs lazily.

He shrugged. "You resisted."

Luna shook her head. "Either way, I'm glad you're home."

"This isn't my home." He didn't have one anymore.

"Then take this as an opportunity to start over," she said. "Maybe get yourself a nice home, finish your degree, start working to establish yourself as the Kingsley—"

"Those are things *you* want, not me."

Her face fell immediately. That seemed to have insulted Valerio.

"Those are things you should want for yourself," Valerio growled. "What did you think you were going to do? Ride around America on that fucking bike for the rest of your life without a care in the world? Stop fucking running."

"You don't fucking know anything," Finn hissed, nearly leaping off the couch.

Valerio's eyes narrowed mockingly. He didn't even attempt to hide the malice on his face. "Oh, I don't? You're not the only one whose daddy dearest died. We all lost someone, but you're the only one who's still running instead of dealing with everything."

"I'm not weak," he spat out.

"He didn't call you weak," Luna cut in. "You're not weak, but you don't have to run either. We're here for you; I'm here for you. And as your sister, I'm not going to see you throw your life away."

He fought the urge to roll his eyes. Of course that was what they thought he was doing. Neither one of them would understand. Luna was the perfect daughter, and Valerio was the perfect son, and together they were the perfect couple. Finn tried too hard to be that person, but all he ever did was disappoint his father. Nothing he ever did was good enough. He was always too weak, too careless, too hot headed.

He would never be the person they wanted him to be—the perfect heir capable of leading the empire that the multiple generations of men before him had created. With him, it would all crumble.

"And what if that is exactly what I want to do? What if I want nothing more than to throw my life away, drink until I can't remember anything? What then?"

Luna's face hardened, showing the viciousness she hid inside her. "Then I'll have no choice but to seriously intervene."

"You'll force me? You'll do exactly what you said you wouldn't do? Become exactly like our father?" he bit back. Watching her face fall should have been satisfying, but it wasn't. It only reminded Finn of how much of an asshole he was for throwing such low blows at the one person in his life that actually gave a shit about him.

Valerio's hand was around his neck instantly, pressing him into the back of the couch with such force that Finn wondered if his neck was about to break. "Don't you ever speak to her like that, do you fucking understand? You should be lucky that there's one person left on this fucking planet that still gives a shit about you. One more word and I won't hesitate to rid her of your undeserving presence. One more word and you'll wish you never learned how to talk in the first place."

"Val," she called out. As if he was in some sort of daze, her voice seemed to snap him out of it.

Valerio pulled away, leaving Finn gasping for air. His throat burned and ached, but he wasn't going to voice it while the douche was still there. Not while he deserved it either.

She cleared her throat, standing. "I think it's best that you stay at the other house for now. I'll visit when I can, but there you'll be surrounded by familiar faces to hopefully bring you back to yourself. You have the option of going back to school if you want, but we'll give you a few days to acclimate before you start getting introduced to the business side of things. Dante will walk you there."

Dante walked over to him, cracking his knuckles. "Let's go, asshole."

The dismissal was final. Luna walked out of the room with Valerio following her immediately. Finn felt the apology clog his throat. The urge to just spit it out overwhelmed him, but he kept it buried instead. He followed Dante out of the house, trying to ignore how much he felt like a stranger since being back.

So much so, he didn't even realize that Luna's new mansion was next door to the one they lived in not too long ago when they worked together to plot against their fathers for a brighter future. It seemed like everyone was living in that better future, all except for him.

Despite the houses being beside each other, the walk still took a couple minutes due to how much land stood between them. It left Dante and him in an awkward silence.

"What happened to my bike?" he asked finally.

"We brought it back because Luna told us to, only because she's such a wonderful person," Dante said. "Should have crushed it with a bulldozer to break your heart the way you broke hers."

"I get it. I'm an asshole."

"No. Asshole is an understatement. You're just bitter."

Finn clenched his fists, fighting the urge to hit him. He needed to plan an escape as soon as possible. "And you're not bitter about a single thing in your life?"

"I got my revenge. I did what I had to. Now, I get to move on," Dante said with a shrug.

How the hell was everyone so nonchalant about everything?

"How do you just move on from killing your father?" he asked.

Dante gave him a hard look. It seemed like Finn finally got under his skin, but it was a valid enough question. He was the Vitali brother who landed the final blow to their father. There was no way he was able to just move on from it that easily, even if it had been five months.

"Do you consider yourself naive, ignorant, or just plain fucking stupid? I didn't just move on from anything. I suffered my entire life and expelled my demon. Now, I'm learning to live without the constant abuse, trauma, and hatred I had known from my father my entire life. I grieved him, I grieved myself, and I grieved the boy I was before. Do you think any of that was easy? It was the hardest thing I've ever had to do in my life," Dante spat out. "Moving on is a fucking blessing."

Finn didn't say a word. Dante was the closest he had come to truly feeling understood—or more correctly, to understanding himself. It was confusing as hell figuring out what the hell he felt when for his entire life he had been told to feel nothing.

"Sorr—"

"Don't apologize to me," Dante snapped. "Apologize to the person who actually gives a shit."

They were all on Luna's side. Why wouldn't they be? She was good and loveable and had built support around herself. She deserved it. Which was why Finn needed to leave. She didn't deserve to deal with his bullshit, not when her life was finally good.

They stopped at the gate so Dante could tell the guards that Finn was permitted in and out. Everything from then on out was a wicked case of déjà vu. The lined driveway with perfectly trimmed bushes and grass on either side. The opulent home for college kids that once again had maids and cooks running through it, though significantly less than before. Most of them must have gone over to the other house to feed Valerio's massive ego.

Once again, Finn felt completely out of place. Everything was the same, but still completely different. It was the vibe that had changed the most. Gone was the depressing and hopeless feeling that once surrounded every inch of the house. Instead, it was replaced with a new lightness and energy that he couldn't describe.

"Do you remember your old room?" Dante asked.

"Hard to forget," he said.

"Then go to it. Shower and shave. You look like shit."

He walked away without another word, leaving Finn standing in the corridor alone. He took the same route from months ago, walking through the long hallways to his old bedroom. They had changed the sheets and bedding for him, dusted months of neglect off the furniture.

His clothes remained—in fact, everything did. His cologne, his books, shoes, and toiletries. The backpack he had on the road was also there, placed on the floor by the bed instead of on top of it. He walked over, opening the bag and retrieving the one item he had grabbed from his old childhood home before he set it ablaze: a family photo.

The picture held Luna as a newborn, his mother, his now deceased father, and him only a couple years old. Finn was the only one smiling. His eyes still held a childish innocence he couldn't remember losing. He stood beside his father who sat on a grand chair fit for a king. His father held a single hand on Finn's shoulder, tight and firm, and he swore he could still feel the ghost of it holding on like an anchor.

His touch had never felt comforting. That was Reece Kingsley. A merciless man.

Finn placed the picture frame on the side table face down, unwilling to feel their haunting stares any longer. He got up and made his way into the bathroom, locking the door behind him.

THREE

GIANNA

NEW BLISTERS WERE FORMING in her pointe shoes. Her legs ached for a break, but Gianna needed to nail down this one move and then she could relax. She leapt across the room, feeling the breeze on her skin. She extended her legs only to land weakly, nearly twisting her ankle in the process.

She fell to the floor, heaving in deep breaths. She wiped the sweat off her forehead, closing her eyes for a moment.

Breathe, breathe, breathe.

She threw her water bottle at the glass mirror in front of her, letting out a scream in frustration. So close, but not perfect. Luckily, the glass didn't shatter, but the sound was loud enough to shock her for a moment. Almost as if she'd been brought back to reality, she ripped the pointe shoes off, throwing them to the side.

The relief was instantaneous. She was correct though—there were new blisters bleeding on her big toe. Gianna had been dancing herself into oblivion because of the showcase in a couple of months. It was a chance for everyone in the dance program at Grand Willow University to demonstrate what they had learned throughout the year, which meant putting together their own choreography for an audience. She chose to perform solo, which meant there was more pressure to make sure everything was perfect.

But after she fell at practice the other day trying to land the grand jeté, she felt humiliated. Ballet was the one thing she knew, and she crumbled like a fool in front of her teachers and the other dancers in the class.

Since then, she had been in the downstairs home studio trying to land the fucking move. She still hadn't.

The music had long stopped playing and she was left in silence as she stretched, her body groaning in painful relief. She looked up into the mirror, catching the reflection of damp brown hair and a look of indifference standing behind her.

It was Finn Kingsley. As in the same one who had been missing for months but was suddenly here as if he had never been gone.

She gasped, turning around in a split second. "What are you doing here?"

"Heard a clash and wondered if you had thrown yourself into the mirrors," Finn said, leaning against the doorframe.

"I don't just mean in the studio—I mean in this house. Or better yet, in New York. I thought you left for good," she said, crossing her arms over her chest. She ignored the way it drew his eyes directly to that part of her body.

"I thought I had as well, but I was kidnapped."

"That doesn't explain why you've been standing there watching me."

He scowled. "Don't flatter yourself."

"Wouldn't want any flattery from you anyways," she said with a sarcastic smile.

"Glad to see you haven't changed."

"And neither have you."

"Can't wait to live here," he muttered before turning and walking out the room.

Gianna's eyes widened. She stood, running after him. "What the hell are you talking about? You're not living here. Why wouldn't you live with your sister? She has a beautiful, big ass house that is perfect for you."

"Well, she tossed me here. Take it up with her, princess."

She followed him up the stairs, appalled by the nickname. "Princess? And what are you? The jester?"

"Has anyone ever told you that you talk a lot?"

"Has anyone ever told you that you're an asshole?"

He stopped his steps, forcing her to slam into his back. Gianna wasn't short by any means—being the tallest one of the friend group—but still, her nose hit the center of his back, leaving him towering over her. From that angle, he should have intimated her. Too bad for him, Gianna wasn't intimidated by anyone.

"Seems you've lost your step."

She wanted to knock the smirk off his face. "I'm going to get this sorted out. You're not living here," she said, walking around him.

"Of course you are. I'm sure there's nothing you haven't gotten just because you asked, princess."

She clenched her jaw. He didn't know half of it. Gianna ignored him, stomping into the living room where Blair was studying. She had her laptop open on the couch beside her and a textbook on her lap as she chewed on the end of the pen in her hand, brows furrowed in concentration while she read. Gianna almost felt bad disturbing her.

"Can you believe that Finn is living here? I'm going to die, Blair. That's three men living here. Three. Four if you count how often Augustus comes here to stalk Cecilia. And he's such an asshole too. Why should he be our problem anyway? We didn't want him home. I say he should go to Luna's house and bother them—I mean, she's the only one who likes him." She slumped on the couch with a huff.

"No, I wasn't busy or anything. Thanks for asking," Blair said, closing the book.

"I'm miserable."

"He hasn't even been here for a day."

"Exactly. I can't handle this for a week, or a month, or God forbid longer," Gianna said, throwing her head into the pillow.

"He's Luna's brother," Blair pointed out. "We have no choice but to be supportive. If she needs him here, then that's where he needs to be."

She shook her head, looking up again. "Something had to have happened. She was so excited for him to come home and then she just dumped him here. I bet she regrets sending Valerio to go get him."

"Doubtful. She probably needs some space. It's been five months since they last saw each other, and last time they did, it was over their father's dead body and sending their mother away."

She both hated and admired Blair's ability to be logical. It was extremely annoying during the times when Gianna wanted to gossip and needed someone to indulge in it with.

"Well, since you're so levelheaded, what do you recommend I do?"

"Ignore him. Go to class, work on your choreography, go to parties, and get ready for the end of the semester," she said, opening her book again.

Gianna nodded her head. She could ignore him. It was a big house, and she had a busy schedule. She could avoid him easily considering he probably didn't have much going on and would probably spend most of his time up in his room.

All she had to do was ignore him. Easy peasy.

FOUR

GIANNA

IT TURNED out that Gianna wasn't so good at ignoring Finn the way she thought she could. For the past week, he was everywhere like a cockroach. When she was in the kitchen preparing her meals, he showed up and obnoxiously shifted through the fridge, and he did it for all three meals. She couldn't enjoy her breakfast, lunch, or dinner anymore. In the living room, he sprawled out on the couch and scrolled through the channels, when everyone knew Thursday nights were reserved for her to watch her reality TV. It even went as far as messing up her workout routine. The day she finally tried getting up before the sun to go to the home gym, he was already there lifting weights. Finn was everywhere.

Enough was enough.

So, she was paying his sister a visit. She entered the bedroom, turning on the light to see they were still sleeping.

Luna and Valerio shot up from the bed, Valerio with a gun in his hand ready to use.

"Gianna? What the fuck are you doing? Have you lost your mind?" he screamed, setting the gun down.

"Do you know what time it is?" Luna asked, sitting up in the oversized bed. "How did you even get in?"

She'd found the spare key months ago, but she wasn't going to tell them about it. When she saw that Finn was in the gym again this morning, she couldn't take it. She didn't think; she just walked over to demand change.

Gianna huffed, throwing herself onto the end of the bed with them. "I can't take it anymore. You need to take your brother back."

"You did not do all this just to fucking talk about Finn," Valerio muttered, running his hands down his face. He moved his feet and pulled the comforter up with him.

"What's going on?" Luna asked.

"He's annoying and he's everywhere. Why isn't he living here?" she asked. She caught the look Valerio and Luna shared with each other.

"Because he's a fucking asshole," he answered.

Luna looked down at the comforter, fidgeting with it. "He compared me to my father for bringing him home. Said I took away his choice." She looked up, her eyes glossed over. "I did what I thought was right. He needs us, not to be out on his own getting drunk to forget about what happened. I went through it too, but he never checked in on me to see how I was. He never considered how I would feel not having him around."

Gianna grabbed her hand, holding it tight. She felt the emotion in her throat, trying to think of something to say that could comfort her best friend. Allister, her brother, was a lifeline. Without him, she wouldn't have been able to get through their mother walking out on them. She could only imagine how Luna felt having to grieve a father she hated, while simultaneously having to say goodbye to a mother she had just begun to really know without her only sibling around. The one person who was there to witness it, who could understand.

Valerio wrapped an arm around her shoulder, pulling her into him. "You're nothing like him. Not even close. Finn can't see the good he has in front of him."

That managed to get a small smile on her face. A twinge of

jealousy swept through Gianna. It wasn't a secret that they all admired the relationship between the newlyweds, but it made her wonder if she would ever find someone who cared enough about her to stay.

Luna turned towards her. "I can ask Finn to come here. I don't want him to bother you."

Gianna waved her off. "Don't worry about it. I'll suck it up."

"You can always stay here."

"No, no, no," Valerio said, shaking his head.

"The offer's out and everyone heard it," Gianna said, jumping off the bed. "And I will be taking advantage of it."

"How did you get in?" he asked. "You never answered that question."

"And I never will." She had a way of sneaking in and out of houses, not that she would ever tell any of them about it.

"You might as well help yourself to one of the guest rooms. It's too early to be awake," Luna told her.

She shook her head. "No, I'll go home."

"Let me have someone drop you off. It's still dark outside and I don't want you walking alone," Valerio said, picking up his phone.

"One of these days I'm going to wake you up like this," Luna promised her.

Gianna could only laugh, leaving the bedroom and going downstairs where a car waited for her. Her impromptu trip had answered some questions for her, enough to let her know that Finn truly had dropped to new depths and that there was no way she could force her best friend to deal with him right now.

So, she was stuck with him. Just her luck.

FIVE

FINN

THE SAME ROUTINE got boring enough after a week. Finn couldn't deny that he missed the wildness and danger of his life from before. Now, he was occupied with working out and sitting on the couch.

He didn't want to go back to school. To be honest, he never did anything while he was there in the first place. His degree was mostly a pass to let him have some fun before he was supposed to seriously start training to take over his father's role as Don, but clearly that never happened.

To say he was bored out of his fucking mind was an understatement. He scrolled through channels on the TV once again, feeling his brain rotting by the minute.

He heard footsteps entering the living room. Immediately, his mind jumped to the possibility of it being a certain blonde that glared whenever she saw him, but instead it was another one of his sister's friends: Cecilia.

She gave him a small nod and smile, which he returned. She didn't say anything, but that was fine by him.

Cecilia went to grab her book from the coffee table when it struck him that she was the one person who might know where Augustus was. He hadn't been answering any phone calls or texts and hadn't been by the house. It stung considering they used to be partners in crime, but things changed.

Still, Augustus was obsessed with her. Their relationship was confusing as fuck, but if anyone would know where he was, it had to be her.

"Hey, has Augustus changed his number or something?" Finn asked, standing. "He hasn't been answering my calls, so I figured you might know."

The small smile slipped off her face instantly and was replaced with narrowed eyes that seemed to hold fire inside of them. "I'm not his secretary."

"Well, do you know where he is these days?"

"Why would I?" she asked, tucking the book under her arm.

"Because you guys have something going on," he said.

Her eyes twitched in irritation, and she clenched her jaw. "No, we don't."

"Listen, I don't give a shit about what you two do. I just need to talk to him. Can you tell him to call me?"

Her voice dropped to a whisper. "I'm going to say something, and this isn't to be repeated to anyone, and I mean anyone. You left him, just disappeared. He was your best friend. You betrayed him after he was there for you through everything. You can't just come back and want to rekindle things. That's not how you treat the people you care about. So no, I'm not going to tell him anything because you don't deserve the loyalty of a friend like him."

The words hit him like a truck, nearly knocking him over. She walked away without another word, leaving him in the silence of his own consequences. He had pushed everyone away. He had left everything and everyone behind. They moved on without him and he was left playing catch up now.

His airway felt suffocatingly tight, a lump of emotion making it hard to get anything through. On the inside, he wanted to claw and rip through his own body to destroy himself and the person he had become. On the outside, there wasn't a single indication of what he was going through. His face remained stoic, but internally it felt like he was on fire.

He pushed it down, further and further, until it was suppressed. Until it didn't hurt anymore.

And that was all he could do to survive.

———

After a vigorous workout session, Finn took a shower and made his way into the garage where Dante had said his bike was. Sure enough, it sat upright supported by the kickstand. Luckily, it didn't look like they had destroyed it in the process of bringing it over to the house.

His bike was the first serious purchase he'd made for himself in college. Simply put, his father would have destroyed it if he ever knew about it, so it was his dirty little secret. The freedom he experienced when he felt the wind on his body while he whipped past cars and went dangerous speeds—there was nothing comparable.

Sex and alcohol couldn't even compare to it, but after a long day of riding, they were close seconds.

He grabbed a rag from the counter and a bucket with water from the sink, taking his time to wash it down. Months on the road had done a beating on it. The bike needed an oil change and other regular maintenance, no doubt. The tires needed to be replaced, but now that Finn had all the money and time in the world, he might as well get the bike prepared for another escape.

Being reunited with the one thing he really did care about almost made him lower his guard. The keyword being 'almost.' The hairs on his neck stood up, letting him know that someone was watching him.

"If you're going to take me out of my misery, doing it when I'm turned around is a dick move," Finn said, still not bothering to turn around to see who it was.

"I don't think you deserve to see my face when I put a knife in your ass."

Now that voice did have him turning. The surprise hit him hard when he saw Augustus standing in front of him and not one of the usual dwellers of the home. He desperately tried to regain his composure, but that seemed futile because this was the one person who was able to read him. They had been best friends— no, more like brothers—since they were eight years old. If anyone knew him, the real him, it was Augustus.

"Why the ass and not my back?"

"I didn't want to bother with the symbolism of stabbing you in the back," he said, shrugging.

Finn stood up, wiping his hands on his jeans. "I've been calling and texting, but you haven't answered. Did Cecilia mention I asked about you?"

"She didn't need to. I hacked into the cameras and watched her myself."

Finn held back his comments. Getting back into Augustus's good graces was his priority, not telling him how batshit crazy it was to follow Cecilia around the house on the camera feed when he wasn't around her.

"The only reason I'm here is because you pushed her to a place where she had to protect me against you, so thanks for being a giant asshole. Also, if you ever talk to her like that again, I'll fucking kill you," Augustus said, the threat clear in his voice.

"Noted." Finn nodded, rubbing a hand on his chin. "I appreciate you coming."

"Where's my apology?"

"I thought you understood why I left," he said. "I didn't realize I owed you one."

"I thought I was never going to see you again, dumbass. It was easier to accept it rather than fight it. Now you're back, so you have to apologize for all the bullshit you put me through," Augustus said.

Finn scoffed. "Everything you've been through? What about what I went through?"

"Can you stop being dense for one fucking second? I'm not undermining what you went through, asshole. I'm trying to make you realize that I'm not disposable. We've known each other for too fucking long for you to just throw me aside—to just throw everyone aside," he said, the vein in his neck popping through at the outburst.

"I didn't throw you aside, or at least I didn't mean to." He shook his head. How could he explain to people that he couldn't have stayed? That the image of his father dead on the floor was so engraved into his head that he had to keep moving to help clear it. That being around all of them was a reminder of his old life, the life with his father in it, and he couldn't decipher whether that was a good or bad thing. He said none of it. Instead, he said the only words he could manage to say, which were easier than anything else. "I'm sorry, okay. You're my brother and you always have been."

That seemed to appease Augustus enough because he nodded his head. "Thank God. I thought I was going to have to beat it out of you." When the smile came onto his face, it seemed that the tension between them had lifted.

"I can admit when I'm wrong."

"Can you? Damn, five months on the road did change you."

Finn shook his head, grinning now. "What's that saying about the road?"

Augustus snorted. "I don't think there is one, dumbass. Now, tell me all about your adventures."

SIX

GIANNA

A PARTY WAS EXACTLY what Gianna needed. A chance to get dressed up, lose her inhibitions, and pretend she didn't remember any of it the next day would cure her from her long dance days and her nightmare house guest.

It also gave her a chance to see Raphael, a boy she had run into at a couple of different parties who also went to Grand Willow University. She refused to bring him home or around anyone she knew, save for her best friends, mainly because Allister, Dante, and Valerio always enacted the third degree on any boy they saw her with. That usually came with an extreme line of questioning and what they called 'roughhousing,' which no boy could ever truly handle. If she brought him home with her, it was serious, but at this point, she was ready enough to take that step with him.

Blair, Cecilia, and Luna were somewhere with the three boys, hopefully keeping them occupied so Gianna could muster up the courage to finally introduce Raphael to them. He seemed keen on making out against the wall, letting his hands wander over her legs, her hips, anywhere he could get them.

She pushed him away slightly, captivated by the daze in his eyes. "What's wrong?" he asked, confused as to why she stopped.

"This is the fifth party we've been to together," she said, running her hands through his dark hair.

"That's awesome." He tried to lean in again for another kiss, but she dodged it.

"My brother is here tonight, and I think you should meet him. I want to be able to go out to places other than just parties and the only way we can do that is if he likes you, so—"

"Whoa, what the fuck? Meet your brother?" He pulled away completely, leaving her cold and empty. "What do you think this is?"

Gianna swallowed harshly, feeling her defenses rising immediately. "Your tongue was down my throat a second ago and we've been seeing each other. What else would I think it is?"

"Yeah, and we've been having fun," Raphael said, raising his voice slightly to be heard over the music. "I thought you knew that's all this was."

"Why would I have thought that?" she asked, bitterness swirling through her.

"Come on, Gianna, you like to have fun."

She narrowed her eyes dangerously. "And you like to dodge questions."

He sighed. "You're not the settle-down-with type of girl. That's not a bad thing either, but I mean, come on, you love to party. Most weekends you're seen with a new guy. I still have a ton of fun with you, don't get me wrong, and you're smoking hot—"

"If you enjoy your life, I recommend you stop talking."

Never in her life had she felt so disrespected. The audacity he had to talk to her that way, as if she wasn't Gianna Moretti. As if she didn't have ties to the most powerful mafia families in the world. And that seemed to snap him out of it because in no time his face was paling, as if he was ready to correct what he'd said.

She walked away without another word, shame and humiliation rocking through every fiber of her being. Was that how people viewed her? Someone to have fun with, but not someone to settle down with?

Not someone to love?

The tears burned at the back of her eyes, but she held them back. She needed to leave before anyone here saw her break down. Nothing would be worse than letting anyone know that boy's words actually got to her.

They didn't. No, his words didn't remind her that maybe that was why her mother had left. Because she was unlovable. She wasn't someone to stay for. She was temporary, not someone's forever.

Cecilia was the first person to spot her. A bright smile on her face that changed immediately when she realized something was wrong. "Are you okay?"

"My stomach is killing me, I think I'm gonna go home," Gianna said. The lie slipped out of her mouth effortlessly.

That seemed to bring everyone else's attention to her. "Do you want us to come with you?" Luna asked, her brows furrowed as she made her way over quickly.

She shook her head quickly. "No, I'll be fine. It was probably the pizza I had for lunch. You know what cheese does to me." Gianna even threw in a small smile to convince them she was fine.

"The car should be outside. If you feel worse, text me and I'll come home immediately," Allister told her, kissing her forehead. He almost managed to break her with that small gesture, but she held out, nodding her head.

"I'll be fine. Seriously, enjoy your night."

With that, she managed to break away, taking deep breaths every step she took through the refreshing spring air. She got into the car and told the driver to head straight home, and as soon as the partition was raised, she let the tears roll down her cheeks.

Not a single sound escaped her lips, though. She had to wait until she was back in her room, in the empty house where no one would be able to hear or see her break down. Only when she was alone could she finally stop being the Gianna that everyone knew her to be.

They didn't know that she'd slowly crumbled away from her

own pressures and that her own demons were constantly trying to take over.

And they would never find out.

The car stopped and she jumped out, thankful that the staff of the house got the weekends and nights off. The lights were off, the house silent.

Perfect.

She ran upstairs to her room, closing the door behind her. She looked at herself in the vanity mirror, staring at a broken girl. Her blonde hair was messy, and her makeup was smeared. She hated what stared back at her.

She turned the mirror around before she got the urge to shatter it. With the little strength she had left, she walked over to the bed, crumbling onto the floor beside it.

There was no use silencing the sobs from there. They left her throat painfully, clawing their way out of her. She gasped for air, nearly suffocating on her own tears, but every time she opened her mouth, another sob would come through, pushing her further into a breakdown she couldn't control.

No one wanted her.

No one needed her.

No one loved her.

Not Raphael.

Not her mother.

Maybe Allister would be next, or her father, or Cecilia, or Blair, or Luna, or Dante, or Valerio.

The thoughts were too painful to bear.

Two hands grabbed her head, forcing her to look into deep brown eyes. She might have been more surprised if she wasn't losing oxygen by the second.

"Breathe," Finn yelled, his eyes wild and filled with worry. "Goddammit, Gianna."

She wanted to tell him that she was trying, but it was impossible to let anything into her lungs. He shook her body, trying to get her body to loosen up, but it was futile.

Without another wasted second, he leaned in, blowing air into her mouth. He then blew air around her face before moving back to her parted lips. Their lips never touched, but even feeling the minty warmth of his breath seemed far too intimate for them.

That thought seemed to snap her out of her daze.

She gasped, finally taking in a deep breath. She coughed and every breath felt like fire, but it felt so good to finally be able to let it in again. He moved away slightly, but kept blowing air, knowing it worked. He allowed her to use him, and she did. She felt her heartbeat slowly return to normal, the air filling her lungs again. Finally, her body relaxed, falling against the bed. Her sobs had stopped, along with her tears.

All because of Finn Kingsley.

"What the fuck was that, Gianna?" he asked, pulling away from her and sitting on the ground. She wasn't sure how much time had passed but she felt loopy. He ran a hand through his hair before running it over his face.

"I had a bad night," she said, wiping under her eyes.

"Are you fucking kidding me? Has that happened before?"

She shook her head. "Never that extreme."

"What if I wasn't here? If you were alone, you could have fucking suffocated. Fucking hell, where is everyone?" He kept going on and on, spewing out questions and curses, but she could only watch him in a daze.

"They're at a party."

"Why aren't you with them? Better yet why are you here having some sort of attack?" he asked.

She didn't know what possessed her to tell him the truth, but she did anyway. "Do you think I'm someone you could settle down with?" Her voice was quiet and vulnerable, but it was hard not to be when already once tonight her heart had been ripped apart. She didn't feel like having the same happen twice.

"Are you asking hypothetically?"

She sniffled, averting her gaze. "I was seeing this guy. I wanted him to meet Allister tonight, but he told me I'm not the type to settle down with. I'm someone you have a good time with and that's all." She felt the tears welling up again. "Am I really unlovable?"

It was silent for a moment. She shouldn't have even asked him. He didn't like her, and she didn't like him, and revealing this much to him was a mistake.

"Don't let yourself get worked up over that asshole," Finn said. "If he had any brain in him, he would realize that settling down and loving you would have been the best thing he could have done in his miserable life. He blew it, and you're better off with someone who isn't going to be ashamed of you."

Gianna turned to look at him now, her heart beating rapidly in her chest. She went to open her mouth, but he wasn't done yet.

"Those assholes don't deserve you, Gianna," he said, his voice holding such strong conviction she almost believed him.

His eyes were darker now, the brown now almost completely black. She didn't even realize they had been so close to each other, but their legs were only a couple inches apart. If she leaned in, she would taste that minty warmth again.

But she didn't. Of course she didn't.

"How will I know who deserves me?"

"I don't think I need to tell you how you'll know if someone worships the ground you walk on, princess."

"Princess? And here I thought you'd become nice," she said, but she still couldn't help the way her lips turned up slightly.

"You've known me long enough to know that'll take a miracle," he said. "Do I get a thanks for helping you tonight?"

"Add that to your list of miracles." She snorted, getting up to stretch her legs before she sat on the edge of the bed. She was awfully aware of his eyes on her, trailing every inch of her exposed skin. She was also aware of how horrendous she must've looked now.

Gianna leaned over to peel the heels off her feet. She threw them across the room, catching the way he shook his head. "What?" she asked.

"I don't understand how you do that."

"Do what?"

"How you went through a breakdown and now you're back to your normal self, as if nothing happened," he said, standing.

She shrugged, leaning back on the palms of her hands. "I had my moment and now it's over. I hope no one outside of this room will find out about it either."

"Is that a threat?"

"I'm not in the business of making threats like you are."

He shook his head. "I don't plan on telling anyone either way. Your secret is safe with me."

A chill ran down her spine at those words. Sharing something with him felt wrong, especially something like a secret. Something that she wouldn't be telling anyone else about.

"Perfect," she said. She rose from the bed when the craziest thought popped into her mind. Maybe it was her testing the waters, or maybe it was her just trying to tease him, but Gianna decided to do something she had never ever considered doing in her life, with her best friend's brother of all people.

She turned around, looking at him over her shoulder. "While you're in here, mind getting the zipper for me? It tends to snag."

The tension in the room turned thick in an instant. She waited for him to tell her to figure it out before stomping out like the asshole he had always been. Finn helping her tonight, being kind, saying the words she needed to hear, was a fluke, a glitch.

Only the opposite happened. He walked up behind her, standing so close she could feel the heat from his body transferring over to hers. With a careful hand, something so unlike him, he grabbed the zipper, using the other hand to hold her lower back. She could feel every single millimeter the zipper moved down her back. Slowly, her back was exposed to the air, and she swore she heard him gasp, or maybe it was her. Shit, she didn't know anymore.

With a long exhale against her shoulder, he pulled it all the way down.

"There," he muttered, pulling himself away entirely.

"Thanks," Gianna said, but he was already walking out the door, closing it behind him.

She caught her gaze in the full body mirror against the closet door, and for some reason, she didn't turn away from it this time.

SEVEN

FINN

WHAT THE FUCK WAS THAT?

Those were the only words that kept coming to Finn's mind the entire time he walked back to his room, scrubbed his hands, and then paced back and forth until he was sure he burned a hole through the fucking floor.

He had never looked or even thought about Gianna in that way. Which way? He wasn't even sure himself. A way that was different to the innocent way he used to look at her. The way that said she was his sister's best friend and that was it.

So then what the fuck was that?

He ran a hand down his face, pausing when he smelt her perfume. Was that his mind playing a trick on him or was it actually there? God, why was he starting to find the sweet strawberry scent that enveloped her being so fucking intoxicating?

He shouldn't have ever come home, that was the problem. He was deprived of everything good in his life—sex included—and the minute an attractive woman showed some interest in him, he completely lost his mind. Finn wasn't even sure she was showing interest. Gianna was a tease and a flirt, but her request for him to unzip her dress was most likely innocent. Yes, that's exactly what it was. An innocent request.

He needed to leave.

He couldn't be lingering around, solving problems for people when he had no intentions of staying. But when she cried—or more like nearly suffocated—he couldn't deny that he sympathized with her. He would have felt the same murderous rage had it been his own sister crying on the floor because some asshole broke her heart.

That made Finn stop pacing. Maybe it wasn't any type of attraction towards Gianna; maybe it was him feeling sympathy towards her. He had known her since they were children—granted, she had been the annoying child that followed her sister around everywhere. But ultimately, had the roles been reversed, he would have wanted Allister to help Luna in the same way—minus unzipping her dress. As an older brother, it was his duty to do what was right.

Maybe it really was that simple. Since he felt bad that she'd had her heart broken, the right thing to do was teach the asshole that did it a lesson. That seemed logical enough; beat up the man that made her cry and then order could be restored. She could move on with someone else, and he could leave the city and never look back.

Besides, he hadn't had a good fight in far too long. He was due for beating the shit out of someone.

The only issue was that he couldn't just come and beat the asshole outright. He had to have some reason for doing it. Something that was accidental or perhaps coincidental. Maybe something that the asshole just so happened to stumble upon.

Finn grabbed his phone to call Augustus. He answered after the third ring. "What?"

"Should I be surprised you're awake this late?"

"Cecilia went out tonight, you know the drill," Augustus said.

"Well, I have a question for you," Finn said, finally taking a seat on the bed.

"What is it?"

"How do you feel about hosting another Fight Night?"

"It's not Initiation Weekend." Augustus sighed. "But you don't give a shit about that, do you?"

"No, I don't. I have some pent-up stuff I have to get out," Finn told him. "Don't tell me you're not willing to beat anyone up."

"Hey, don't get ahead of yourself. You know I'm always down for a fight. Who are the opponents then?" he asked.

"Let's make it a special invitation for whoever dares to step in the ring with us." Finn couldn't help but grin.

There was something exciting about stepping into the ring, letting his body and instinct take over to annihilate the person in front of him. It had been far too long since he'd had a good fight. Actually, the last time was last Fight Night when he and Valerio got into it, but no one won that fight. Finn still wasn't sure why he left the ring in the middle of the fight, but something told him he didn't want to know.

"Where do you plan on hosting it?" Augustus asked.

"What do you mean? The same place we always do."

"Yeah idiot, the arena is now under the Vitali's since you left and refused to handle anything related to the Kingsley name."

Fuck.

"So, if I want to use the space?"

Augustus snorted. "Then you better start kissing your brother-in-law's ass."

Then he hung up the phone, leaving Finn in his own silence. He groaned, falling back on the bed.

Why the fuck was nothing ever simple?

EIGHT

FINN

MAYBE BRINGING over coffee and pastries was overkill, but the last time Finn had talked to Luna, he was quite possibly the worst fucking brother in the world. To be fair, he had been in a shitty headspace. And to be fair, he still was in one. But she did have him kidnapped and brought back home, so really the entire situation was complicated.

He still needed to use the arena, which was under the Vitali name. Valerio wouldn't allow it until Luna forgave him, so if coffee and pastries could warm her heart, he would try it.

Getting past the gates was a hassle on its own. The guards patted him down as if he was smuggling something under his T-shirt, but he knew it was strict orders from Valerio to have him roughed up if he ever showed up again. They spared no expense checking his ID, looking into his shoes, his pockets, even opening the fucking coffee cup.

At least the money on the security detail was being well spent.

Finn knocked on the front door, waiting a second before it was pulled open. It wasn't a maid or any of the staff he was expecting to see so he could build up some courage. Instead, it was Valerio.

Of course, he had been alerted about Finn's presence.

"Could I interest you in some muffins?" Finn asked.

"I have a sniper aimed at your head waiting to unleash on you at my word. Give me one good reason I shouldn't give him the signal," Valerio said, his voice menacing.

"I'm here to apologize." Finn held up the food in his hand. "I have her favorite pastries, and I would hate for her to go hungry all because you won't let me in."

"She's never gone hungry with me, and she never will," he spat out. "Your apology is long overdue. I wonder what finally brought you to your fucking senses."

Finn clenched his jaw, resisting the urge to say something that would land him a bullet to the head. "I made a mistake, okay?"

"Mistakes are accidental. What you said to her was geared with every intention to hurt."

The asshole was right. He did want it to hurt. Finn wasn't denying that, but he was here to apologize now.

"Val? Where are you?" Luna's voice called out from somewhere in the house.

Immediately, Valerio tensed. "If one fucking bad thing comes out of your mouth, I'll kill you," he hissed, finally letting Finn into the home.

He resisted rolling his eyes and followed Valerio, who led him into the kitchen. Luna sat on a barstool, looking like she had just rolled out of bed still in her pajamas and her hair messy. It had to have been nearly eleven in the morning at that point, but then again, she was never a morning person.

Hearing their footsteps, she turned around, but her smile fell immediately. "What is this?" she asked.

Valerio walked up to her, pressing a kiss to her forehead. "He came to the door, begging and crying."

Finn stood there for a minute, not sure if he should move. Even though Valerio was the Don, it was clear who controlled everything. Luna commanded a power he had never seen from her before, especially not after the life they'd lived with their father.

She had always been muted, not literally, but she might as well have been. The Luna he knew before was never sure of herself, always crippled by her own mind overthinking the worst possibilities. This Luna was different. He hated to admit it, but it had to do with the death of their father and the addition of Valerio in her life.

Why hadn't the death of their father impacted him in some grand way that actually helped him?

"I brought those strawberry Danishes you like from that one cafe in the city," Finn said, holding up the bag. "I also got you an iced coffee, which is now more room temperature because it's been thawing in my hand all morning."

Luna looked at him suspiciously. "Why?"

Valerio stood behind her, giving Finn a hard look that reminded him of the threat from earlier. He sighed. "Because I'm sorry. I'm an asshole, though I'm sure you already knew that."

"I did." Still, she patted the seat next to her at the counter. "Might as well enjoy what you brought even though your apology doesn't mean anything."

He took the seat, handing her the bag and the drink. "I didn't mean any of it."

"Which part? That I'm exactly like our father for forcing you home?"

"Yeah, that part."

The awkward tension covered every inch of the room. Neither Valerio nor Luna did anything to help expel it or to help make him more comfortable, so it was up to him to navigate the entire apology. Something he had absolutely no experience doing.

She opened the bag, pulling out a Danish with aggression. Valerio watched her with a careful eye, as if he was worried that she was going to break.

Maybe it was a bad idea for Finn to come here after all.

"So what? Have you come to tell me you're leaving? Don't let the door hit you on the way out," she said, taking a bite. "As a matter of fact, I'm not sure why you stopped by in the first place.

You left the first time without a word. A second time wouldn't have mattered."

"I'm not going anywhere," Finn said.

"Oh, what a new development." Her voice was laced with sarcasm, and it shocked him to hear it. She threw the pastry back in the bag.

"Maybe we should have this conversation a different time," Valerio suggested.

For once, Finn agreed with him.

"No. If Finn wants to come here to apologize for comparing me to our abuser, then he can listen to what I have to say." Her hands shook as she talked and the emotion was thick in her throat, but she continued. "You know what I've been through—what he put me through—because you saw it all. The fact that you could even go there, after everything, is disturbing. No, it's worse than that, I just don't have the words to express it."

He swallowed harshly. There was an ache in his chest that got worse with every word she said. "I said it in the heat of the moment. There wasn't any truth to it."

"There's always a little bit of truth."

Valerio gripped the counter until his knuckles turned white as if it pained him to see Luna in that much anguish. Was that what love was? Willing to do anything to take her pain away? The thought was just another painful reminder that Finn might not have ever truly loved anyone in his life. Not really. He didn't know if he ever truly could.

He shook his head. "I didn't want to be found, Luna. You have to understand that. After what we saw, after everything—I needed to get lost. I couldn't be here."

"I needed my brother."

And there was her own selfish reason for bringing him home. The only family she had—well, blood family—skipped town the moment he could. He hadn't thought twice about it because he was in a state of fight or flight. He ran while she held on with all her strength. That was the type of people they were. She couldn't fault him for that, just like he couldn't fault her for wanting him home.

"I'm sorry for not being here when you needed me," he told her. This time, he actually meant it.

"I'm sorry for bringing you home when you weren't ready," she told him. "I seriously won't blame you if you want to leave."

"I'm not planning on going anywhere for a while," he said. The words came out of his mouth without him even registering them. It seemed like his mind was made up then. He was hunkering down here for a little bit longer than he'd intended.

"Oh, great," Valerio said, his sarcastic tone cutting through the room.

It brought a smile to Luna's face, which seemed to have been the intended effect. It was interesting to see how they interacted with each other. Maybe that was why Finn hadn't hesitated to leave; he knew Valerio would always take care of her no matter what. Not that he would ever tell them.

"Sorry to burst that cold heart of yours."

"He'll live," Luna told him, leaning into Valerio. She reached for the bag again, sliding them over to Finn. "By the way, these are the wrong Danishes."

Finn shrugged, grabbing the bag and taking one out for himself. "I tried."

Valerio shook his head, moving to the fridge. "Useless."

"How has your stay been over at the house?" Luna asked him.

"It's been fine. I mostly keep to myself, which seems to be working out."

"Gianna came here not that long ago complaining about you," Valerio said.

Finn swore his heart stopped at the mention of her name. For a short period of time, he had been able to forget about her, but just like that, he was thrown back into her orbit.

"What was she saying?" he asked, trying to sound unaffected.

"Said you were an asshole," Luna said. "I hope you guys are being friendly now."

Finn shook his head. "No, I'm still an asshole."

"Be nice to her. She's still my best friend."

Exactly what he had to remember. She was Luna's best friend. Someone to be friendly with. That was all. He needed to be done with Fight Night as soon as possible so he could put all this bullshit to rest.

"I need access to the arena, and I heard it's in your name now," Finn said, this time looking at Valerio's back as he cooked something on the stove.

"Yeah, remember you were gone? Someone had to do something with the properties."

"Why do you need it?" Luna asked.

"I want to host another Fight Night."

"What a productive use of time," Valerio said, turning around.

"Sign it back over in my name," Finn said.

"On one condition," Luna said.

"What?"

"That we can come."

"You want to come to Fight Night?" Finn asked, snorting at the thought. She hated fights and hesitated to come in the past. Why the hell did she want to come now?

"Sure. Let's see if you're still worth betting on." She grinned.

"I want to fight," Valerio said, immediately speaking up. "I don't care who it's against."

"You want to fight?" Luna asked him, her brows raised.

"What? You care to make a bet again?" He had a smirk on his lips.

Finn watched the interaction in complete disgust. He for sure did not want to know what happened at the last Fight Night.

"Come if you want, fight if you want, I don't care. Is the arena mine again?" Finn asked.

"Sure," Valerio said, not bothering to look over at him.

The two still looked at each other with sick grins on their

faces, a conversation happening between them without words. Finn stood, taking the pastry bag with him.

"I'll text you the details."

Neither one replied, so he let himself out of the house. Sure, it was an emotional morning, but he felt lighter than he had in so long. Dare he say he felt optimistic.

He walked back home, heading straight to the gym to train.

NINE

GIANNA

THERE WERE a lot of things that Gianna truly loved in the world. One was the bottomless mimosas at her favorite brunch spot in the city with her best friends. After all the grueling dance practices she'd put herself through during the week, and the worst weekend of her life, she needed all the mimosas she could get.

Waffles didn't hurt either.

"You never told us what ended up happening with that one guy you were seeing, Gianna," Blair said, stirring her coffee around.

It broke her out of her happy daze and sent the miserable chill right back through her. "What is there to talk about?"

"Didn't he end up meeting you at the club?" Cecilia asked. "You seemed to really like him and after that night you just stopped talking about him completely."

"I realized I was too good for him," she said quickly. "He was boring and cheap, not my type at all. I mean, complaining about a twenty-dollar cocktail, who does that?"

The lies slipped out of her mouth so effortlessly she almost believed them herself. It worked out better if they were able to believe her standards were over the top instead of hashing out her spiral over how no one would ever truly love her. There were some things her best friends didn't need to know, and unfortunately, that night was one of them.

"He always seemed like an asshole to me," Luna said, cutting into her eggs Benedict. "I don't think you should ever have to settle for anything."

Cecilia snorted. "Easy for you to say."

"What is that supposed to mean?" she asked, confused.

"You're married now to a man who is obsessed with you. You don't know how terrible the dating scene is out here," Blair said. "It's like a war zone, just constantly dodging missiles left and right."

"Believe me, I realize how much worse I could have it," Luna said, shaking her head. "But all I know is that you all deserve the world."

Now Luna was in on believing Gianna deserved better, just like Finn. If only she could believe it herself, but it seemed that no matter how many people tried to repeat those words to her, her mind was unwilling to truly hear it.

"Having someone obsessed with you isn't all great," Cecilia said, pointing her fork around in the air. "I'd rather be alone."

"You have a stalker. There's a huge difference," Gianna told her, patting her back in condolence.

She still didn't really know what the hell went on between her and Augustus, and she didn't want to know. Hell, her own life was too complicated at the moment to get caught up in whatever was going on there.

"Oh, I almost forgot to tell you guys that Finn came over the other day," Luna said.

Gianna froze but covered it up swiftly. She reached for her mimosa, taking a big drink.

Finn Kingsley.

Perhaps her long dance practices had to do with her also trying to forget his hands on her, his minty breath, his warmth.

She didn't know what it was but those moments with him had been replaying in her mind on a loop.

Maybe it was a moment of desperation that made them seem far more intimate than they actually had been. She tried to convince herself that it was just him trying to help her out, that there was nothing romantic or sensual in the way he let her breathe from him.

Nothing at all.

Nope.

"And what happened with that?" Blair asked.

"Well, he apologized for everything. We ended up having a heart to heart, which was so needed. Everything was weighing on me so heavily, I think we both needed to just let everything out," Luna said. She had a smile on her face that showed she meant what she said.

"I'm really happy for you," Gianna told her.

"Thanks. He seems to be warming up to staying here now too. He even asked for the arena back so he could host another Fight Night," she said.

Gianna couldn't help the swirl of excitement that swept through her. She loved a good fight more than she was willing to admit, but why the sudden change in his attitude? He seemed so adamant about leaving, and now it seemed like he was trying to set up a life for himself here.

"I thought he was completely against being here?" Cecilia asked.

"I thought so too, but something seemed to have swayed his mind," Luna said. "Do you think he's met someone?"

Gianna's eyes widened. "Met someone?"

"I know it sounds stupid. I don't think he's the type to settle down, but one minute he's ready to pack up and never look back, then the next he's wanting property back. The only thing I could think of is that he's trying to impress someone, maybe get his life together for her." Luna shrugged so casually that it was completely juxtaposed with the rapid beating of Gianna's heart.

Did he have someone else?

If he did, that would mean everything that had happened that night meant nothing. It couldn't mean anything because he already had a girlfriend or something equivalent.

She should have felt relieved. Having any sort of feeling towards her best friend's brother was wrong on every level possible.

But why did her heart ache?

Maybe it was because her mind created scenarios and over-thought everything, creating delusions of what she wanted rather than what was reality. Reality was that he wanted nothing to do with her, and another rejection stung. Bad.

"Well, good luck to whoever that girl is. No offense to you, Luna, but I think all women could strive to do better than him," Gianna said, her tone nonchalant.

"That's harsh, G," Blair said.

"The truth usually is."

"We know no one can match your standards," Cecilia said. She turned to Luna. "He could have finally knocked some sense into that stubborn ass of his."

"Well, whatever it is, I just hope he stays around for a while," Luna said, ending the conversation with that.

Gianna didn't miss the way Luna kicked her shin under the table, but she deserved it. And Finn probably deserved worse for even being around her that night if he had someone already.

But that wasn't Gianna's problem to worry about anymore.

"So, when is this Fight Night happening?" Gianna asked.

"Next Friday," Luna said. "And this time it's me forcing you all to go, not the other way around."

"The student becomes the master." Cecilia grinned. "It's about damn time too."

Luna threw her napkin at her, making Blair screech at not getting hollandaise sauce on her new skirt.

Things always worked out for the best, it seemed, no matter

how much it burned in the moment. Men sucked, but at least Gianna could enjoy a good fight now without any kind of drama following.

The thought brought a smile to her face.

TEN

GIANNA

THERE WAS ALWAYS a reason to dress-up and Fight Night was no different. While most people tried to stick to black and a more badass look, Gianna wore whatever she wanted whenever she wanted. That was why she threw on a sparkly pink miniskirt and a matching cropped long sleeved top. She wore heels that only accentuated her long legs and curled her hair so that it would bounce with every step she took.

She demanded attention wherever she went, and tonight was no exception. She would be lying if she said she hated it because she honestly didn't. Knowing that people watched her, hated her, wanted to be her, wanted to *fuck* her—it filled the void for a second. And as long as it filled it, she was going to enjoy it.

The arena was packed with people hungry for a good fight. The dome shape allowed everyone a view, all the way from the back of the building to the seats right by the ring. They always sat right up front, mostly so the boys could keep an eye on them, but it was the best spot in the house.

The past couple of Fight Nights had always included Gianna and the other girls, but now they were joined by Allister, Valerio, and Dante—who attended by invite this time and weren't crashing it. She still didn't know why they were all fighting, but she assumed that since it was an unofficial Fight Night and not being used to bait new recruits for the Kingsley family, that rules could be broken.

Either way, it was easy to guess who would be winning all the fights tonight and she was hoping to leave rich by betting on them.

She took her seat right beside Blair after everyone had placed their drink orders. The event felt fancier than previous Fight Nights, with waitresses and better chairs. Immediately, she knew that was Valerio's influence. God forbid his wife sit on anything uncomfortable or have to get up to order her own drinks.

The lights dimmed in the arena, indicating that the first fight was going to begin. The waitress came back with Gianna's drink and immediately she took a big sip, letting the burn warm up her body as it traveled down her throat.

"Ladies and gentlemen, welcome one and welcome all, to the return of Fight Night," the announcer said, letting his voice carry out an echo with the last syllables. The cheers from the crowd were deafening. Gianna couldn't help but scream with them.

"For the first match of the night, we have the reckless, the wild, the life of the party—Dante Vitali!"

He came out already shirtless and his body glistening as if he'd poured oil all over himself. She wouldn't have been surprised if he actually had. The grin on his face showed his confidence, and it only grew bigger once his opponent came out. He had a similar build to Dante, but the match was unfair on the basis of no one being able to win against the Vitali boys in the first place.

The bell rang and the other man threw the first punch, but Dante let him. They went back and forth, trading punches and kicks, but with one last hit to the neck, Dante had the match.

Allister was the next one on. By then, Gianna had finished her drink and was onto her next. She knew her brother could hold his own, but there was still a strike of anxiety that tore through her when he entered the ring and smacked his gloves together. It only got worse when his opponent stepped in and was considerably larger than him.

Gianna's eyes widened and she stood up to get closer to the ring, chewing on her nail. When the bell rang, Allister struck first, moving with a speed that the other man couldn't match. He might have had a larger build, but he had no agility to help him against Allister.

Her brother stepped around the larger man, managing to kick his knees down to push him down to the ground. With one more punch to the head, Allister was declared the winner.

Gianna felt her shoulders relax. She cheered loudly, cupping her hands around her mouth to make sure he heard her. He sent her a grin, jumping out of the ring and giving her a hug.

"How did I do?"

"Surprisingly well," she told him.

"Asshole," he said, laughing. "That dude was no match against me."

She snorted. "Yeah, he just had like 150 pounds on you."

Allister shook her hair and messed it up, knowing it would annoy the hell out of her—and it did. He walked back over to where Dante stood now, watching as Valerio entered the ring. He took his time, keeping his gaze on Luna as she did the same to him.

Gianna walked over to her, knowing the last time they were in this situation, Luna was a wreck. This time, it seemed like there was some kind of secret going on between the two of them. Something gross, probably.

The moment the opponent entered the ring, Luna's eyes widened. It was a big man, bigger than Valerio and bigger that the man Allister had just fought. Valerio didn't let his smirk fall, even as he sized up his opponent for a moment before returning his gaze to Luna once again.

She went to open her mouth to say something, but as soon as the bell rang, it was too late. Valerio dodged the punch that was headed his way and sent one back, meeting the man's head with such strength it sent him flying back.

A total knockout.

Valerio stood there for a moment, looking down at the man lying on the floor unconscious in front of him. The cheers started all at once, but it was like he didn't care at all. Valerio jumped out of the ring and walked over to his wife. Gianna was sure the shock on her face matched the one on Luna's, but it didn't matter because he whisked her away without another word.

She shook her head, heading back to Blair and Cecilia now.

"Well, that was quick."

"I don't even want to know what they had going on with that," Blair said, shaking her head.

"Well, this was a good night," Cecilia said, standing up now. "I think I'm ready to go home."

"What are you talking about?" Gianna asked, scrunching her nose in confusion. "It's not over yet."

"Trying to avoid the next fight?" Blair asked.

"Geez, what a lucky guess," Cecilia said, her voice full of sarcasm.

Then that meant Augustus was on next. He walked out with a sick grin on his face. The way he enjoyed violence always made Gianna uncomfortable, but he wasn't obsessed with her. He was obsessed with the girl with black hair that did everything she could to try to avoid his gaze.

He didn't head straight for the ring. Instead, he made a pitstop by Cecilia, leaning close to her ear to whisper something. Judging Cecilia's heated cheeks, and the way her mouth and eyes sprung open in shock, it was probably something vulgar.

"I hope you choke," Cecilia spat out.

"Only if it's on you," he said before finally entering the ring.

There was no point in asking what was said because she wouldn't tell. Gianna shared a look with Blair, before squeezing Cecilia's shoulder in comfort. The bell rang once again.

Augustus lunged like a madman, tearing into his opponent

and beating him with such ferocity it was frightening. Gianna looked away from the sight, going back to the drink that was still on her chair. She waited for them to call the winner before she turned around.

She wasn't normally so squeamish around the blood and violence that Fight Night brought, but something about seeing so many fights and so much blood back-to-back left her feeling unsettled. Thankfully, there was only one more fight left of the night and then they could go to whatever after parties were being thrown around campus.

Augustus jumped out of the ring covered in blood as his opponent was carried out. The sight didn't deter the crowd from losing their minds at the entertainment they witnessed moments before. He took his seat right beside Cecilia without bothering to clean himself up, forcing her to look forward the entire time.

Gianna caught her gaze for a second, and all she gave was a brief nod to tell her she was okay. She accepted it for now but still kept an eye out. Allister and Dante were still there too. If anything happened, they would jump in without a moment's hesitation.

That was when it struck her. She managed to see everyone throughout the night but Finn. Hell, the night managed to distract her so well that she hadn't even thought about him. Her brief lapse in sanity questioning whether something could happen between her and Finn was completely gone, it seemed. For all she knew, he was probably cozying it up with the secret girl Luna thought he was keeping before his big fight. Maybe Gianna would even get to see her.

For her sake, she hoped the girl was at least somewhat as pretty as Gianna. More was impossible, but significantly less attractive—although that was the most likely scenario—would just be tragic.

Gianna adjusted her outfit and ordered herself another drink. She took her seat next to Blair, who sat scrolling on her phone.

"What are you doing?" Gianna asked.

"Studying," Blair said.

"How are you studying right now? We're in the middle of a fight," Gianna asked, completely dumbfounded.

"Actually, we're in the middle of them wiping the ring clean of blood," Blair said. "And I have an exam on Monday."

"Allister's not studying right now."

"Exactly."

Gianna rolled her eyes. "You can have fun sometimes."

"I am having fun, but also that A isn't going to happen by itself," Blair said, waving her off.

Gianna huffed, leaning back in her seat. She was officially bored now. She needed something to really make Fight Night end with a bang now that Luna was gone, Cecilia was being held hostage, and Blair was studying. Something dramatic needed to happen.

The lights flickered on and off, directing all the attention back to the ring once again.

Gianna ignored it, instead accepting her drink from the waitress beside her. Considering how easy the other fights had been, this one was sure to be the same. She was rich now, yes, but all of them, even Augustus's, were boring. They were sure wins and had no mystery in them.

Maybe she should call it a night and take Cecilia and Blair home with her.

She swallowed her drink, standing when her eyes caught someone familiar in the ring. It was Raphael. The same one that broke her heart in the club and left her nearly suffocating from a panic attack.

She felt the air get knocked out of her lungs. What was he doing here? Shirtless? With gloves on? Looking like he was going to fight someone?

This was supposed to be the last fight of the night. That didn't make any sense. The last fight was reserved for the main event, for the person who was hosting, which would be Finn. Maybe there was another fight happening before the last one?

"Now, to introduce the man, the legend, the one you all came out to see tonight—Finn Kingsley!"

He stalked out from the locker room, his shorts hanging low on his hips and she hated the way her eyes immediately traced his body. There was a scowl on his face, one that promised destruction in his path. The cheers were louder than they had been all night as everyone knew a good show was coming, but that wasn't what Gianna was focused on.

She was still stuck on the fact that Finn was headed straight into the ring towards Raphael.

Finn was fighting Raphael.

Why?

Ding. Ding. Ding.

ELEVEN

GIANNA

GIANNA'S LEGS had a mind of their own when they carried her directly in front of the ring. She was so close now she could see the small hairs that covered Finn's body under the bright lights.

Neither fighter went for the immediate first punch. Instead, they took their time assessing the situation. Raphael had told her that he used to box recreationally, and maybe that would come to benefit him now. But she wasn't rooting for him.

No, she still rooted for the brunette boy who was far more toned than she cared to admit. Admittedly, she had always bet on Finn during every single Fight Night for the past couple of years. It got to the point where she didn't even bother asking who his opponent was; she just placed her money on him.

It would have been stupid not to because he knew the ring. The way his eyes moved over his opponent to weigh out every option, and the way his muscles flexed and extended all proved that he was a professional.

When he fought, it wasn't archaic like Augustus. It was art.

Finn seemed to find the opening he had been waiting for because he dove a punch in, landing it directly against Raphael's ribs. He doubled over in pain for a moment, but that was long enough to have Finn launching another hit, against his cheek this time. She could hear every time skin hit skin. The hits he gave were full of power and aggression.

She was fascinated, so much so that her eyes never once drifted over to Raphael. They stayed on Finn the entire time. This was the first time she was seeing him since the incident in her room and now she couldn't get enough of him. Her eyes ate up every movement he made. Almost like she was the predator stalking its prey now. It was humiliating, but she couldn't help it.

Finn pushed his hair back, looking up for a moment and locking eyes with her. Her heart shouldn't have picked up the way it did, nor should she have found satisfaction in the way his eyes widened a fraction when he saw her.

In a split second, he broke their eye contact, landing another painful punch to Raphael's nose. Blood splattered the already stained ring, nearly getting on her outfit in the process. She would have cursed Finn out, but he managed to get kicked in the stomach unexpectedly.

He groaned, taking a couple steps back. Worry etched in her body. Did Finn know that Raphael knew how to fight? Dammit, she sure hoped he did.

His few seconds of recovery ended quickly when Raphael was back up landing another hard hit against his temple. It didn't seem to faze Finn, luckily.

They exchanged hits in a heated exchange, each more brutal than the one before. Finn overpowered Raphael, towering over him in a show of pure dominance.

What was this feeling inside of her? Attraction? Sure. Admiration? Maybe.

Pure and raw lust? Absolutely.

It only became more intense when he ripped off his gloves before wrapping a hand around Raphael's throat. Finn lifted him off the ground, letting him choke and plead for air before slamming him onto the ring.

A gasp left her lips at the absolute show of strength. Raphael didn't move after that. He could have been dead for all anyone knew, but from the small rise and fall of his chest, Gianna knew he was alive.

Finn stood there for a moment, letting the sweat roll down his body and mix with the other liquids already covering the ring.

He raised his arm, naming himself the winner.

For once in her life, she was truly at a loss for words.

His dark brown eyes connected with hers in a way that had her stumbling back. She wanted to question why he did it, why he fought Raphael, but she already knew the answer. The look on his face, the intensity in his eyes, it told her everything she needed to know.

He did it for her.

That was all she knew and maybe she didn't need to know any more than that.

Someone grabbing her hand was the only thing that pulled her out of the nauseating gaze.

"Are you ready to go? I think we're still going to hit up a party with Dante," Blair told her, seemingly unaware of what was happening. "Luna and Valerio said they would meet us, but I highly doubt it."

If Blair didn't notice the intensity of the moment, maybe there wasn't anything to it in the first place. Was Gianna just imagining it?

She shook her head. She couldn't decide if a party was exactly what she needed or the last place she should have been at. "I'm not sure."

"Are you serious? You're turning down a party?" Blair asked. She raised her brow and had a look in her eyes that said she didn't buy it for a single moment.

Gianna placed her hand on her forehead, trying to feign sickness the best she could. "I think the mixing of the alcohol plus all this yelling really did a number on me. My head is killing me."

"You're sure?"

"I'm sure," she said.

She wasn't sure about anything anymore, actually.

"Okay, well tell Allister so he can get a car for you," Blair said. "And text us if you change your mind or if you need us to come home."

She nodded. "Of course."

Gianna did exactly that but had to work a little more thoroughly to convince Allister she was fine.

"You've been sick a lot lately," he said, walking her out to the car. "I think you should get in to see the doctor."

She shook her head. "I doubt it's anything serious. I've been working hard at the studio, it's probably all catching up to me now."

"Well, if you feel worse, you know my number."

"Take care of Blair while you're out," Gianna said, getting into the car.

Allister looked taken aback for a moment, before leaning down in confusion. "Why didn't you tell me to take care of all the girls?"

"Because they have their boys with them," she said innocently.

He seemed to accept that answer but still didn't wipe the stunned look off his face. He closed the door for her, letting her finally leave. She let a heavy sigh leave her lips, more confused than she had ever been in her life.

She needed a new boy in her life. Something casual to get herself to stop thinking about Finn.

And quick.

TWELVE

FINN

FINN COULD REMEMBER his first fight like it happened yesterday. He was sixteen and had stumbled upon some street fight with Augustus. He didn't know where they were other than outside of the city and they were drunk out of their minds.

It was an escape more than anything. His father had put his hands on him once again, nearly breaking his fucking arm, but stopping just before he did. Finn didn't care where he went, he just needed to leave for a moment. So, he and Augustus grabbed the bikes they had hidden in the forest so his father wouldn't find them, and they drove until they stumbled onto a group of people fighting like madmen beside a big bonfire.

They blended in with the crowd easily, drinking the cheap liquor and watching as the grown men beat each other mercilessly. He was fascinated. And when enough of the alcohol had numbed the bruises on his body, he stepped forward when they called for volunteers for the next fight. Augustus tried to stop him, but there was no use.

He needed that fight more than he had ever needed anything in his life.

When a grown man a little bit larger than his father stepped up, he forced himself to stand even taller instead of cowering down. He remembered every hit, every kick, every drop of blood he had ever bled in his life. The grown man sent a punch towards him, and Finn snapped. He attacked the man with something he didn't know he had inside of him.

It was like he fell into a blackout because when he finally came to, the grown man was on the ground unconscious. He felt disgusted with himself for hurting someone else, but there was something better deep inside that he chased instead.

Control.

He wasn't the scared child forced to take a beating from his father. He was the future mafia Don controlling his own destiny.

That feeling was an addiction. Fight Night became a celebration, but fighting for him became a necessity.

It cleansed him of his demons for a little bit and usually left him with a sense of clarity.

Not tonight though.

Tonight, all fighting Raphael did was push Finn towards something else—something dangerous that he wasn't supposed to even attempt to move towards.

Gianna Moretti.

He couldn't stop thinking about her wide blue eyes and the small gasp that left her mouth when he slammed the useless waste of space onto the ring.

Finn was supposed to get revenge for her and be done with it. He was supposed to have cleared his mind and conscience after the fight, but for some reason, his heart still beat rapidly as if he hadn't even fought at all.

His body was still craving a high and it seemed to have become resistant to the normal treatments.

Going to the gym to burn off the energy by beating the shit out of the punching bag did nothing. If anything, it made him even more antsy. He needed to move; he couldn't stay stagnant. He considered going out to the party that everyone else seemed to be at, but that seemed like a disaster. In his current state, he felt like he could pick a fight with anyone that even looked in his direction the wrong way. He considered leaving the house for a drive, but it still felt like something was missing.

Something pink and blonde.

Maybe a cold fucking shower would do it.

He left the gym, still in the shorts he fought in with no T-shirt to cover the rest of his body. They had specks of blood on them, as did his arms, but his first thought hadn't been to shower when he got home.

He ran like a coward up to his room, making his way into the shower. The water was cold, but he needed it. It shocked his entire system for a few seconds as he worked on fixing his breathing so his body could relax. Eventually, he was able to and soon the cold water felt refreshing on his feverish skin.

That was exactly what he needed.

Until pink lips, blue eyes, and blonde hair entered his mind. His brain had to be completely rotten for him to be sitting there thinking about his sister's best friend the way he was. A girl he had known for years, and a girl he hadn't even looked at in that way ever before in his life.

But now that was all that consumed him.

Finn needed to stay as far away from her as he could. He needed to make sure he didn't look at her, didn't talk to her, didn't even breathe in her direction. The next thing on his list had to be looking for an apartment. He would talk to Luna and Valerio about getting some money so he could get a place far enough away from this house so he could escape the bullshit.

Maybe that would solve it all. Once he moved out and they weren't forced to be under the same roof anymore, he wouldn't be stuck in his current predicament.

He let his shoulders relax for a moment, but the raging hard-on between his thighs stood as stiff as ever. When was the last time he had fucked someone? Months ago?

That could have been another reason for why he was so pent up. He hadn't had a good fuck in so long. That was going on his list too. Finding an apartment and someone to fuck. Both things would get his mind back in order, he was sure of it.

He got out of the shower, unwilling to let himself get anywhere near his dick while Gianna was still swirling his mind. That was a cliff he wasn't willing to jump off.

Finn dried off before walking over to his closet, throwing on black jeans and a black hoodie. It was warm enough that he wouldn't need much else for his ride tonight. He laced up his boots and walked out of the room, keeping his steps light.

All he needed to do was head straight for the stairs and grab his bike to get away for the night. As long as he could do that, he would be fine.

But a weird tingling started at the base of his spine when he realized that she might have been home. Her door was at the very end of the hall, two doors down from his. One of the rooms between them was occupied by Blair and the other was an empty guest room that had been used by Augustus once upon a time. It was a blessing that there was so much space keeping them apart.

If he turned around, he could get to it in a couple of quick steps, which would be a horrible idea. She had either gone out with everyone else, or she was sleeping—considering how late it was into the night—so it was a good idea for him to mind his own business either way.

But his legs seemed to have a mind of their own.

He shouldn't have felt so giddy walking up to her door. He leaned in to see if he could hear anything. It was silent. Not a single thing could be heard.

Perfect chance to walk away.

Instead, he grabbed the doorknob and twisted it open. One look to see if she was home or not. It was a good enough excuse in case anyone asked him what he was doing. Or perhaps it was just good enough to convince himself.

The door squeaked slightly as he pushed it open. His eyes found the bed instantly and saw a body there.

She was home then. She hadn't gone out with everyone else.

There didn't seem to be any movement to indicate that the sound woke her, so he took that as his chance to enter fully, once again surrounded by all the pink and white in the room. She had a small flower night light plugged into the wall beside her bed that lit only that small corner of the room in a warm light.

It was ... *cute*.

She laid on the bed, nearly buried under the pile of blankets she had. Her eyes were closed, and her lips were slightly parted.

She was fine. He was good to leave.

But he stayed standing there, looking at her. Despite her hair being blonde, her eyelashes and eyebrows were still darker. They stood out on her pale skin. Completely makeup-less, he could see the small freckles on her face, how they traced up her forehead, over her nose, and even onto her chin. Finn even noticed the small mole by the side of her nose. He could see just how pink her lips really were and that she didn't always have that aggressive bite to her. She could be serene and peaceful like she was at that moment.

He realized just how close he had gotten to her. The strawberry smell from whatever perfume or lotion she used was stronger now, as if she had just put it on.

Finn looked up at the ceiling, letting out a long sigh. What the fuck was he doing?

"Finn?"

His head snapped over to where her groggy voice came from. Gianna's brows were furrowed as she squinted at him, trying to decipher if he was really there or not. She sat up, rubbing her eyes as Finn moved back.

Shit.

"What are you doing here?" she asked.

He cleared his throat. "I was just making sure you were okay. After the last party, you were kind of a wreck."

"I didn't go to any parties tonight."

He knew that, but did she know he had been home all night?

"Oh, I wasn't sure." He could have done a better job lying, he just hoped that in her loopiness she wouldn't question it any further. "I'll let you sleep then. Sorry for waking you up."

"Wait ..." She reached for his arm. Her hand was cold compared to his, and his skin shouldn't have lit up in goosebumps the way it did when she touched him. "I need to ask you something before you go."

"What?"

She opened and closed her mouth a couple times as if she couldn't come up with the right words. If he had to guess, she was probably going to ask about the fight.

His excuse? Shit, he wasn't sure he had a good answer for it.

"Why?" she started.

"Why what?"

"Why did you fight Raphael? And please, don't lie to me."

Finn couldn't help the snort that left his lips. "Since when do we only tell each other the truth?"

"I trusted you with my breakdown, I think we're beyond having to lie about trivial matters," she said. As if realizing she was still holding his hand, she let go, letting her hands grab the blanket instead.

He ignored the feeling of loss and instead tried to think of an answer. Why had he fought Raphael? He told himself it was for revenge, so maybe he could start there.

"He hurt you and you were upset. I would have done it for anyone," he said.

"You didn't have to do it at all. It wasn't your problem to deal with," Gianna said.

He knew that.

"But I did and it's over and done with now. Just let it go." He turned around to leave, but the sound of her jumping off the bed had him stopping in the middle of the room.

"Just let it go? I can't just let it go. You publicly fought someone that I was seeing because he hurt me. That has implications to it," she said.

Finn turned around now, nearly groaning when he saw what she was wearing. A matching pink tank top and shorts set. Nothing else. She should have stayed bundled up under her blankets.

"What sort of implications does it have?" he asked, raising his brow in question.

She shrugged. "I don't know. That there might be something going on between us or that you're a little too involved in your sister's best friend's life."

"Well, anyone who thinks that is a fucking idiot."

Her eyes narrowed at him. "Why would they be an idiot to think that?"

"Because there isn't anything going on between us."

"Of course not because rumor has it, you're off the market." The snarl on her face was apparent, but he was more hung up on what she'd said than anything else.

"What are you talking about?"

"Luna thinks you're seeing someone and that's why you chose to stay around," Gianna said, crossing her arms. "So, if that's true, not only do I feel bad for that obviously miserable girl, but I would rather not get involved in some weird throuple scandal with you and her."

This time Finn couldn't help the sweep of anger that rushed through him. "That is exactly why I didn't want to come back. The bullshit rumors and the stupid judgmental comments. I don't have any secret girlfriend, so you can run back to my sister with that information and let her know, which I know you will. I can also promise that any girl with me isn't miserable, princess. If you haven't been fucked right in so long that you're left feeling miserable, then just say that."

"Excuse me?" she asked, her cheeks burning red.

Finn stalked up to her, leaning in close so she could hear every word that came out of his mouth. "If that's the case, you should be thanking me for what I did to Raphael. Obviously, he hasn't been doing it right."

"You're disgusting. Even if that was the case, I wouldn't fuck you even if you begged me for it," she hissed, her eyes glazed over.

"Princess, if I ever fucked you, all you would be doing is begging."

"Is that why you came into my room? Hoping I'd beg you?"

This time Finn was the one at a loss for words. Anyone would have backed down by now, given in or walked away from the conversation completely. But Gianna hadn't. She pushed and pushed and drove him fucking wild.

From the way she pushed up against his body, he knew she could feel just how hard his cock was in his jeans. Her eyes were a darker shade of blue, the pupils huge and her tone taunting. She didn't back off though—she kept her body against him to make sure he felt every single heavenly curve she had.

And fuck did she have them.

"Too bad that'll never happen," she whispered, giving him a little grin.

"You're sure about that?" he asked.

"Positive."

He watched the way her tongue came out, sliding over the smooth skin of her lips. His eyes followed the movement like a moth to a flame, completely mesmerized.

Nothing would ever happen between them. Not in the future, at least. But right now? Shit, why not?

"Fuck it," Finn growled.

He wrapped his hands in her hair, pushing his lips against hers. The spark that ignited when they met scared the shit out of him, but it felt too good to pull away. Her lips were soft, and expecting her kiss to be gentle was completely wrong because she met every single bit of heat and anger that he gave her.

She pulled at his hair, wrapping her hands in it the same way he did to her. But he let his hands wander down the length of her neck, her spine, and the curve of her ass. Perfection. Every inch of her was absolutely perfect.

Had he ever been kissed like this? He didn't think so. There wasn't a single moment he could think of that compared to the thrill he had from her kiss, other than his first fight. The rush of adrenaline, of excitement, of feeling alive.

And when she pulled back, lips swollen and eyes wide, he knew he'd fucked up.

One kiss wasn't enough. That was a high he needed to chase again.

THIRTEEN

GIANNA

HUMANS WERE FLAWED INDIVIDUALS. Or at least that was what the self-help book Gianna purchased said. She had never been a reader, always choosing to watch a movie or show instead, but she was having a life crisis. No one had made a book about what to do if you kissed your best friend's brother and liked it, so instead she stuck to how to become a better person.

She couldn't undo her mistake, but she could stop herself from making any more in the future.

To be completely honest, she had been a mess. Not a small manageable mess, but a huge 'need to call a cleanup crew' mess. She couldn't figure out why he leaned in and kissed her. They were fighting, which to her meant they disliked each other. Sure, maybe she had a small little crush on him, but that wasn't supposed to go anywhere. Gianna sure as hell wasn't planning on kissing him either.

The words on the page slowly started to blend into gibberish and her mind drifted off into thinking about how Finn's hands wrapped up in her hair, his mouth devouring hers. She slammed the book closed.

He was a damn good kisser. Too good. Where did he learn to kiss like that?

She shut down the jealousy that swept through her at the thought. She needed extensive therapy, or some sort of retreat away from this house to clear her mind. Being here wasn't helping her, especially when she could sense his presence down the hall.

It was like her body was hyperaware of him, immediately lining her body up with goosebumps and wanting to repeat what happened the other night all over again.

She grabbed her phone off the side table, immediately scrolling through her messages on social media from boys who wanted her, but she never gave the time of day to. She ignored the disgusting ones and instead focused on the ones from boys she knew. Gianna eliminated the ones that were annoying, the ones she had already been with, and the ones she knew had girlfriends. It left her with a decent selection to go through.

One stood out to her. His name was Dylan. He was cute, looked sporty, and went to their school. He had blonde hair and more of a boy next door vibe, which she might have been into before if her mind wasn't corrupted by someone else. She didn't hesitate to message him, getting a response back asking if she wanted to meet up for coffee later in the week.

Perfect. A date on the books meant she had something and someone else to focus on, so her mind wasn't rotting on Finn anymore. For all she knew, Dylan could be the love of her life.

Something in her gut told her he wasn't, but she ignored it anyway.

Gianna got up from her bed, practically skipping downstairs with a new pep in her step. She made her way into the kitchen where both Cecilia and Blair were sitting, eating a bowl of pasta.

"There's some dinner if you want it," Blair said, motioning to the stove.

"I think I will have some," she said with a grin, grabbing a bowl.

"Why do you seem so joyful?" Cecilia asked.

"No reason." She shrugged, pouring herself some of the pasta.

"She's probably on something," Dante said, pushing her to the side to grab the entire pot for himself.

"Excuse me, I was still trying to grab some," she said, hitting him with her fork.

He gave her the middle finger, stealing her fork and sitting down at the counter. "Be quicker next time, Barbie."

"So really, why are you so happy?" Blair asked.

Gianna turned around, a grin on her face. She set her bowl down, pausing for dramatics. "I have a date."

"Congrats, who's the lucky boy?" Cecilia asked, raising her brow in question.

"His name is Dylan and he's on the soccer team," she said.

"Since when are you into sporty?" Dante asked, snorting.

"Since always. Shut up."

"When's the date?" Blair asked.

"It's on Thursday. He's taking me to get coffee like a gentleman," Gianna said.

"Coffee? That's it?" a deep voice asked.

Gianna's face fell. She knew it was Finn. Her body could sense him.

He walked in with Augustus, the latter immediately walking over to Cecilia.

"I'm surprised security let you in," Cecilia said, her face immediately turning sour when he sat beside her. "I thought I put your picture on the enemy list so they would have no choice but to tackle you down."

"I hacked the system and changed it back," Augustus said. "You're gonna have to try harder to keep me out."

"You didn't answer my question," Finn said, directing Gianna's attention back to him. If it was up to her, she would rather watch Cecilia and Augustus fight for the rest of the day.

She turned to face him, trying hard to keep her face neutral, or at least she assumed she did. The butterflies in her stomach fluttered so rapidly she thought she might throw up.

"I didn't hear it."

He gave her a sarcastic smile. "You're settling for a coffee date? I thought you had higher standards."

"It's a first date."

"Are you worried about him being able to pay for you?"

She clenched her jaw. What the hell was he doing? "I hadn't even thought about it."

"Hmm." Finn walked over to the fridge, forcing Gianna to watch him in confusion.

"What does that mean?"

"I didn't say anything."

"What do you guys think?" Gianna asked.

Blair shrugged. "I honestly didn't care."

Cecilia shrugged sheepishly. "Well, to be honest I was surprised. I mean, you have really strict standards for guys to meet on your first dates."

"I do not," Gianna hissed, sending Cecilia a glare. "Maybe I did before, but I'm a changed woman now."

"Enlighten us on what changed your life." Dante snorted, shoveling another mouthful of pasta into his mouth.

Finn turned around, a smirk on his face. "Yeah, what's made you change?"

Gianna returned it with her own. "I had the worst kiss of my life."

Cecilia gasped. "You're joking!"

Gianna shook her head. "Made me consider celibacy."

Watching Finn's face change from amusement to pure anger was worth tarnishing the moment they had shared. Of course it was a complete lie, but he wouldn't get the satisfaction of knowing that.

"That is tragic," Augustus muttered.

"When was this?" Blair asked.

Gianna paused for a moment. She hadn't been out anywhere considering she bailed on going out with them this past time and she had been beyond busy with practice lately, which they all knew. So, when did it happen?

She cleared her throat. "Fight Night. I skipped the party to meet up with someone, but it was the worst decision of my life."

"Let your brother hear you say that, and he'll never let you out of his sight again," Dante told her, shaking his head in amusement.

Allister was the least of her worries. Not when Finn looked at her in a way that told her he was going to get her back. His eyes were darker than usual and the smile on his face was full of malice. She swallowed harshly.

"Looks like you dodged a bullet with that one," Finn said, shaking his head.

Gianna shrugged nonchalantly. "You're right about that."

It was a miracle that no one else seemed to pick up on the tension between them, and she couldn't be more thankful for it. Especially when he walked past her, letting his hand skim past her lower back as he did so.

She tensed up completely and couldn't relax until he had walked out of the kitchen with Augustus. Only once she was sure he was far enough away did the air return to her lungs. She grabbed another fork from the drawer and finally started to eat the pasta.

Their words made it sound like they had ended everything between them.

So why did it feel he was just getting started?

FOURTEEN

GIANNA

THE MUSIC FLOWED through the studio and sweat dripped off Gianna's face as she leaped and spun to hit every single one of her moves. As soon as her last class for the day ended, she headed straight to the studio to make sure she had enough time to practice. Her performance was still a bit away, but every time she went to hit the *grand jeté*, she stumbled and looked like a giraffe just beginning to walk rather than an experienced dancer. She desperately wanted to get it down already.

She didn't know how long she'd been at the studio for, but all her classmates were already gone and so were her instructors. Gianna had decided to practice on campus rather than at home, mostly to avoid the plague that seemed to linger there more often than not.

She hadn't seen him since she revealed to everyone in the kitchen that she was going on a date, but she could *feel* him everywhere. His presence was so ominous, leaving her with sickening anxiety constantly.

She couldn't handle it, so staying out of the house for as long as possible was the best solution.

Gianna stopped, feeling the soreness in her calves. She was overdoing her body and if she didn't stop now, she would no doubt be entering into injury territory, which was the last thing she needed. Icing her feet and sitting with some cereal sounded like the best way to end her night. Plus, she still needed to do all her date prep for her coffee meet-up tomorrow.

Sure, she was excited, but the date didn't spark the same thrill that others had in the past and she wasn't sure why.

You know why.

Nope. She had no idea.

She took off the pointe shoes and the tape from her toes, letting them stretch and breathe. She rolled out her legs briefly, letting out groans from how good the pain felt before she rolled out her foot. The stretches were equally her least favorite and her most favorite part of her routine. She stood up, stretching out her spine in the process, and tugged on a pair of sweatpants over her tights and a pair of fuzzy boots that were more like slippers.

With everything thrown into her bag haphazardly, she hoisted it over her shoulder and walked out of her studio. Her time walking to the car was usually when she caught up on her phone. She refused to let herself get distracted with it during practice, especially if someone decided to send something horrible.

Like Allister texting that their mother was coming back for another visit soon and they would have to go back home to see her.

Gianna stopped walking, her heart halting.

For the life of her, she couldn't understand why her mother even bothered seeing them once a year or why their father made them show up to the visits. She left them when they were children, abandoning them because she didn't want to be a mother anymore. She'd only decided on it after she had Gianna, though.

They had been raised by their father and nannies, seeing their mother as often as they saw Santa.

Maybe calling that woman her mother was too strong of a word because that was something she had never been and never would be.

Gianna shoved her phone back into her bag, taking a deep

breath as she started walking again. She needed to push it down for now. Bury it deep, deep inside of her where she could pretend that her mother leaving when she was three years old didn't make her feel like she was the problem.

You are unlovable.

There it was. That nasty voice again. The one that came at the worst times but told her the truth.

She lifted her hand, biting on the skin around her fingers. She hated being alone for this reason. When she was alone, that was when she felt the most abandoned, even if she knew she had a whole network of people at home who supported her.

She would be home soon and then she would find Allister and Blair and Cecilia, maybe even Luna and Valerio and Dante, and then she could rest her mind.

She dropped her hand, going to reach for her phone again. Maybe she could call one of them while she walked. That would ease her mind.

A hand wrapped around her mouth, pulling her against a firm body. She gasped, her body tensing. Then she started to fight, thrashing her body against the unknown assailant, trying to scream for anyone to help her.

"You seriously need to be more aware of your surroundings, princess."

Her brows furrowed. Why the hell did that voice sound so familiar?

"Look how easily you recognize my voice," he said, leaning close to her ear. "You know who it is."

Finn.

He turned her around, still keeping his hand covering her mouth tightly. She desperately tried to ignore the way his arm held her waist, the way he pushed her body up against his.

She was getting distracted.

"I'm going to remove my hand. Don't scream—or do, I don't give a shit," Finn said, a wicked grin on his face.

Gianna frowned, pushing him as soon as he removed his

hand, but he didn't move an inch. "What the hell is wrong with you? Why would you do something like that? You scared the hell out of me."

"You're so careless, you didn't notice that I have been following you since you left the studio."

"What are you doing here?"

"Giving you a ride home like the sweet man I am."

She looked at him skeptically. It was hard to believe a single word that left that beautiful mouth of his. "I have a car waiting for me."

"I sent it home."

"You don't have a car."

"I have my bike."

"I'm not getting on that death trap," she screeched, trying to pull away.

"I have a helmet for you." He grabbed her arm and pulled her along. "You'll be fine."

Gianna looked at the bike that was parked by the sidewalk. It was one of those that people raced obnoxiously fast, not the type that biker gangs had.

"Nope. I can't do it," she said, putting all her strength into tensing her body so he couldn't pull her along.

It didn't matter when all he needed to do was lift her and carry her over to the bike. He held her awkwardly, as if he didn't know where to put his hands, but it was such a short walk that she was back standing in no time.

He grabbed a helmet, handing it over to her. She crossed her arms. "I'm not putting that on."

Finn simply shrugged. "Okay."

He sat the helmet on her head, pushing it down without a moment of hesitation. She stumbled at the action.

"Asshole. You could have let me undo my bun first."

"I gave you the option. You didn't take it."

She slid up the visor, looking at him with narrowed eyes.

"Where am I supposed to put my bag, genius? It's not like your bike has a trunk."

He glared at her. "Don't insult my bike."

He opened a small compartment where another helmet sat, taking it out. He grabbed the bag off her shoulder and placed it inside. He closed it with a look on his face that dared her to try to make another complaint.

"I'm still not getting on."

Finn threw one leg over the bike, hopping on like it was completely natural for him. It almost looked like second nature. He turned it on, revving the engine.

"Then I guess you'll have to find a way home without your phone."

She was confused until she realized that her phone was in the bag that he was now sitting on. She let out a growl, pushing down the visor and getting on the bike behind him. It was uncomfortable to say the least. She tried to keep as much space between them as she could, but every time she did, her body slipped down until she was flush against him.

She kept her hands beside her, waiting for this nightmare to be over. They lived close to campus so it would hopefully be a quick ride.

Finn put on his helmet and kicked up the stand. Without a moment to waste, he took off full speed onto the road. Gianna screamed, wrapping her arms around his body to keep from flying off. That was exactly what it was. To protect herself, nothing more.

She hadn't realized she closed her eyes, but when she opened them, she saw they had already passed their neighborhood. In fact, they weren't anywhere near it.

The trees around them had become denser, the lights and access to the world scarcer.

She swallowed harshly, finally understanding the predicament she was in.

He had set his trap, and she had fallen into it completely.

FIFTEEN

GIANNA

WHETHER HE HEARD her calling his name to slow down during the ride or not, Gianna wasn't sure. What she did know was that they were in the middle of the woods. Alone. At night.

Finn drove for a little bit longer until he pulled up to what looked like a dock that extended several feet into the nearly invisible lake. She wouldn't have even known there was a lake if it wasn't for the moon that lit up enough of the sky to allow for the reflection to be seen.

It was creepy, no doubt, but there was also something serene about it.

A perfect place to die, it seemed.

He cut off the bike, and the moment he did, Gianna leapt off. She took off the helmet, holding it in front of her like some sort of weapon.

"Why did you bring me here?" she asked, her voice strong despite how scared she was.

He stared at her for a moment, not making a single sound. She couldn't even see his face to see what he was thinking. He was like a shell of a person, devoid of everything for that one moment.

Until he let out a loud laugh that had him throwing his head back.

She frowned, furrowing her eyebrows in confusion.

What the hell was so funny?

"Do you really think that helmet could do something to me?" he asked, getting off the bike.

"Come here so we can find out," she told him. "Now, answer my question. Why did you bring me here?"

He shook his head, taking off his helmet and setting it on the seat. "Why do you think I brought you here?"

"I don't know. To kill me?"

"Wow. If you had that much intuition while you were walking alone on campus, you probably wouldn't have gotten kidnapped."

Gianna threw the helmet at him, but he caught it with ease. "That's not funny."

"Neither is the wild shit you come up with in that pretty little head of yours." He put the other helmet on the seat as well, crossing his arms as he looked at her. "If you're finished with your little freakout, I'd like to have a chance to talk."

Her shoulders fell. "Talk? About what?"

Finn didn't say anything. He just started walking towards the dock, forcing her to follow him. The old wood creaked and groaned under them as they walked, and there were missing parts that showed the dark water underneath, but he seemed to know exactly where to step. It was like he had been there before.

He got to the very end of the dock, taking a seat at the edge and letting his legs dangle. Gianna looked at him suspiciously, wondering if he would push her in and hold her down if she took a seat too.

"You're safe to sit," he finally said, letting her mind rest.

She did, keeping a good amount of distance between them. It was so silent. Usually the silence scared her, left her feeling completely alone and sent her mind whirling. But for some reason, sitting here in this silence, she felt relaxed. Other than the occasional owl and Finn's breathing, there was nothing else out there.

"Finn, why are we here? It's late, I'm hungry, and to be honest, I'm really not in the mood for whatever game you're trying to play."

She turned to look at him, but his dark brown eyes were already staring at her. His gaze was too intense; it made her want to look away, but she forced herself to stare back. In situations with guys, she was the one who held the upper hand, who played them like puppets and had them falling on their knees for her. Not him. He played her and she hated it.

But it wasn't in the same way Raphael—the dumbass—had broken her heart out of his own selfishness and desire for being an asshole. Finn played the game *with* her. He matched her moves before she even realized it.

"I wanted to know if you were still going on that date tomorrow."

Immediately the same walls she had up earlier were back.

"Why?"

"Just asking. Now that we're friends and all."

"We're not friends."

"Since when?"

"Since always."

"Well, didn't seem that way when you had your tongue down my throat—"

"That was all you!" she screeched, pointing her finger at him. "You kissed me."

Finn leaned in closer, his smirk growing. "You kissed me back, though of course it was apparently the worst kiss you have ever had in your life. I would say by the little moans that escaped your mouth and how tightly you held onto me that you enjoyed it more than you're letting on. Hell, I would even bet that you went to bed with a soaking wet pussy, princess."

Gianna's mouth dropped open. The filthy words leaving his mouth shouldn't have sounded so fucking delicious, but they did. And all it did was remind her of how good that kiss was—how often she had thought about it since then.

"You're disgusting," she said, trying to make the words sound aggressive. Instead, they came out of her mouth sounding more breathless than she had intended.

"Tell me, did you slip your hand into those tiny little shorts and play with yourself before you went to bed, or did you leave yourself frustrated?" Finn asked.

The words sounded like honey leaving his mouth, but they were wrong. All of it was so fucking wrong. He was her best friend's brother. She had known him forever; she had never even thought about him in that way.

And she still didn't.

No, she didn't.

"Shut up," she growled, pushing him away.

He grabbed her hands, pulling her body closer to his. His warmth surrounded every single inch of her skin, and she hated how much she liked it.

She needed to hate it; she needed to snap out of it. For God's sake, she needed to get a grip.

"Did you think it was me doing it for you? What did you imagine? My tongue or my fingers?" His eyes were dark, matching the thickness of his voice. "Is that why you're going on that date tomorrow? Because you're hoping that boy will get you off? Let me tell you, princess, no one will give you the same feeling I did, and I haven't even touched your pussy yet."

His hand drifted from her wrist, stroking up her arm and over her shoulder before it reached the back of her neck. Her lips parted, suddenly so aware of how close he was, how good his touch felt, and how fucking wet she was.

"Too bad you pissed me off with your words the other day," he said, shrugging. Then, he pulled away from her completely, leaving her feeling cold and empty once again.

Gianna blinked, coming out of her daze. "What the fuck?"

"Let's go. Don't want people to start wondering where you went."

He stood, holding his hand out for her. She ignored it,

standing without his help. She swore she could feel steam leaving her ears, her cheeks most likely a bright shade of red.

Once again, he trapped her. He lured her in, and she fell for it completely.

She stomped back to the bike, not willing to look at him. One glimpse at that arrogant face and she was scared she might actually attack him.

How could she have let him get a leg up on her again? She needed to focus. Gianna wasn't the type that let any man play her and that was what she was forgetting. She was becoming too soft, too easy to play with.

If Finn wanted to play, she would beat him at his own game.

SIXTEEN

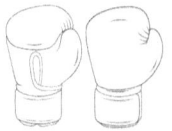

FINN

HANGING around Augustus again was proving to be a bad idea because here Finn was, following Gianna to her date. At this point, he might as well have been following Augustus's handbook on how to stalk because Finn was out of control, hacking into her phone to find the boy she was going on a date with, running a full background check on him, and showing up to the cafe even before she did.

At the dock, he saw how much she wanted him. From her wide pupils that replaced the blues of her eyes, to her parted lips, to even how much she hung onto every word he said. He teased the hell out of her, but as a result he was left driving home with the hardest fucking dick he'd had in years. He so badly wanted to lean over and make her crumble, but her words hurt his feelings.

Finn got her back, or at least he thought he did. Honestly, it seemed like he was just punishing himself because he wanted a taste of her. She seemed willing to give in, but after last night, that was doubtful.

Even more so because she had actually shown up to the date. Gianna giggled and laughed at everything Dylan said even though it wasn't funny. Finn couldn't hear them, but after finding out

LEJLA MURIC

what a dumbass the boy was, there was no doubt in his mind he wasn't saying anything profound.

He knew she wasn't enjoying the date either. She kept fidgeting as if she was already prepared for it to end and her eyes kept looking at her phone. She even stuck to a hot chocolate instead of ordering her usual coffee that somehow ended up costing an absurd amount of money because of all her substitutions and add-ons.

Why?

Because his words had gotten to her. She probably hated that they did. That he was able to get under her skin.

Good. She was finally able to see what Finn had been dealing with for weeks now. Once Gianna got under his skin, it was impossible to get her to leave. The only difference was that he didn't want her to go anywhere, which was why he was stalking.

God forbid it actually went well, and she fell for the sorry son-of-a-bitch. She would be mourning him just as quickly.

The Dylan boy stood from the table, heading towards the bathroom. Gianna's shoulders fell and the mask slipped off her face. She took another sip of the hot chocolate, grimacing at the taste. Finally, a frown settled on those perfect, plump lips.

She looked miserable.

Good.

She needed to see that no one else could make her feel the way he did and no matter how wild it drove her, she would just have to accept it.

Did he accept it?

Heh, fuck it. Finn was beyond caring about much now because it seemed like nothing ever truly made sense in his life anyways. He ran away and then was forced back home. He hated his father and was even willing to kill him, but then he grieved his death. He was an asshole and then felt immediate remorse. He knew feeling anything towards Gianna was wrong, but he also knew that nothing had ever felt more fucking right.

His mind and his life were full of contradictions.

Dylan came back from the bathroom, a big smile on his face. Gianna looked up at him, standing in an awkward way to let him know that she was done with the date. He grabbed her arm, saying something to her, but if he was smart, he would let her go before he lost that arm completely.

Gianna leaned in, placing her lips on his cheek before leaving the cafe.

If Finn had been in therapy, he would have known to count to ten and to breathe before he did anything irrational. But he wasn't.

His feet carried him over to Dylan and without a moment of hesitation, he grabbed him by the scruff of the neck, slamming him against the table. Customers and the cafe workers let out startled screams, but they didn't need to be alarmed. He wasn't coming for them.

Finn leaned down, his voice full of malice. A raw threat to the boy who trembled underneath him. "If you ever talk to Gianna again, I'll make sure no one ever finds you. Are we understood?"

Dylan nodded his head like a coward, the fear in his eyes appeasing Finn enough to let him go. Without a second thought, he ran out of the cafe, his feet squeaking against the floor. Finn took his time, not bothering to look at the staff or anyone as he left. They knew who he was. If they were smart, they would stay out of it and most of the people on campus knew to do exactly that.

He felt accomplished for the day now that he didn't have to worry about Gianna finding another boyfriend. Dare he say that he even had a little pep in his step, though his face wouldn't show it.

Finn decided to head back to the house, knowing that was exactly where she would be going since she didn't have class today and she didn't have her dance bag with her to practice with. Perhaps he had dived a little too far into her files once he realized he could, but it was harmless.

She must have taken a car home because he couldn't spot her

anywhere. He couldn't blame her; a disaster of a date like that would leave him wanting a quick escape too.

His bike still waited in the same parking space, so he jumped on and reared it to life. He put the helmet on that she wore the other night because it was stamped with that strawberry perfume she used. The smell was addicting and when he pulled into the garage, he had to rip it off his head or he would have kept it on for the rest of his life.

The house was silent when he walked in. It was more common than not that it was empty, which Finn had actually come to appreciate, but that would end as soon as the semester did. With most of the house still in class and the others who fucking knew where, Finn had time to relax during the day. Living with other people like this was hell. He needed to get his own place, and he could now, but something held him back.

Or someone.

He walked around the house, finding every single light off and every room empty. Even the staff were out for the day, it seemed. Finn went upstairs, purely curious to see if she had made it home or not. Keeping his footsteps light, he made his way to her door and saw the lights were on from underneath the door.

Gianna was home and so was Finn. It was just the two of them now. At home, alone. That felt dangerous.

He walked back to his room, seeing the door was slightly ajar. Immediately, he knew something was up. He always closed his door completely, no matter what. Someone had been in there without his permission.

Finn pushed the door open and walked inside. At first glance, everything looked normal. Nothing was destroyed or out of place. He didn't have much in the room in the first place, but the things he did have remained where they were. The books on the desk were still in the same order, the picture frame on the bedside table was still face down, even his laptop remained unmoved and closed.

He checked the closet. Clear. Then the bathroom. Also, clear.

Was this just someone playing a trick on him knowing it would drive him mad if he couldn't figure out why someone came into his room?

He was close to running into Gianna's room to ask her if she was up to it when he finally saw it. On the bed was delicate lacy pink material laid out perfectly in the center with a small note right beside it. He walked towards it, grabbing the underwear in one hand and the note in the other.

Wore these on my date. I guess you can say I had a great time!

Even her handwriting was fucking perfect and pristine, but what stood out to him was the wet spot on the underwear. She was lying. He watched her that whole fucking date. She was miserable the entire time. That boy hadn't even touched her.

This had to have been from after the date, not during.

He groaned, throwing his head back. The fucking tease was getting him back for last night.

He ran out of the room, going straight to her door and not bothering to knock before he let himself in. She wasn't there, but he heard the shower running in the bathroom. He shut the door behind him, making his way to her. Steam and humidity hit him from whatever hellish temperature she kept the water at.

Her back was turned to him inside the all-glass shower, and he didn't bother to stop himself from admiring every single curve of her body. She turned around with her hands still in her hair, letting out a gasp at his intrusion. It took her a moment to make the connection between what was in his hand and the snarl on his face, but once she did, a smirk set on her lips. "I see you found my gift."

"What is this?" he asked, his voice sounding more like a growl.

"What? Never seen a pair of women's underwear before? Huh, I should have guessed that was the case," she told him, crossing her arms. All it did was bring attention to her breasts, making him her puppet as she guided his attention wherever she wanted it and he let her.

Finn stalked closer to the shower, feeling the heat of it seeping into his already feverish skin. "What the fuck were they doing on my bed?"

She gave him an innocent smile, showing off her perfectly white teeth. "Well, since you were so curious about it last night, I fucked myself with my fingers after my date and left the evidence all over my underwear for you to see. Want to know who I was thinking about while I was doing it?"

He could feel himself getting really close to snapping. She knew it too. She was playing a dangerous game, and maybe she didn't know what she was getting herself into. Finn Kingsley at his core was a selfish bastard. Once an heir to the Kingsley empire, that throne was now waiting for him to fill it. He knew how to be ruthless; he knew how to be terrifying—it was in his blood.

And yet, she didn't back down for a moment. It was like she didn't care or maybe it excited her to play with such danger, with so much *fire*.

"Choose your next words very fucking wisely, Gianna," he snarled.

"I was thinking about—"

Finn didn't let her finish. He ripped open the door of the shower, soaking himself in the process, but it didn't matter as soon as his lips were on hers once again.

He could feel the electricity sparking between them all over again, somehow making this kiss feel even more explosive than the last. His hands found her waist, picking her up and pushing her back against the tiled wall. Her nails raked down his back, leaving marks in their wake that would last for a couple days, but for some reason the thought drove him wild.

His tongue found hers, fighting and devouring every inch that it could, leaving them out of breath and dizzy. Fuck, she tasted delicious. She tasted perfect. Maybe he wasn't the one to be wary of; she was.

She was the danger; she was the fire.

His hands traced every inch of skin they could, grabbing her ass painfully, forcing her to gasp against him. He pulled away for a moment, panting and staring at her wide eyes. She looked upset at their loss of contact, and it almost made him smile. A real genuine one, not the fake bullshit he learned to put on over the years.

"Don't tell me you're going to leave me hanging again," she said.

"Wouldn't dream of it, princess."

He leaned down, leaving bruising kisses along her neck and biting the skin to leave marks on her. An opportunity for any asshole out there to know that she wasn't available, that they had no chance in hell with her.

The thought of her going on some date with another asshole had him leaving them everywhere he could, following a trail down her collarbone, the top of her left tit, before he finally wrapped his mouth around her nipple. He knew he would never get into Heaven, but hearing her moan the way she did seemed the closest to it.

His cock pulsed, reminding him of how fucking suffocated it was inside the soaked pants while her pussy grinded against it, back and forth.

He slid one hand between them, finding her soaking pussy. He ran a finger through her slit, dragging it up slowly to her clit. With slow circles he pushed against it, working moans from her lips that had her arching her back in need.

"You're so fucking wet," he said, moving to her other breast. He worked his finger quicker before slowing down, eliciting a groan from her just like he wanted.

"Stop teasing me," she growled, pulling his hair. She undid the button of his pants and tried to push them down his hips.

"Don't tell me what to do." He bit her nipple slightly, forcing another breathless gasp out of her lips. "Do you have a condom in here?"

"No, usually the guy brings them," she said. "I've never slept with anyone without one."

"Fucking hell," he said. "I've never fucked anyone without one, but I haven't been with anyone in months. I didn't think to get any."

"I'm on the pill," Gianna told him, her eyes dazed as he pushed the finger inside of her now. "We'll get some later, just fuck me now."

He let his jeans slip down his legs, his cock springing up against his stomach. She didn't hesitate to grab it, surrounding it with her hand, moving it up and down. Finn groaned, throwing his head back. "Who's the fucking tease now?"

He bent his finger, fucking her with it before he took it out completely. She went to complain but stopped the moment he guided his dick to her pussy, letting it rub against her clit. She looked at him with glazed eyes, a look of content on her face that changed the moment he slammed inside of her.

She gasped, her eyes widening. Finn groaned, leaning his forehead against hers. She squeezed him impossibly tight, suffocating his cock like she was made for him. Fuck, there was no doubt in his mind anymore that she was.

He grabbed onto her thighs, holding her tightly before he began really fucking her, thrusting with every single bit of energy he had left in him. She held onto him, her eyes closed as she let breathless moan after moan escape her.

"I wonder who you're going to think about after this," Finn said, biting her ear as he made sure she heard every single word. "I wonder if you're still gonna try to entertain any of those worthless fucking boys knowing that you're going to be filled with my cum, knowing that you're going to be covered in my marks, princess."

He picked up the speed of his thrusts, lifting her hips so he hit a part inside of her that had her gasping for air.

"Answer me, princess, or I'll stop right now."

"No, don't," she begged, leaning her forehead against his.

"Are you gonna go on any more dates? Entertain any more boys?" he asked.

He could feel her squeezing around him, almost as if she liked when he talked this way to her.

"Fuck," she groaned.

"Gianna," he warned. He began slowing down, just to prove a point.

"No," she cried out, shaking her head. "I won't."

"Then, I think my princess deserves to come."

If she was waiting for his permission, he wasn't sure, but at those words she came harshly, biting down on his shoulder to keep from screaming out. She rested there for a moment, finally lifting her head just as he was about to come.

And when he did, he connected their lips, making sure he filled her with every last drop he had to offer her. The kiss was still full of hunger, as if they hadn't just fucked and were ready to do it all over again.

Shit, he probably would.

Instead, he put her down, holding her up on wobbly legs. He finally took off his soaking wet clothes, leaving both of them in the shower, completely naked, and freshly fucked.

Then it hit him.

He'd just had sex with Gianna Moretti.

SEVENTEEN

GIANNA

"OH MY GOD," Gianna screeched, pushing Finn away. She couldn't believe she had let herself get seduced by him, that she had slept with him. She really screwed up, beyond anything that was able to be fixed or amended.

"What the hell is wrong with you?" he asked, trying to rinse off.

"Nothing much, other than the fact that I have your cum sliding down my leg," she whisper-screamed. She wanted to rip out her hair, or maybe rip out his, or maybe sleep with him again.

What the hell was happening to her?

"We're adults, it's not like we're doing something illegal," he said.

"You are Luna's brother, who is my best friend, who is married to my cousin, who is going to tell my brother, who will all hate me and kill you if anyone ever found out," she said, the panic thick in her throat. "It's girl code. How could I do that to Luna?"

"What exactly did you do to her? I'm my own person," he said.

"Did you not hear a single thing I just said?" she asked, throwing her hands up in the air. "I just betrayed my friendship."

"That's dramatic. She'll understand."

Gianna scoffed, shoving a finger into his chest. "She will absolutely not understand a single thing because no one will ever hear about this literally ever. Do you understand me?"

He smirked, wrapping his hands around her waist and pulling her closer. "So what? I'm your dirty little secret now?"

"You're insufferable," she muttered, pulling away. "How are you planning on getting out of here, by the way? Your clothes are soaking wet."

He shrugged. "I'll walk down the hall naked."

Gianna let out a sarcastic laugh. "Oh, yeah. I'm sure that'll go over perfectly with everyone who lives here."

She turned off the water, finally getting out herself. Her skin was pruney and the bathroom was covered in a thick layer of moisture and heat. She needed to get some fresh air. Maybe that would help her think a little bit more logically about everything.

After wrapping a towel around herself, she threw him one before marching out of the bathroom. The cool air of the bedroom hit her immediately and it felt like a relief until he came barreling after her with the towel around his waist hardly covering anything.

She walked to her closet, grabbing the first clothes she saw, which happened to be a sweatshirt and shorts, before throwing them on and wrapping the towel around her hair instead. Stepping out of the closet, she saw Finn eyeing his back in her vanity mirror.

His back was scratched up by her nails, but there were also plenty of little white scars that lined the surface of his skin. They looked like past scars that had been healed, but the fact that they covered the entirety of his back was concerning. From the crisscross appearance of them, she knew it couldn't have been past lovers or even her doing this time. She hated to even think about it, but it almost looked like lashings from a whip or something. If it was, who the hell would have done that to him?

"Do you have claws on your hands?" he asked, giving her a

mischievous look. She felt her face turn red, her thoughts getting averted for the moment.

"You can keep staring at yourself or you can tell me where your clothes are so you're not standing around naked all day," Gianna said, walking towards the door.

"I thought you would have preferred me this way," he said, motioning to his half naked body.

She rolled her eyes, walking out of the room and quickly making her way to his. Thankfully, it didn't seem like anyone was home yet. She tried being quiet earlier, but if no one was home then it was fine. No witnesses to the crime.

She entered his room, remembering how good it smelled when she was in there earlier. To think that putting her panties on the bed would have led to what happened in the bathroom. She shook her head.

She went to the closet, which was surprisingly organized. The first things she saw were a pair of black sweats and a gray T-shirt. With those in tow, she closed the door to his room and made her way back to hers, locking up as soon as she entered.

"Here," she said, tossing the clothes on the bed for him. "Get dressed and get out."

"You're kicking me out? No post-fuck cuddle?" Finn asked.

He dropped the towel, exposing himself completely. He didn't seem insecure in the slightest and he had no reason to be. Though Gianna would never admit it to his face, he had an amazing body. He knew how to use all parts of himself, but she would never experience it again, so it didn't matter.

"What happened between us will never happen again. Ever," Gianna said, shaking her head.

Finn pulled the shirt over his head. "You promise, princess?"

She rolled her eyes. "I'm being serious."

"I am too. This was bound to happen." He crossed his arms.

"Well, just because it happened once doesn't mean it has to keep happening," she told him. "This isn't going to go anywhere and I'm trying to get past the whole casual hookups part of my life, hence why I went on a date with Dylan in the first place."

"Don't bring up his fucking name," Finn growled. She was stunned at how quickly his whole demeanor was able to change in the blink of an eye at the mention of something he didn't like. "You said you were done with all of those assholes."

"What I said while you were inside of me doesn't count."

He was in front of her in a second, holding her chin in his hand. "It does to me, so maybe you should watch what you say next time."

She frowned. "Well, I'm not going to be a nun and not date just because you don't like it."

"You won't be."

"I don't get it."

"You'll be dating me."

Gianna's eyes shot open. She was rarely ever at a loss for words —actually, she could count on her hand how many times she had been left without a good comeback or left in silence. She loved to talk. It was actually one of her favorite hobbies. And yet, there wasn't a single reply she could come up with now.

So, she laughed.

She laughed so hard that she snorted and leaned over, grabbing onto his arm for support before she was able to regain her composure after a moment.

"Are you kidding me? Have you not listened to a single thing I've been saying? I just said no one can know about us ever, and now you're suggesting we date? Are you sure you've never fallen off your bike or anything?" she asked, her voice still joking until she realized that his face still held the same stoic, emotionless look.

"Don't be a fucking brat."

"You can't say you want to date and then call me a brat."

"Then what should I call you, princess? My girlfriend?"

She narrowed her eyes. "You're really frustrating."

Finn shrugged. "I've been called worse."

"I'll call you worse."

"I'm sure you will. Call me whatever you want, but if you go around any of those little boys again, I will fucking kill them."

Gianna's mouth fell open before it snapped closed in anger. "So, you can still see whoever you want but I can't?"

"You sound jealous." He grinned, pulling her closer.

"I am not jealous," she hissed.

"You don't have to be because I'm not seeing anyone other than you," Finn said.

He was delusional. This was not going to be a relationship or whatever he was trying to turn it into. It was madness, complete and utter madness, and yet, he still spoke as if he was so sure that he wanted to date her.

Gianna had never seen Finn date a single girl in her life. He had never been the type to commit to anyone, and she sincerely doubted that he'd be starting with her. Hell, she wasn't going to let him experiment with his newfound love of monogamy on her.

"Finn?"

"Hmmm?"

"Get out of my room."

EIGHTEEN

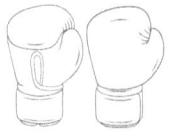

FINN

FINN SAT IN THE GARAGE, a can of beer in his hand and a frown on his face. He truly did not understand women because he and Gianna had a wonderful fucking time in the shower—amazing, the best sex of his life—and then she turned a complete cold shoulder to him.

He said he wanted to date her, that he wouldn't see anyone else, and she wanted nothing to do with him. What the hell was he doing wrong?

This was why he had never been in a relationship before. It always got too complicated, and he never gave a shit to work anything out or to commit to anyone. Everyone was always so *boring*.

Not Gianna. She was a firecracker and drove him up a wall, and he was wild with need. The number of times he had caught himself thinking about her perfect fucking body in the shower, her plump lips, her dazed look, her small smile—fuck, Finn had lost count.

"Have you been listening to me at all?" Augustus asked, throwing the rag at him. He was hunched over some older car, fixing it up as if he gave a shit about it, or maybe he did. Finn thought it was just an excuse for him to be here closer to Cecilia.

"Sorry, I zoned out," Finn said, sitting up. He sat the beer on the counter and walked over to the car, leaning against the side and looking in. "What the hell are you doing there?"

"Fixing the motor."

"Really? Looks like you're breaking it."

"Then it looks like I'll have to be here all the time to fix it." Augustus grinned, taking a drink of his beer.

"Speaking of, how do you deal with a girl not wanting anything to do with you?" Finn asked.

"Why? You have someone in your life now?"

Finn sighed. "Something like that. She's been fucking ignoring me since I said we were dating."

"You asked or you said?" Augustus asked, his brow cocked.

"Are you supposed to ask? I thought it was just like a statement type of thing."

"Dumbass, have you even gone on a date? Been romantic at all?" Augustus asked.

"Why are you asking these questions like it's something I should have fucking known? Seems to me like you don't practice what you preach," he said, getting defensive.

"Me and Cecilia are different." It was left at that. "Who is the girl?"

"I don't know if I should tell you," Finn said, scratching his chin.

Augustus shrugged. "I have cameras all around this house, so I know exactly who it is. I was just giving you a chance to tell me yourself."

Finn waited for some kind of panic or worry to hit him, but neither came. Instead, he nodded his head, making a mental note to find where all those cameras were and to get rid of them. At least any that were obviously harmful to him.

"And what?"

Augustus snorted. "That's all you have to say? I just told you that I know you're fucking Gianna Moretti and you're acting that calm?" He shook his head. "The old you would've been strangling me by now."

"I know you won't say shit because one word and I'll let Cecilia know that you have cameras watching her," he said.

That seemed to do it because Augustus held his hands up in surrender. "You got me there. Seriously though, do you know what you're getting yourself into? She's high maintenance, dramatic, and seems like everything you wouldn't fucking want. How did this even happen?"

Maybe Finn had changed because he felt his blood boiling when Augustus went on and on about Gianna in that way. "It happened because it happened."

"Wise words."

"Fuck off."

"Whatever, man. Maybe if you're dating Gianna, Cecilia will want to do double dates or something," Augustus suggested.

Finn let out a loud laugh. "Did you forget that they both hate us?"

"That's what they say," he said, drinking the rest of his beer. "That doesn't last forever."

He really hoped it didn't because it felt like he was already starting to lose his mind without seeing Gianna. He couldn't even have a simple conversation without it revolving around her. She bulldozed her way in, left her mark, and then tried to leave just like that.

Unfortunately for her, that didn't work for Finn. He hadn't had a reason to stick around before. To settle down and actually create a life for himself in the place where it felt like he was haunted by the reminders of his past. But now he did. Suddenly, he had a reason to stay, he had people in his life he would miss too much.

So, try as she might, but he wasn't going anywhere.

And dare he say, he was finally getting everything his father told him he would never have.

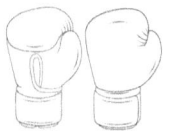

NINETEEN

FINN

ONE WHOLE WEEK. It had been one whole week since Finn had seen Gianna. She ran to her room or surrounded herself with her best friends and brother any chance she got to avoid being around him. If he was worse, he would have simply thrown her over his shoulder and left, but as it stood, most of them still hated him so that would not have gone over well with anyone.

Actually, he didn't know where his relationship with Allister stood. They never really talked. Mostly because he was up Valerio's ass and Finn couldn't have cared less what the loser was doing before. Maybe he needed to care more now. Gianna would want him to have a good relationship with Allister if they ever went public with their relationship.

But where one idiot went, another followed by the name of Dante Vitali. By associating with one, Finn would have to associate with the other. This was exactly why he didn't date—too much fucking work. But when it came to Gianna, he didn't hesitate to do it. He even felt compelled to do it, took the initiative, which was wild in his opinion.

Still, her avoidance was why he approached Allister and Dante as they sat in the study, talking about something that he couldn't care less about. The moment they saw him enter they stopped talking. Dante's eyes narrowed immediately as if he couldn't believe that Finn was in his space. Allister, on the other hand, raised his brow in question.

"Hi," Finn said awkwardly, standing by the entrance. When he couldn't be an asshole, he wasn't sure how to act.

"What are you doing here, Kingsley?" Dante asked, taking a sip of whatever drink he held in his hand.

"Thought I would come here to extend a hand to you both considering I live here, and I don't talk to either of you," Finn said.

Dante went to open his mouth, but Allister was the one to talk first. "Take a seat."

He did. He leaned back on the couch, getting comfortable while they eyed every single movement he made. They all sat there for a moment in silence. Was Finn supposed to say something? How the hell did people even become friends? Should he compliment them?

"Do you want something to drink?" Allister asked.

Thank God.

"Sure," Finn said. Allister grabbed a glass from the center of the table and poured him some scotch, handing it over. He grabbed the glass, swallowing nearly half of it at once. "Thanks."

"How are you liking being back home?" he asked, getting comfortable again. "I know the circumstances weren't necessarily your favorite."

Right, where they drugged him and then Dante knocked him out by hitting him in the head with a gun. No, it really wasn't his favorite.

"Every day gets better," he said. "It's weird being back in this house with everyone considering the last time we all lived together, we were in the middle of a war."

"Well, that's over now," Dante said. His eyes were harsh. "So there's no point in reliving the past."

"Not reliving it, just making an observation," Finn said.

"I can't imagine the transition has been easy for you," Allister said.

"Thanks for saying that," he said, and he genuinely meant it.

Since he had been back, it felt like he was constantly trying to convince everyone of how hard it was for him to be there, but hearing someone acknowledge it themselves felt refreshing. It seemed like Allister was the logical one amidst the wild Vitalis.

"I know that neither of you have to let me stay here, so I want to take you both out. Treat you to drinks," Finn said. He knew they liked their parties, and so if there was one way to get them to tolerate him, or maybe even be friendly, it would be through a wild night out.

Immediately, Dante's eyes lit up. "If you want to treat us with that big fat Kingsley inheritance, then I'm not complaining. Just a heads up, we're expensive."

Finn resisted the urge to roll his eyes. "I think I can handle it."

Allister stood, a grin on his face. "Then I think you have yourself a deal, Kingsley."

Gianna popped into his head. That was who he was doing this for. All for her.

Fuck his life.

When he brought up the idea, Finn thought they would plan for something a few weeks from then. But Allister and Dante had jumped up and dragged him out to some fucking club that night.

They were at some club in the city that was obviously owned by the Vitalis, and yet, they had no issue creating a tab under Finn's name and ordering bottles to it. The club was three stories tall. Each floor was open, acting like a balcony that looked down onto the main dance area at the center of the first floor. Red lighting covered the entire building, making it difficult to see anything clearly, but he assumed that was the point. This seemed like the type of club people hid out at to be as wild as they wanted to be.

They were currently on the third floor, which seemed completely reserved for VIPs because it was decked out with red velvet sofas and a glass table. Dante had invited people up with them, so Finn didn't recognize a single person except the duo he came with.

He used to be the type of person who would have enjoyed this very environment, but now, it seemed like this was the last place he should have been. Things had changed so much in such a short time, and it was hard for him to wrap his fucking head around it.

He sat on one of the sofas with a drink in one hand and his phone in the other. His text conversation with Gianna stared back at him.

Gianna

> Are you awake?
>
> I can't stop thinking about you.
>
> Stop ignoring me, princess.

Yeah, he kept texting, and she kept not responding. He didn't give a shit. It didn't change the fact that she was his now and no matter how much she tried to ignore him, he would make sure he lingered around just to remind her of his presence.

He turned off his phone, sighing. Allister sat down next to him, handing him one of the many bottles on the table.

"Need a refill?" he asked.

"I think I do," Finn said, grabbing it and pouring himself another drink. He didn't know what number this was, but it didn't matter anymore. The burn going down his throat was all that was helping him get through this night.

"You didn't have to do all of this, by the way," Allister said.

He shrugged. "I've been an asshole. It felt like the right thing to do."

"You've been through a lot, and sure the way you handle things is horrible, but I don't think any of us process things in a healthy way. If we did, none of us would be the way we are now." Allister grinned, grabbing a different bottle off the table and refilling his glass.

Finn snorted. "Yeah. You're probably right about that."

They were quiet for a moment, but it wasn't an awkward silence like before. It was comfortable, like two friends just sitting beside each other observing the scene in front of them. Said scene being Dante with his tongue down some dude's throat, but it was still a scene. Finn turned his head away.

"Why aren't you out there partying right now?" Finn asked.

Allister sighed. "It's fucking complicated. You?"

"Same fucking thing."

"You know, Luna suspected there was someone in your life," he said. "We were all trying to figure out if it was true or not."

"I've heard." Finn rolled his eyes. "I love her, but sometimes she really drives me insane."

"Those are sisters for you. A fucking headache, but still, I would die for her."

"Are you and Gianna close?" Finn asked, taking his chance to learn more about her.

Allister nodded. "We've always been. With only us two and our father, we relied on each other a lot. She acts so strong, but deep down she's so fragile. That's why I'm happy she has the girls and all of us as her support; she needs it even if she pretends that she doesn't."

"You're a good brother." That was the truth. It made him question his own relationship with Luna; how much he had been willing to put up with, how little he had done with everything that was going on between them and their father. He tried his best to protect her, but he hadn't realized she had already been past the point of protecting. That it was a life-or-death situation.

"You are too," Allister said. "You stood by your sister when you could have walked away."

"I didn't have a choice," Finn said.

His father wanted him dead towards the end; Finn knew that to be a fact. Sticking with Luna had been a matter of preservation as much as it was out of protection.

"We always have a choice."

Finn swallowed harshly, desperately trying to push down every painful reminder of everything that had happened. Now was not the time to dive into any of that.

"Is this you choosing to be nice to me when you could be an asshole?" Finn asked him.

"Being an asshole isn't really my style."

"I think I know someone who might beg to differ," Finn muttered. Too many times, he had heard the very phrase come out of Blair's mouth when she was complaining to Luna throughout the years.

Allister's eyes lit up, but he covered it up with a small laugh instead. "I think we should celebrate this moment with a picture."

"A picture? You don't seem like the monumental type," Finn said. Then it struck him. A picture was exactly what he needed. "On second thought, that sounds perfect."

Allister took the first one on his phone and then Finn took one on his. They plastered on big grins as if they were the best friends in the world. Whatever Allister's motivations were for taking the picture, Finn didn't really care. All he knew was that he felt so giddy sending the picture off to the very girl who was so keen on ignoring him but wouldn't be once she saw it.

GIANNA

Thought you might enjoy seeing me and your
big bro being best buds!

Sleep tight, princess.

He turned off his phone just as the bubbles from her typing came
up, a true and genuine smile on his face now.

TWENTY

GIANNA

WHAT WAS SUPPOSED to be a relaxing night of reality TV and popcorn ended up being a night full of anxiety and horror for Gianna. What the hell was Finn doing with Allister? Why were they smiling? And why did he look so fucking good in the picture?

She could have sworn that her heart actually stopped the moment the picture popped up on her screen. After rubbing her eyes frantically, pitching her arm, and even slapping her cheek, she confirmed that it was in fact not a nightmare. It was reality.

Finn hadn't answered a single one of her texts, which was convenient considering he couldn't stop texting her a couple hours ago. It was nearly one in the morning, and they still weren't home. She could only imagine what they were talking about, how Finn was managing to weasel his way into Allister's mind to poke and pry into their lives and find out anything he could about her.

She had multiple different names she could use to describe Finn, and not one reigned positive at the moment.

Gianna chewed on her nail, watching the clock in anticipation when she finally heard the front door open and loud voices disturb the peace of the house.

She tiptoed to the door, holding her ear up against it to listen. Dante shouted something, but it was too slurred for her to fully understand what he was saying. Putting him to bed was going to be a nightmare, especially when he got to that level. After a while though, she heard the closing of doors followed by footsteps up the hall. Dante and Allister stayed on the opposite side of the house, meaning that the only person coming to this end would be the one person she needed to talk to.

She gave it a few more minutes just to be sure everyone was down and settled for the night before she carefully opened the door, tiptoeing through the hallway. She avoided every little creak after years of memorizing that very hall when she used to sneak out more often. Now, she didn't need to. Part of her missed the thrill of the secret nighttime rendezvous when the darkness covered her and she could do whatever she wanted before the sun came up and no one ever found out.

They always left her cranky as hell though, having to wake up early and never getting enough sleep. After everything that had happened the previous year with the war, she had to stop it for her own safety and everyone else's. Maybe it was time to start it back up again.

She walked past Cecilia's and Blair's rooms, both on opposite sides of each other. They were both home and hopefully both dead asleep at this point.

His door was closed, and the lights were off, but she didn't care. She turned the knob carefully, pushing it open and sliding in before anyone could see her. She closed it behind her just as quickly, looking around the room to see where he was.

He laid in bed, already snoring, but the smell of his shampoo and bodywash lingered strongly in the air like he'd just used it. She approached the bed, getting on it and straddling his waist carefully. He didn't move a single muscle, which had to mean he was either deep asleep or seriously drunk.

She ignored how good the position between them would have

felt despite how risky it was. There was a deep power that swept through her being on top now. How she held the upper hand in that moment.

Gianna placed her hand on his mouth, leaning down before muttering, "Wake the hell up."

His eyes snapped open, confusion filling his core and he went to push her off until he saw who it was. She saw the gleam in his eyes, the excitement, but she ignored it.

"I don't know what the hell you were doing around my brother tonight, but that's going to stop. Do you understand me?" she asked, keeping her voice sturdy and hard.

A tongue swept against her hand, forcing her to let go of him. She let out a disgusted sound, wiping her hand against his comforter.

"I was just getting to know him. I figured you would be happy if your boyfriend and your brother were good friends," he said, tucking his hands behind his head.

"Boyfriend? You are not my boyfriend and you better not have told him that you are," Gianna whisper-screamed, desperately trying to contain the panic in her voice.

Finn shrugged. "Hmm. I can't remember if it came up or not. We spent a couple hours together talking about everything and anything, so I'm really not sure."

She reached her hands out, slapping them against his chest. "I'm going to kill you."

"I would have filled you in on the plans, but you weren't responding to my texts," Finn said nonchalantly. He paid no mind to her idle threat, which only frustrated her more.

"And I'm not going to respond, so you can stop texting."

"Would you prefer I called you then?"

She clenched her jaw. "I would prefer zero contact."

He shook his head, using his hands to trail the freshly shaved skin of her thighs before they landed on her hips. He squeezed before slipping his hands under her silk tank top. "That's not going to happen. You know it. I know it. Hell, even the devil knows it, princess."

Gianna swallowed hard, feeling him hardening under her. It sent her mind right back to the night in the shower and she hated how easily her body answered to him.

Both of his hands slid up her stomach, igniting goosebumps in their wake. She held her breath, her eyes locked with his. When he finally reached her breasts, he traced his fingertips over the sensitive nipples for only a moment before he held them firmly in his grasp. She gasped, looking at him with wide eyes.

"What? Nothing to say now, princess?" Finn asked, his voice full of mockery.

She frowned, opening her mouth but his fingers grabbed her nipples, pulling at them painfully before rubbing to soothe them. Her underwear was already damp, and she was so grateful that there was a comforter separating them.

"You know what I'm in the mood for?" he asked.

"What?" Gianna responded, breathless.

"I'm in the mood to finally have a taste of your pussy."

Heat soared through her body. There was nothing she wanted more in the world.

"But I need to hear you ask me," he said. His lips pulled into a grin, and it only pissed Gianna off, but the more he played with her nipples, the more turned on she got.

"No," she said immediately. "I'm not going to beg you."

"That's too bad," Finn said. "Because you're not going to come otherwise."

He lifted his lips, rocking them against hers. A long moan left her mouth the moment she felt his hard cock brush against her swollen pussy. Was he wearing anything underneath the covers? She didn't know, but the stimulation of her nipples with his grinding was sending her mind reeling.

And then he stopped completely.

Gianna let out a frustrated groan, grabbing his cheeks. "Why did you stop?"

"You know the deal."

She bit her lip, trying to find a way around it. She could leave right then and there, go back to her room and finish herself off, but it wouldn't feel the same. She just knew it wouldn't. Not when he was offering his mouth.

She pressed a kiss to his lips, praying it would make him forget about the begging and he would give her what she needed anyway. His tongue slipped into her mouth, fighting with hers before he pulled back too soon.

"Don't be a brat," he said. "Beg and I'll give you what you want."

This never happened to her. Men never held back from her in bed, making her beg for anything. But Finn wasn't like everyone else.

She swallowed harshly. "Please," she mumbled.

"What was that?"

"Please," she repeated, louder this time. She so badly wanted to smack the smirk off his face, especially when the brown in his eyes turned black from how wide his pupils were.

"Be specific, princess."

"Please, eat my pussy," she said, but the words sounded more like a hiss.

"Well, when you beg so nicely."

He flipped her over, barely letting her back hit the mattress before he pulled the shorts and underwear down her legs. His lips left a trail up her thigh as he slowly inched his way up to the one spot that ached uncontrollably for him.

He moved with such precision and ease that she couldn't help but watch him in complete awe. Every single inch of her body was awake, shaking with need.

"You have such a pretty pussy, princess," he said, looking up at her with a devilish grin.

Fuck. Why did such vulgar words sound so good coming out of his mouth?

The teasing was becoming unbearable, so much so that she

was sure she was going to explode if he didn't do something, anything. She begged, she was open for him, what more could he possibly want?

Finn leaned in, and just when she thought he was going to give her what she wanted, he left soft kisses on her pussy, eliciting a groan of frustration from her.

Gianna grabbed his hair, pulling at it. "Stop teasing me."

"Fuck. I shouldn't like it when you're a brat, but here I am, rock hard," he said. Her mouth was suddenly dry when he reached down, cupping himself through the boxers he had on. Acting like he had all the time in the world, he moved his hand along his dick, playing with himself right in front of her.

"You're supposed to be paying attention to me," she said, suddenly so aware of the words that left her mouth. Did she really just say that?

Grinning, he leaned back in. "My greedy princess."

Finally, with a swipe of his tongue, he tasted her from her slit to her clit. Gianna gasped. Her hips bucked off the bed when he did it again, this time focusing his tongue over her clit. The pressure was a consistent, gentle touch—so light that it had her grinding her hips up to meet his mouth, but he held her down.

"So fucking delicious," he groaned.

In a sudden change of pace, his mouth wrapped around her clit, forcing a squeal out of her lips. He pressed a hand against her mouth, pulling away from her for a moment.

"Shhh, someone's gonna hear us, princess."

Let them hear. She was so far into her own pleasure, withering against his tongue that she didn't give a shit who heard or saw them together. All she cared about was chasing the high that he was giving her. The one that was so close she could taste it.

With one hand occupied trying to keep her quiet, the other one slipped two fingers inside of her, curling up to hit the spot that had her eyes closing. She held his hair in her hands, forcing him against her pussy, nearly suffocating him while he kept licking and sucking on her clit, still thrusting his fingers inside of her.

Had she ever felt like this? Only one other time came to mind, and it was when Finn fucked her in the shower.

She knew she was going to come. She felt it growing and growing inside of her, but when her orgasm finally came, it hit her like a semi-truck, shocking every single nerve in her body. Her legs shook and she truly had never been more grateful for Finn's hand on her mouth, or his hand inside of her.

Wave after wave ripped through her and only when it was over, when she was completely overstimulated, did he pull away. He replaced his hand with his lips, letting her taste the way he had devoured her.

It shouldn't have been hot. God, none of this with him should have been as hot as it was. But it was. Everything with him was driving her fucking wild, and unfortunately, she had no problem wrapping her arms around his neck to kiss him back.

When he pulled away, she finally opened her eyes, blinded by his grin and soft eyes looking down at her.

She cleared her throat, uncomfortable by his warmth. "So, I'm guessing you want me to reciprocate."

He shook his head. "Sure, one day. But not tonight."

Gianna's eyebrows shot up. "Are you sure?"

"I didn't eat your pussy so you would have to return the favor. I did it because I wanted to," Finn said, kissing her again.

"Okay." Again, she was at a loss for words. Her vocabulary, or maybe more accurately, her ability to speak, was dwindling more and more as she spent time with him.

"Don't sound so shocked."

She ignored him, instead going back to the reason she came into his room in the first place. "What did you and Allister talk about?"

"Wouldn't you like to know," he said with a grin.

"You're infuriating."

"I've been called worse."

She shook her head, pushing his heavy body off. It was hard to ignore the tingles that rushed up her hands when they made contact with his bare chest, but she managed anyway. His body didn't move an inch, but his lips fell into a frown.

"I'm being serious," Gianna said.

"Where are you going?" he asked.

"To my room." The confusion was clear in her voice. Where else was she going to go? Exhaustion swept through her body and her eyes were burning with the need to sleep. Her bed was the only place she truly wanted to go.

"Just stay here."

"Are you serious?"

"Why would I joke about that?" Finn asked. His tone was serious enough, but she still couldn't tell if he was being serious. She could only assume he had to be joking because they had a full house that could walk in on them at any moment.

"I don't know," she answered honestly.

"Just spend the night. Don't think too much about it."

She couldn't help the snort-chuckle that slipped past her lips. "Well, that's easy to do."

"Try it, you might be surprised to find that you like it," he said.

"You must be an expert in not thinking."

"Fucking brat," he muttered. He pinched her butt cheek, moving to lay beside her now.

She turned on her side, staring at him and he stared back at her. It wasn't awkward. No, there was something almost comforting about it. He pulled the covers over himself, surrounding them both in warmth and silence.

It felt nice. Too nice. Nice to the point where she felt like she shouldn't be enjoying it. Like it would get pulled away from her, like most things usually did.

Gianna sat up in a panic. "I have to go to the restroom," she told him, quickly getting out of bed. He stared at her in confusion, but she ignored it, rushing to the ensuite and closing the door behind her.

She used the restroom and washed her hands, staring at

herself in the mirror. The image that stared back wasn't one that she hated, which was rare. Flushed cheeks and the glow on her skin looked good on her. Why then did she feel this panic settling deep inside of her?

It wasn't her first time lying in a bed with a man. Well, not without them wanting to fuck. Usually, the lying in bed part only happened as they took breaks, but then they picked back up where they left off before whoever she was with snuck out sometime in the early hours of the morning. So no, she had never *slept* with anyone like that before. Innocently, at least. Was that why she was freaked out? The intimacy of sleeping in bed right beside someone and how much she might like it?

Or was it because she knew she would crave it again? The only issue was that once she left herself wanting something, *craving* it, she set herself up for disappointment when it was taken away from her.

If she wanted real intimacy—or worse, started needing it— what would happen if he just left? One day, if Finn decided that he wanted to be free and hop on his bike and run away again, she wouldn't be able to stop him.

Hell, she couldn't even keep her own mother from leaving. She couldn't expect anyone to stay just for her. Not her best friends, or her brother, or even her cousins.

Gianna hadn't even realized that she was chewing on her nail, biting the skin beside it raw until she tasted blood. She turned away from the mirror, suddenly disgusted by what stared back at her.

Opening the door to the bathroom, she was stunned to see Finn standing right outside of it. His hand was lifted as if he was going to knock but she beat him to it.

"I came to see if you were okay," he said.

She cleared her throat. "I am."

"Are you going to spend the night?"

The question was simple. Not a big deal. And when she looked into his brown eyes, the same ones that seemed to bring a newfound comfort into her soul, it made her long for something she hadn't dared to long for in forever. Made her yearn for something she saw in Luna and Valerio, in the shows she watched, in the dreams she dreamt.

Someone who would choose her and stay.

Gianna nodded her head. "Yes."

TWENTY-ONE

FINN

FINN HADN'T EXPECTED her to agree. He was so sure she was going to run out of the room, say that everything they did was a mistake, and demand he never talk to her again. He had expected it, waited for it, but it never came.

Instead, she crawled into bed and went to sleep. Granted, she turned away from him and pushed her body towards the complete edge of the bed while using the comforter as a makeshift wall between them, but still, she stayed.

Finn expected sleep to come to him, but it didn't. He was hyperaware of her body next to him and instead of soothing him, it made his body go crazy. It was as if there was an electrical pull that kept shocking him, reminding him that he wasn't alone.

He had always preferred his isolation, especially with sexual partners. They would fuck, but there was no cuddling afterward or spending the night. It was a one and done thing for him. Hell, he usually didn't bring anyone into his bed to fuck either. It was either somewhere public or in their bed. His space was his. He still wasn't cuddling with Gianna, and she had barged in, but this was different.

He *wanted* to fucking cuddle. He *wanted* her to stay.

So, when he was sure that she was sleeping from the even

breaths escaping her perfect lips, he shifted her body, pulling her into his arms. She was so fucking light, it was scary how easily he was able to move her body around.

She was strict with her regime. He saw it when he was doing his *research*. She worked out like crazy and then pushed her body to extreme lengths while she practiced her dance. God, she reminded him of himself in so many ways.

Gianna shot up, looking around the room in confusion. "Where am I?" she asked groggily.

"You're sleeping in my room. At least you were sleeping like two seconds ago," he said, letting out a huff. "You freaked me the fuck out."

"What am I supposed to think when someone just starts moving my body?"

"Oh, so now you have situational awareness?"

She pushed his chest, forcing him to fall back on the mattress. "What were you even doing?"

He thought about it for a moment. The truth was honestly more humiliating now that she was awake.

"You were about to fall off the bed," he lied.

"I didn't feel myself falling."

"Yeah, because I caught you."

She huffed, lying back down, this time on her back. "Whatever."

He took note of how much closer she was this time but didn't voice it out loud. He didn't need her moving right back to the same spot she was in before only to have the same situation happen again.

"What time is it?" she asked.

"Almost five."

"I should probably leave soon, before they start waking up."

"If you want."

She rolled her eyes. "It's not if I want, it's a must. Could you imagine what would happen if they caught us in here together? I have no idea where my shorts and underwear are and all you're wearing is a pair of boxers. There's no lie in the world that would be able to get either of us out of that one."

"Why would I need to lie?" he asked. "I would simply just tell them I ate your pussy."

She slapped her hands over her face, muttering something he couldn't hear. She ran them through her hair before turning her body, so she was now on her side facing him. "Do you mean to be this infuriating or is this really how you are?"

"I thought you knew me well enough by this point to know the answer to that." Finn couldn't help his grin. "You know, for someone who swears they don't want anything to do with me, you have no issue finding yourself in compromising situations with me time and time again."

"I came in here for answers."

Her voice wavered as if she didn't believe herself fully either. Hell, she was smart. Of course she knew that wasn't the real reason she had come in.

"I'm sure you did, princess, but you seemed to stay for something else."

Gianna's face fell. Her lips pushed out into the cutest pout—unintentionally, it seemed. Finn had to stop himself from leaning in to press a kiss to her lips.

"I'm confused, okay?"

Had he been standing, his legs would have given out. Finn was dumbstruck. Gianna was finally admitting something to him. Something he already knew—still, something she probably had never shared with anyone else.

"What are you confused about?" He kept his voice soft and supportive. It surprised her, judging by the look on her face, and it even surprised himself. He had never heard himself speak that way in his life.

Her hand waved around in the air. "All of this."

"The room?" he asked, trying to crack a joke.

Her lips lifted in the smallest smile. "You know what I'm talking about."

"What about it confuses you so much?"

"You're Finn Kingsley. I've known you for years as Luna's annoying, overbearing older brother. Suddenly, we're in the shower having sex and you're saying we're dating and it's all so quick. Actually, quick is an understatement. It's moving faster than the speed of light."

"I've always known you as Luna's annoying little best friend who was a brat. Wait, that's still true."

"Finn, I'm being serious."

He groaned. "I see what your point is, princess. We can't change how we used to know each other though. You're not going to stop being friends with Luna, and I'm not going to stop being her brother. Get to know me as me, without any of that shit getting in the way."

Gianna looked reluctant, then let out a loud groan. "You're not going to leave me alone, are you?"

"Hell no."

TWENTY-TWO

GIANNA

IT SEEMED like the more Gianna pushed, the more Finn latched onto her and refused to let go. He was driving her insane, but she couldn't stop thinking about him either. When she said she was confused, she wasn't lying.

Whenever she got into these moods, there was only one place to go: the studio. Tonight, she chose the home studio instead of the one at school. The more she danced and tried to force herself to nail down the stupid leap she kept messing up, the more she began uncovering that confusion.

One part of it came from the possibility of losing Luna if she ever found out about the stupid relationship. She didn't exactly know Luna's opinions on the matter, not that she could ask her outright. God, she didn't even want to think about how that conversation would go if it ever did happen.

Gianna knew that Luna loved her and only wanted to see her happy. She also knew that Finn's happiness meant the world to Luna. Now, whether she would want to see them happy together was a whole different question. The point was, she wasn't ready to risk it. There was a possibility of everything going right and working out, but just the same was the possibility of everything going wrong. Luna could find the relationship uncomfortable and never support it, which would put Cecilia and Blair in an awkward place. Gianna would never make them choose a side; she didn't even want sides to exist. However, that would be the natural consequence. Who would they pick? God, making them pick would be awful.

Valerio would definitely choose Luna, Dante would choose his brother, and Allister would be stuck between his loyalty towards his best friend or his little sister, unless he hated her for breaking everyone up like she did to their family.

Now she was spiraling.

This was why she hated thinking about these things and why she couldn't risk it for Finn. She couldn't lose everyone and everything on the small chance of it working out with him.

Which brought her to the second part. She didn't think Finn was fully into the whole concept of monogamy. Hell, he only just started thinking about girlfriends. He didn't know anything about relationships and had never been in one. Not to mention, he had just been kidnapped home. He hadn't come willingly. There was a big chance he could leave at a moment's notice and an almost sure chance that he would break her heart in one way or another.

No matter what, she would be losing someone.

Was it worth it to lose Finn though, or to lose her entire group of friends and the only family she had left?

She would have thought that the choice was obvious enough, but when she thought about it, there was a horrible ache in her chest. It had already happened, it seemed. He had managed to break his way in.

"Do you always dance this aggressively?" Allister asked from behind her.

She screamed, turning around in a panic. Thank God it wasn't Finn, but still the sudden intrusion was enough to freak her out.

"What are you doing here?"

She walked over to the music, pausing it so she would be able to hear him clearly.

He took a seat on one of the wooden stools against the back wall. His glasses were perched on his nose and his hair was messy, meaning that he was either studying or was getting work done for Valerio.

"I heard the music and thought I would come check on you. I haven't seen you a lot lately," Allister said.

She shrugged, sitting on the floor across from him to remove her pointe shoes. "I've been busy trying to prepare for the recital coming up. There's one move that's been impossible to nail."

"I'm sure you'll end up getting it," he said. "You always do."

She gave him a genuine smile. "I really hope so."

"I wanted to see if any of this aggression has to do with the text I sent you. About Mom's visit?"

The smile slipped off her face in an instant. She swallowed harshly, trying to avoid the way his blue eyes stared back into hers.

To be fair, with everything going on with Finn, it provided the perfect distraction, so she didn't have to think about everything going on with her mother. Maybe subconsciously, part of her frustration was because of it, but not all. Not like it would usually be.

At least not until he reminded her.

"Do you know why she's coming back so soon?"

He shook his head. "No idea. Dad told me about it the other day. Imagine his surprise when he got the call early this time."

Gianna exhaled. When her mother decided to visit for the first time after she abandoned them, she came unannounced. Gianna had been too young to really know what happened during that visit, but from what her father had told her, he never let her show up again without calling. She couldn't blame him. One year wasn't nearly enough time to pick up his life after his wife had just left.

The fact that she even got yearly visits was something Gianna still didn't fully understand to this day. There were plenty of times throughout the years that she fought the idea of them—she hid in her room, spent the night at Cecilia's, and once even ran away from home just to avoid the visit.

But her dad always made her come home. He knew it was painful for her and for Allister, but every year he told them the same thing: *"It hurts, but you get to sleep knowing you did everything in your power."*

The first time she'd heard it, she had no idea what he was talking about. She had been a child. Over the years, she knew he didn't want them to live with any regrets or wonder what could have happened had they never seen their mother. The lack of relationship wasn't on them if they showed up to the visits; it was on her.

Now, as a grown woman, Gianna knew she didn't want any relationship with her mother. Not the yearly visits, not a healthy steady relationship—though that was impossible now—nothing. She wanted nothing to do with the woman who gave birth to her.

And yet, she still showed up to the yearly visits.

"I'm assuming we'll be riding back home together?" Gianna asked.

Allister gave her a grin. "Only if I get to choose the music this time."

"Hell no. I'm not listening to your classical bullshit the entire way," she said immediately.

He rolled his eyes. "I don't listen to classical music. Who do you think I am?"

"You complain that my music sucks. What am I supposed to think?"

"Yeah, because you play the same things over and over again."

"Blah blah blah." She waved him off.

He rolled his shoulders, sitting up on the stool. "Oh, you're never going to believe who I went out with the other night."

Gianna froze. She tried to play it off, extending her left leg and bending over it to stretch. "Who?" she asked, trying to keep her voice as neutral as possible.

"Finn. To be honest, I never thought much about him, but he doesn't seem that bad."

She snorted. "Are we talking about the same Finn?"

"You sound just like Valerio."

"Maybe we see something you don't."

Allister shook his head. "No, I think it's the other way around. Seriously, I think he's misunderstood. Just really messed up after everything that happened with his parents."

Huh, that sounded a little too familiar.

"You guys got that deep at the club? Are you going to be his best friend now?" she asked, moving onto her other leg.

"Now you sound like Dante," he said. "We just chatted about things. I asked him about that one rumor Luna came up with."

Gianna lifted her head. "Which one?"

"The one about him seeing someone. He didn't confirm or deny, just said something about it being 'complicated.'"

"What do you think?"

"I think it's true."

She swallowed harshly. "What makes you say that?"

"He didn't move from the couch once. Didn't look at anyone, didn't touch anyone, didn't talk to anyone. A whole club of women and he didn't do anything." Allister shook his head, almost as if he was analyzing something deeper, and if Gianna was paying more attention she would have tried to get to the bottom of it. All she could think about though were his words.

Or more specifically, Finn's actions.

"I guess we'll never know for sure," Gianna said.

He shrugged, standing. "I guess not. Don't go blabbering to Luna about it. The last thing I need is her questioning me a million times over to find out if he's actually seeing someone."

She swiped her finger over her lips as if zipping them shut. "No point in feeding a stupid rumor."

"I have more work to do. Try not to stay up too late dancing."

Gianna could only nod her head, watching as Allister left the studio to head back up the steps. She fell against the floor, her heart pounding against her chest. People were starting to notice, which was extremely dangerous for both her and Finn. Whatever they had going on needed to get nipped in the butt because curious minds never just stayed curious.

So then why did she have a big smile on her face thinking about Finn staying loyal to her at the club, texting her nonstop, and then begging her to spend the night?

He needed a big fat warning sign stapled to his head. One that read: *Danger!*

TWENTY-THREE

GIANNA

GIANNA GASPED AWAKE, fighting against the body that was currently on top of her. It was convenient that there was a hand over her mouth, keeping her silent while she tried to scream for help.

"Relax." The voice was smooth in her ear. "It's me."

She could barely make out his figure in the darkness, but she recognized his voice immediately. It was Finn, and for some reason he was in her room in the middle of the night.

When her body relaxed, he moved his hand away but remained hovering over her.

"What the hell are you doing in here?" she asked, agitated.

"Paying you back for the other night."

She let out a frustrated groan, pushing him. "I have not slept a full night in forever. You are not going to mess that up for me again."

"Are you asking me to sleep with you?" He beamed.

"I'm threatening you to let me sleep or I'm going to seriously hurt you."

Finn sat up, pulling the covers off Gianna. "Come on, let's go on a drive."

"You need to get better listening skills. I'm not going anywhere. It's the middle of the night."

"It's only midnight."

"If it has the word night in it, I shouldn't be awake."

"Oh, come on, princess. Live a little." He tried to be convincing, but the argument was futile. There was no explanation for why he was up and awake at this time of night, trying to drag her along for a ride.

"You'll have more fun without me," she told him.

"I need you there."

She froze at his words. He said it lightly, but just the thought of being needed stunned her. "Why are you awake right now? What happened that you're suddenly in a rush to go?"

The joking mood slipped off his face completely. A haunted look found him instead. It was bizarre watching his eyes turn devoid of the warmth she was used to them having. Something told her that whatever it was that kept him awake tonight was probably the very thing that had him always trying to run.

"Please, Gianna."

She pursed her lips, but still nodded, nonetheless. "Fine, but I'm not staying out long."

He moved away, letting her slip off the bed. She threw on the first hoodie and sweatpants set she could find, slipping on some warm boots with it. If she was going to be forced onto a bike in the middle of the night, she wanted to be warm.

"Here, put this on too," he said, handing her a leather jacket.

She hadn't even noticed he had another one with him, but she slipped it on, equally hating and enjoying how they matched.

Finn moved to open the door to her room, but she stopped him. Instead, she walked over to her balcony doors, unlocking and carefully opening it.

"What's this?" he asked, surprised.

"We're not going through the front door," she said.

"So you're telling me I could have been sneaking in through

the balcony this whole time instead of using the door? Why do I like that idea so much more?"

"Probably because you're demented."

"You like that I am."

She rolled her eyes, motioning for him to walk out first so she could close the doors behind them.

Admittedly, her balcony was pretty nice. She spent the time decorating it with a pink outdoor couch, a small wooden table, and a hammock chair for when she really wanted to lounge out. On warm summer nights, she would turn on the outdoor lights she strung along the roof and just relax there, letting her mind wander, but usually turning on a show to keep her occupied.

"What now? You expect me to jump down and then catch you?" Finn asked, looking over the railing.

"Jump if you want, I think I'll use the ladder."

She slid it out from under the couch, using her strength to hoist it over the railing and let it down slowly. Once it was leaning against the brick wall, she turned to face him.

"What the hell is that?" he asked, his voice mocking.

"A ladder."

"That flimsy little shit looks like it's going to snap at any second."

"It's served me well." Gianna left out the part where plenty of men had also used it and been fine, thinking it might kill the mood. "You'll be fine."

"Is this really easier than just using the front door?" Finn threw one leg over the railing, letting his foot grab hold of the first step on the ladder before he threw his other leg over.

"Consider this your punishment for waking me up," Gianna said. "Now hurry."

He took his time going down the ladder, and admittedly, it was way too small for his large build. He was definitely a lot bigger than most of the guys she had been with in the past, which was probably why they had never struggled with the ladder while he did.

He let out a loud breath of relief when his feet finally touched the ground. He then held onto the bottom to steady it as she began coming down. Once she was safely on the ground as well, she had him hide the ladder in the bushes so that no one would be able to see that it was there.

"Where's your bike?" she asked him, wrapping her arms around herself. Convenient that he had picked a windy night to go for a ride.

"Are you cold?" he asked her.

She nodded. "A little bit, but I should be fine."

Finn grabbed her hand, walking them to the garage. It was far enough away from any of the rooms in the house for anyone to hear the garage door opening or to hear them leaving.

His bike stood there freshly polished, it seemed. Two helmets sat on the seat, but Finn didn't walk towards it. Instead, he approached one of the many cars in the garage, pulling Gianna along with him.

"What are you doing? Your bike is over there," she said.

"It's too cold for you to go on a bike ride right now, so we'll just take a car," he said, opening the door for her.

She frowned. "I thought the whole point was because you needed the bike ride."

"I'll live."

He looked at her expectantly, still holding the door open. Gianna entered the car, getting comfortable while he grabbed the keys from the wall. Him choosing her comfort over what he needed did something to her. It made her stomach flip violently in the most pleasant way possible.

Finn got into the driver's side, starting the car up.

Gianna cleared her throat. "I can handle the cold. Seriously, it wasn't that bad."

He shook his head. "I'm not going to risk you getting sick. You agreeing to come out with me is what I needed, not the ride."

They pulled off into the darkness, staying in silence. She leaned her head against the window, letting out a loud yawn. Her body was unbelievably warm and cozy with the combination of the heaters and the heated seat.

She only closed her eyes for a couple of moments when she felt the car stop completely. They were at the lake again; the wind having picked up even more now as the trees shook violently. Thunder cracked in the distance and lightning sliced through the sky, letting her know that a storm was on its way.

Finn turned off the headlights, keeping them in darkness. Gianna took off her seatbelt and boots, folding her legs under her. Her feet had been killing her more than usual lately, and any chance she had not to wear shoes she was taking.

He took off his seatbelt, leaning back. A loud sigh left his lips, and she couldn't tell if it was out of exhaustion or relief.

"Are you going to tell me what's wrong?" Her voice cut through the silence.

He didn't answer right away, and for a second, she almost thought he wouldn't tell her at all. But then he cleared his throat, shifting in his seat.

"I had a nightmare."

"You don't have to tell me about it if you don't want to."

He shook his head. "I was ten years old again and my father was standing over me, the sickest fucking look on his face. It was worse than anger; it was like he was a monster. That's how I remember him looking my entire childhood. This time, me stuttering when his coworker asked a question sent him off. He kept hitting and hitting until I was a puddle of blood. And then I woke up," Finn said. His voice was emotionless as if he had removed himself from the story completely.

Gianna swallowed down her nausea. "That sounds oddly specific to just be a random nightmare."

A bitter chuckle left his lips. "My whole life has been a nightmare."

Gianna heard the rumors. She knew Reece Kingsley was a horrible man, that was no secret. She knew of the things he did to Luna, like forcing her into marriages and threatening to hit her at the engagement party, which was luckily stopped by Valerio. But no one knew just how extreme the horrors in the Kingsley household were.

It made her wonder how Luna kept it from them all those years, how either sibling ever dealt with it.

"I saw the scars on your back the other day," she said. "Were those from him?"

"From one of the many times he whipped me. Takes forever to fucking heal."

"Why didn't you tell anyone?" Gianna asked quietly.

"I don't know," he said, authenticity coating his voice. "Maybe it was because I thought it would make me tougher or I thought I deserved it, or because I had already dealt with it for that long, I knew it wouldn't be able to last forever. I don't fucking know."

"And you were hesitant to kill him," she said. "When everything was happening last year, you hesitated."

"I know I'm fucked up." He gripped the wheel in his hand, turning his knuckles white. "You don't have to remind me."

"I didn't say that."

"But you think it like everyone else."

"No, I don't," she said, grabbing his hand. It took some effort to pull it off the steering wheel, but he let her hold it anyway. "I'm trying to understand you."

Finn looked at her, and in the moonlight, she caught the glazed-over look in his eyes. The unshed tears, it seemed.

"Why?" His voice was soft, small even. It lacked the confidence that he always seemed to carry, the one that now seemed to be a facade.

She swallowed harshly. "I don't know. But you should know that I would never judge you, especially over how you feel about your parents."

"Your mother?"

"Ding ding ding," she said, laughing sarcastically. It sounded strained and forced rather than her usual authentic laugh.

"I'll kill her for you if you want," he said out of nowhere. "No one who makes you feel like shit should take another breath."

Her eyes widened in shock, but she shook her head immediately. "No, that's okay. Like I said, it's complicated."

He shrugged, intertwining his fingers with hers. "If you change your mind, the offer stands."

She couldn't do anything but laugh in disbelief. If that was his way of trying to be sweet and romantic, it certainly was flawed and wrong, but the sentiment was there. And it showed her that maybe she was just as fucked up because even with the option available, she wouldn't take it because in the back of her mind she still thought about the 'what if' of a better relationship with her mother.

They had been so deep in their conversation, she hadn't even realized that it was raining now, pounding against the windows and the roof of the car.

"It's a good thing we didn't take the bike," Finn said, just as another crack of thunder cut through.

"You and that damn bike." She rolled her eyes, trying to hide the smile on her face.

He grinned, poking her side. "Don't be jealous. You can be my favorite girl; she can come second."

"Oh God. Tell me, does she have a name too?"

"FiFi."

She gasped. "That's terrible."

"I think it's cute."

"What's that supposed to be a play on? Finn?"

"She's my daughter."

Gianna let out a loud laugh, the cackle filling the small space. "Remind me to never let you name anything."

His eyes lit up. "Oh yeah? Like what? Our kids?"

She shut up immediately. "I didn't say that."

Finn shrugged. "I'll have a baby with you, but I'm more interested in the creating, if I'm being honest."

Him holding a baby, *their* baby, popped into her head for a split second. It warmed her heart, for a second. No, a millisecond. So quick that it was almost like it didn't even happen. She ignored the way her heart beat erratically, blaming it on the weird night and nothing else.

"You'll be getting neither from me."

"Such big words."

"With lots of truth in them."

He shook his head, still beaming. "Oh, I'm sure."

Gianna bit her lip. She was having an oddly good time with him, and it only reminded her of the conversation she had with Allister the other night. How he was starting to get suspicious of Finn's dating status and how it was probably best that they cut it off.

"I talked to Allister the other night," she said.

"Great way to change the conversation."

She ignored him. "He said that you guys brought up dating?"

"It was brief."

Gianna exhaled. "He said that you said it was complicated and that you didn't interact with anyone else all night. He's convinced that you're seeing someone."

"I am." He was confused. She could tell by his furrowed eyebrows.

"And when they start asking you questions or when they start getting really curious, then what?"

"You want me to lie to them? Is that it?" Finn asked. "Do you want me to be seen with someone else in public? Do you want me to fuck someone else in front of them to make sure no trails lead to you?"

White hot jealousy traveled through her body. She was surprised by how visceral the reaction to just his words were, let alone if he actually did it. God, she might lose it.

He shook his head. "That's what you're alluding to, right? That you want me to have someone in public and what, you in private?"

She couldn't take it. She hopped over the center console, holding his face in her hands.

"Shut the fuck up," she hissed.

"Would that make you happy? For me to parade someone else around at my fights? To let someone else on my bike? To have someone else spend the night in my bed? To listen to me fuck someone else all night? Or maybe to bring someone else here, to my special spot where I've never taken anyone else?" The words sounded like venom leaving his mouth and it only fed the fire that was inside of her.

Gianna couldn't believe her increasing frustration. It was just pulling her further and further into his inferno.

Finn leaned in closer, pulling her hands down from his face, and instead letting her wrap them around his neck.

"Do you want me to call someone else a brat?" he asked, his voice a careless whisper. "What if I called them my princess instead?"

That broke Gianna.

She pushed her lips onto his, pouring all of her frustration and bitterness into the kiss. She didn't know where he got the audacity, but she couldn't fathom it. Any of it. The thought of hearing him call anyone else princess—a growl escaped her throat.

His lips were violent, kissing her with the same ferocity that she had. One hand wrapped up in her hair, the other hand on her hip, pulling her closer into him. The console dug into her stomach, forcing her to pull back for a moment.

He pushed the seat back, giving more space between the steering wheel and his body before he lifted her over so she could straddle his lap.

She ground against his hips hard, pressing against his hard cock every single time. Finn connected their lips again, slipping his tongue in.

His hands worked in a frenzy, pushing the leather jacket off her shoulders and throwing it somewhere in the car before he lifted the hoodie off her. She did the same, pulling his jacket off and then the T-shirt he wore, leaving his chiseled body on display for her. She ran her nails down his chest, beaming at the groan that escaped his lips and the goosebumps that rose on his skin.

Heavy breaths escaped her lips, but her body felt alive. Even more, she was wet beyond belief. She found herself craving him far too often and too intensely than she should.

Finn's lips found her neck, biting the skin harshly and then soothing it with his tongue, repeating the action over and over again. Her hands found the buckle of his jeans, undoing the button. He lifted his hips slightly, pressing against her aching pussy on accident, but allowing him to lower them enough to free his cock from its restrain.

She wrapped her hand around him, swiping her thumb over the bead of cum at the head of his dick before jerking him off. Finn was vocal, and fuck did she love it. Every moan and groan that escaped his lips only added to her own pleasure, highlighting just how good she was making him feel.

"Fucking perfect," he said, pulling her back in for a kiss.

Heat swirled in her core. She needed more friction, touches, something, anything. She slipped her hand inside her sweatpants, still keeping the other one wrapped around him. With no issue she found her clit, swirling her fingers around the nerves, moaning against his lips.

He pulled back, looking between them before looking back up at her. Finn's eyes were almost completely black, his pupils huge. "Don't be a brat, let me have a taste."

She looked at him in confusion until he grabbed her wrist, pulling her hand out. He dipped her fingers into his mouth, swirling his tongue over them, keeping his eyes on her the entire time.

Oh God.

"I need you inside me," she said breathlessly.

He lifted her again, helping her slide her underwear and sweatpants off. She was completely bare, the rain still pounded against the windows, and here she was fucking Finn in a car in the middle of nowhere.

He guided his cock inside of her, letting her sink down on him. He felt better than he did the first time. Hell, he would probably feel better every time they fucked. She sat all the way down, letting the gasp leave her lips.

She felt full. Completely and utterly full. And not alone.

She ground her hips, rotating them, riding him, and chasing her pleasure while she held onto his shoulders. It all felt so fucking good.

His eyes were on her, a smirk on his face. "What?" she asked him, barely keeping her eyes open.

"I love to see you claiming my cock as yours," he said.

"And if I said it was mine, then what?"

"I would say take it." He grabbed her breast in his hand. "I would say use me however you want."

She let out a moan, her pussy pulsing at his words. "And if I said that if I ever see you with anyone else, or if you call anyone else a brat—or worse, princess—that I'll kill you, then what?"

He wrapped his hands around her body, pulling her into him so they were flush to each other. He smiled like a Cheshire cat, leading her to believe that he had gotten exactly what he wanted.

"Then I would say you're just as fucking obsessed with me as I am with you," Finn said, leaning in close. "And it's about fucking time because you're mine, *princess.*"

And then he lifted his hips, thrusting into her like a madman. She opened her mouth, but not a single sound came out. She was overstimulated from pleasure, from his words, from his touch, from *him*.

"Don't come yet," he told her. "Wait for me."

"Please," she begged.

"Wait for me, princess."

And as if her body was now attuned to only him, she waited to come. She waited, teetering on the edge of her pleasure until she could fall over the edge.

Finn's hand wrapped in her hair, holding her forehead to his. It was intimate, more than just fucking. That was exactly what this had become. More than just sex. He knew it. She knew it.

"Come with me, princess." The groan left his lips, and at his command, she came, her body crashing completely.

He held her against him and all she could do was relish in the warmth, in his arms. Finn pressed kisses against her head, running a hand up and down her back. "My princess," he muttered against her hair.

She didn't fight it. Gianna closed her eyes, imagining a world where she could have it all.

TWENTY-FOUR

FINN

FINN LET GO of her so she could get dressed, but surprisingly, she still let him hold her afterwards. It felt so right being there, holding her in his arms. And maybe he was jumping to conclusions, but something seemed different in her.

When she lifted her head, looking up at him, he almost thought she was going to do it all over again. That she was going to convince them that they couldn't be together, that they needed to be a secret. Blah blah blah, whatever bullshit she was convincing herself they needed to do.

But instead, Gianna surprised him.

"Are you going to take me on a real date?"

He couldn't help but laugh. He had never been on a date in his life. Ever.

"Here I thought I was being romantic taking you to the lake."

"You want all this," she motioned down her body, "you need to understand I'm high maintenance."

"Are you? Geez, I couldn't tell." From the slap on his chest, she didn't appreciate his sarcasm.

"I'm being serious."

"You want a date, so we're going on a date."

She sat up. "Where?"

"Aren't they supposed to be surprises?"

Gianna frowned. "Is this date going to suck?"

Finn held his chest in faux hurt. "Have some hope in me, princess."

"Well, can you at least tell me how I should dress for it?"

"You could wear a sack, and you would still be the most beautiful girl in the world," he said. It was true. Gianna's beauty was a force to be reckoned with. She was perfect in those dresses she loved to wear, when she slept without a care in the world, and even when she screamed at him.

He was whipped.

She rolled her eyes, but there was still a small blush on her cheeks. "I'm not going to wear a sack. If I have a chance to dress up, I'm going to take it."

"If you're wondering if we'll be going anywhere nice enough so you can get dressed up, the answer is yes. I'll take you somewhere nice," Finn said.

Even though he lived five months on the road in dodgy motels, he wasn't a stranger to the finer things in life. Growing up in the life he did, he was used to galas, fancy restaurants, and splurging on wines. He hadn't preferred it before, but he didn't hate it.

Even now, rejecting what was supposed to be his with the estates and businesses was more of an act of rebellion than it was him actually hating it. Truthfully, he didn't hate the lifestyle, he hated the way his father chose to live. He hated the abuse, the unnecessary violence, the disloyalty that seemed to exist at every turn. But that was because of his father, that didn't need to exist in the lifestyle.

If he was Don, he wouldn't need to live or rule that way.

"Are we going to take your bike?" she asked, successfully pulling him out of his thoughts.

"If I didn't know better, I would think you missed it, princess."

"I can't exactly wear a dress on a bike," she said. "Not appropriately anyway."

An image of her in one of her little pink dresses sitting on his bike popped into his brain. Holy shit, now that was a sight to see. On second thought, maybe they needed to take the bike so that he could make the image a reality, have something to engrave into his mind.

But he wanted to give her a nice first date, so he could save that fantasy for another night. Or at the very least for after dinner.

"We'll take a car there."

"Anything else I should know?"

Finn leaned down, pressing a kiss to her nose. "Stop stressing, it's going to be fine."

She rolled her eyes. "I'm trusting you."

And for some reason, her willingness to put any trust into him made his heart squeeze painfully. He had never had someone trust him in such an intimate way before, and although it seemed so mundane, it screamed volumes on how much she was willing to try for him. He had changed too because as soon as she uttered the words, he found himself locking in that trust, creating a plan in his head to ensure that nothing would go wrong for their date.

TWENTY-FIVE

GIANNA

"YOU NEVER SAID who you were going on a date with," Cecilia said, flicking through dresses on the rack in front of her. "You actually haven't said anything."

Gianna shrugged, pulling out a dress from one of the racks and holding it against her body. "Does this one look good on me?"

"Stop ignoring me."

"I'm not ignoring you, I'm just choosing not to answer you."

"Who is this person and why can't you say a word about them to me?" Cecilia asked, standing in front of Gianna now. "You know I would never judge you. I mean, you've seen some of the dudes I've gone on dates with."

Gianna should have gone shopping by herself, but to be honest, she never went shopping alone. Luna and Blair were busy, thank God, because seeing how much Cecilia was grilling her, she wouldn't have survived it if all three of them were asking questions.

She hadn't even mentioned any date to Cecilia, but her best friend knew her well enough to know that whenever she came shopping for a new dress or outfit like this, there had to be some kind of event involved. The bitch had to have narrowed down the possibilities because once she got it, she hadn't stopped asking questions.

"It's not about you judging them or anything like that. It's just not serious enough yet to tell anyone about it," Gianna said. "The last time I got invested and told you all, it ended up in a shit show. I want to make sure this is going somewhere before I introduce you all to him."

Lie. Lie. Lie.

She was getting good at it. First of all, she would never need to introduce any of them to Finn because *duh*. And it would never get to that point. Ever. Secondly, what happened with the asshole from the club was a disaster, but it wasn't her fault. Still, there was truth there. She wouldn't be introducing anyone to her best friends or her brother until it was *serious*. Gianna was not risking it.

"At least tell me his name. Is he cute? How have you been seeing him? How *long* have you been seeing him? I need some details," Cecilia said, groaning.

"It's a new thing, I see him at school, yes he's cute, and no you cannot know his name because I know you share the same stalkerish tendencies as Mr. Augustus Larson."

Her face fell. "Don't ever compare me to him."

"Wouldn't have to if you two weren't such soulmates," Gianna said mockingly.

That did the trick of sending Cecilia down a tangent about how annoying her stalker was. If it stopped the questions for the time being, then Gianna would handle it.

They wandered around the store, trying on different dresses and shoes. Like always, the simple task of finding one dress turned into shopping for other things that she definitely did not need. It was her form of relaxation. She regularly subscribed to retail therapy as a way to get her mind off everything that was going on in her life. It left her with an overflowing closet and unresolved issues, but it worked for the time being.

Gianna checked her phone, seeing that Finn had texted her.

FINN

I have an update on our date night.

What could it possibly be?

Pack an overnight bag and your outfit so you can get ready out of the house.

I'm taking you to the city for the night. I'll pick you up after your dance practice Friday night.

Uh, yeah that's not going to work.

I can't spend the night anywhere.

Go ahead and change the plans.

Hello?

Finn!

I can see you reading every single one of these texts.

Answer your phone!

I'm so glad you're on board, princess ;) See you on Friday.

Gianna held the phone with a death grip, letting out a frustrated exhale of breath. She looked up, locking eyes with Cecilia who seemed to have been watching her the whole time.

"I'm afraid to ask what just happened, but I'm also extremely curious," she said with wide eyes.

Gianna shook her head. "Men are stupid. That's what happened. I need to ask you for a favor, though."

"Of course."

"You need to be my alibi for Friday night," Gianna said. "I don't know how this is going to fucking work because I'm convinced he doesn't use his brain, but I need us to come up with something so I can get out for the night."

"All night? I'm going to need a name then because if you're going through this much effort for a man, it must be some man." Cecilia's eyes bore into her own, and Gianna felt herself cracking under the pressure.

"Fine," she said, letting out an exasperated huff. "It's Finn."

"It's who?" Cecilia screamed.

Gianna jumped on her, putting her hand over her mouth. "Are you out of your mind? Shut up!"

She ripped it off. "Are you out of your mind? You're fucking Luna's brother?" She shook her head, laughing in disbelief. "This is crazy."

"Don't say that."

"How did this happen?"

"I don't know," Gianna groaned. "It just kind of did, I guess. God, I don't know. We're still figuring it out. I'm trying to stop it."

"Oh, I'm sure you are." Cecilia laughed again, running her hands down her face. "This is wild."

"Don't tell anyone. Please," she begged. "Especially not my brother or Luna."

"I'm not going to tell anyone."

"Thank you."

It was silent for a moment.

"Is the sex good?"

"Oh my God," Gianna exclaimed, walking away.

Cecilia followed closely behind her. "You can't tell me something like that and then not give me any details."

"Obviously it's good enough if I'm telling you about it."

"Obviously it's good enough if you're running off to have a sleepover."

Gianna gave her a death glare. "I'm done with this conversation."

"Oh, come on. You know I'm playing with you. If you're into him and it works, then who the hell am I to judge?"

"Don't say things like that."

Cecilia's brows furrowed. "Why?"

She shrugged, guilt filling her. "Because it makes it feel like me and Finn are dating and that makes it worse. I don't like hiding things from you or Luna or Blair or anyone."

"It's wrong, but it feels so right. I know that feeling," Cecilia said. "Who cares? If it's a secret, live in the secret. Care if you decide to make it public. Deal with it then but live in the now."

"If only it was that easy."

"It can be. You'll be going to whatever date he has on Friday and I'm going to help cover for you," Cecilia said, grabbing her hand. "Don't think about anything else. See if that's really a relationship you want to explore and then take the time to worry about everything else when you get home if you have to."

The intense gratitude that swept through Gianna had her pulling Cecilia into the tightest hug she'd ever had before. Maybe there was also a small bit of relief knowing that she could confide in someone about the relationship now, someone who wouldn't judge her. She felt relieved even if for a small moment.

But Cecilia was right. She needed to take the chance to experience the relationship, see how they could function, and if there really was something there before she tried to complicate it with everything else. For the night, she would let all that go. All the worries about betraying her brother, Luna, and everyone else in her life. She would see who Finn was and let him see who she was.

Her eyes landed on the dress that was right behind Cecilia that seemed to shine down from the Gods above. A pink mini dress that had jewels in every shade of pink hanging off it, mixing a flapper-esque style with something that was more of Gianna's style.

It was perfect.

Like a sign from the universe, Gianna knew everything would be okay. At least for her date night.

TWENTY-SIX

GIANNA

AS PROMISED, Finn was at the dance studio on Friday afternoon to pick Gianna up from her practice. She made sure to end earlier than she normally would, wanting adequate time to get to wherever they were going so she could get ready for their date.

She had her overnight bag with her, the dress, and her dance bag. Luckily the studio was empty when Finn came marching in, looking around the room like he had never seen so many mirrors in his life.

"What are you doing in here?" Gianna asked, throwing her pointe shoes in her dance bag. "I was coming outside."

"I figured you probably had a lot to carry," he said. He was still wearing a pair of jeans and a T-shirt, more casual than what she'd assumed he would be wearing for their actual date. "How was your practice?"

"It was alright." Other than the fact that she had tripped twice and was distracted more than usual. "I could have done better."

"I know you're the best in your class."

"Why would you think that?"

"Because you don't seem like the type to let yourself be

second in anything," he said, grinning. "Are your practices open to the public?"

"Why do you ask?"

"I want to come watch you."

"You want to see me practice?" she asked, her eyes widening in shock.

"I really want to come see you dance, but I'll take a practice too," Finn said. He grabbed her dance bag and overnight bag, leaving her to carry the dress that was still in the special packaging from the store.

Gianna swallowed, feeling her skin heat up. "Okay."

"Perfect."

She stood up, her legs suddenly shaky. She never had a boy interested in her dancing before. Like ever. It was something she usually kept to herself because of how vulnerable she felt while she did it. The raw emotion that came with every movement of her muscles and body, it was something she didn't like to share with just anyone.

But something about him being interested in it made her hot.

"Are you ready to head out?" he asked.

Gianna nodded. They walked out of the studio and to the SUV that waited for them. He placed her bags in the back with what she assumed was his overnight duffle and his suit. She placed her dress down on the seat, letting him close the door. She grabbed the door handle for the passenger side, but he was quick to push her hand off, opening it instead.

"What a gentleman." She snorted, getting in. The slap to her ass was quick and unexpected, forcing a yelp out of her lips.

"Can't help being a brat, can you?" He closed the door, moving to the other side to get into the driver's seat. He turned on the car and they began their drive.

"I was just complimenting your helpfulness."

"I'm sure you were. By the way, I have to say I quite like those little ballerina outfits you wear," he said, looking down at her.

She was still wearing a black leotard, light pink tights, and a pink wrap top with a matching ballet skirt. It was what she wore during practice, and she had meant to at least change into some sweatpants, but his comments in the studio made everything completely slip her mind.

Gianna rolled her eyes. "Of course you do."

"Is that what you wear during every practice?" he asked.

She shrugged. "Different variations."

"Are there boys in that class?"

She turned to face him, a grin on her now. "Are you jealous?"

"I have nothing to be jealous of. I'm fucking you, they're not." Finn looked over at her, and she caught the darkening of his eyes. "I will say though, if any of them ever do anything inappropriate to you, I will fucking kill them."

"Careful, you're starting to sound like Valerio."

"God, don't compare me to him of all people."

She laughed, shaking her head. "Where are you taking me? This could be classified as kidnapping."

"We're going to the city," Finn said. "And that's all you're going to get for now."

"That's it? I need more than that. It was a lot of work to be able to have tonight covered. Somehow, me and Cecilia managed to convince everyone we're doing a wellness night at some spa."

"I know, she's with Augustus tonight," Finn said causally.

Gianna's eyes went wide. "She's with Augustus?"

She felt horrible. Gianna hadn't known where Cecilia was going for the night, all she kept saying was that she had it covered and not to worry about it. Had she known that meant Augustus, Gianna absolutely would not have agreed to it.

"I feel horrible. I had no idea she was going there. Wait, does Augustus know about us?" Gianna asked.

"Yes, he does. I told him, and she'll be fine with him. He would never hurt her," Finn said. "That's probably why she didn't tell you about it."

She frowned, thinking about Cecilia. Immediately, she began chewing on her nail in worry.

Finn looked over at her, grabbing her hand. "Don't think about it now. She's fine."

"Maybe I should just call her."

And she did, but Cecilia didn't answer. She did, however, end up sending a text saying not to worry about her and to have a good time. It seemed to be Cecilia and not some kidnapped version of her, so it soothed Gianna's worries enough. She owed her best friend everything and more.

The spring weather was in full bloom. The sun shined brightly, but it wasn't overbearingly hot or freezing cold. It was the perfect amount of warmth coupled with the emergence of bugs and flowers that made Gianna love spring as much as she did. Though it was May now and she only had a month or so left of it, spring in the city reminded her that she needed to spend more time outside instead of letting the studio swallow up so much of it.

"What are you thinking about?" Finn asked.

"Just how much I love this time of year. The flowers, the rain, how everything just comes back to life after the harsh winter."

"Seems fitting that you would enjoy spring."

She crinkled her nose. "Why is that so fitting?"

"You're so bright. If I had to match any season to you it would have been either that one or summer," Finn said, giving her a smile.

"Summer is probably my second favorite, but it gets a little too hot for me."

"Figured you spend most of your time in a bikini on a beach somewhere."

"Oh, I do," Gianna said with a grin. "I love to travel."

"I only started to enjoy it recently."

"When you were on your backpacking trip?" She couldn't help the little quip.

He shot her an unamused look. "Yes. I know it doesn't match

your level of expectations, but it was probably one of the best experiences I've ever had in my life."

Gianna was silent for a moment. It hurt—his sting. His belief that she couldn't enjoy something like that because of what he thought about her, what most people thought about her, it hit her in a way she hadn't expected it to. She liked the finer things, sure. But the way he assumed it, so quickly too, it hurt weirdly enough.

"I wasn't trying to be malicious."

Finn sighed, scratching at his chin. "And I didn't mean to get so defensive. I'm used to people shitting on my decisions. Hell, shitting on me."

She shrugged. "I'm used to people assuming that I'm thinking the worst about them. That I'm judging them."

He grabbed her hand, pulling it onto his lap and holding onto it tightly. Gianna continued staring out the front windshield, feeling overly exposed.

"And you don't?" he asked.

She bit the inside of her lip. "I do. I'm not perfect. It just sucks when that's the first thing everyone expects of me."

"I make shitty decisions all the time. Because of that, people expect me to fail, to make mistakes. They expect it, but I've stopped giving a shit. You want to know why?"

"Why?" She turned to face him now, noticing they were at a red light.

"Because the best decision I've made is sitting in the car with me right now and that proves to me that I can do the impossible. I haven't failed with you and that makes me really fucking happy. So, I'm actively proving them, and even that part of myself that believed them, wrong. And you being here with me does the same for you. Shows that you have an open and welcoming heart, because I know if you didn't, you wouldn't be here with me right now."

The way he stared back at her, with an intensity she had never seen from him before, was enough to leave her speechless. The way he understood her was the way she'd wanted to be under-stood her entire life. It made her reconsider every way she had ever looked at him. All the times she had been harsh, unforgiving, and relentless in her mild torture towards him. Maybe one day she would be able to tell him that she hadn't meant to do it, but from the way his brown eyes became so soft when they stared back at her, she didn't think she needed to. It was like he already under-stood her. Maybe more so than she knew herself.

"I'm really happy you made that choice," Gianna said, swal-lowing harshly.

"Me fucking too."

Honking behind them took them out of the daze. Finn muttered some words under his breath, but Gianna was too high up in the clouds to hear any of it. She felt giddy and dare she say *shy*. Even as they pulled up to the fancy hotel and he beat the valet to open her door, she still felt so unsure of what to do, how to act.

They didn't need to check in because he had made sure every-thing was set up ahead of time, so he led her straight to the elevator and they were off up to the top floor. She wished she could have spent more time admiring the stretch of windows that covered the penthouse, giving an open view of the city or the obviously beautiful master bedroom that held a king-size bed and was adorned with the exact white bedding and sheets she had at home and absolutely loved. Or how the hotel bathroom was lined with the shower products she used regularly, and the kitchen was stocked with her favorite snacks. She wished she could have admired the material items that usually she would have gone crazy about, but instead her heart beat uncontrollably when Finn approached her with two glasses of champagne.

She admired his brown eyes, his thick brows, his messy hair, the small mole he had next to his left ear, his rough and calloused hands, and his plump lips that once used to scowl so often but only seemed to smile these days.

Gianna beamed at him, taking one of the glasses from him and clinking them together.

"Oh, you never told me what your favorite season was," she said, taking a sip.

He stared at her for a moment. "You know, it used to be fall, but now I think it might be spring."

Yes, that was what she truly cared about.

TWENTY-SEVEN

FINN

FINN PRACTICALLY HAD to peel himself away from Gianna to let her shower and get ready for their date. If it was up to him, he would have preferred a shower together, but when he told her the reservation was in an hour and a half, she screamed and ran to the master bedroom.

He went to the other bedroom to shower himself, then shaved, and made sure he was fresh. He set the suit out in the closet to air out before he had to put it on, but it was still too early. Instead, he paced around the living room like a fucking madman.

He was nervous. Actually, nervous was an understatement. He was anxious, jittery, and completely stressing himself out. Sure, he had never been on a date. But goddamn, he was losing it. He used to act so fucking cool around women, but Gianna wasn't just anyone. She wasn't someone he wanted to put on a front for.

She was someone he could open up to, and he did so unintentionally. It confused the hell out of him how easily he could talk to her; how quick he was to console her and explain himself. Like in the car, when her face fell, he needed her to know that it wasn't a dig towards her. God, he wouldn't dream of it. It was towards himself. His own insecurities about how often people brought up his fuckups. Considering that she might have felt the same way ignited his defenses so quickly, it was out of instinct.

But Gianna was so much like himself. She understood what it was like to be misunderstood. To have the world not truly know the real her. She put on a front the same way he had for so long, and finally her mask was starting to slip. Finn had seen it.

Fuck it. He couldn't wait in the living room alone for another hour.

His impatience led him to the master bathroom where she had the door open and stood in front of the mirror with the robe around her body and her hair freshly blow-dried. She looked up at him, her eyes wide in panic.

"Don't you dare come in here to rush me," she threatened, opening what he assumed was her makeup bag.

Finn held his hands up in surrender. "Wouldn't dream of it. You still have time. I got bored out there, so I came in here."

Her shoulders fell in relief. "Oh, well I'm just getting ready."

"Can I watch?"

"If you want." Her voice was full of hesitation. "I don't think you'll find it very interesting."

He shrugged, sitting on the closed toilet anyway. She took out her creams and tubes of things, applying them each to her face with precision. Every so often, she looked over at him in the mirror, but his eyes never left her. Even while getting ready, she moved with such precision and elegance, executing every step perfectly.

"You look beautiful," he said. "I meant to say it earlier, but I just got lost watching you."

A small laugh escaped her lips. "I'm halfway through my makeup. I look wild right now."

Finn shook his head. "I don't think it's possible for you to ever look bad."

"What about when you found me on the floor having a panic attack that night? I doubt I was the image of beauty."

His mind rushed back to that night. When he saw her tear-stained face that was nearly blue from lack of oxygen. She was in some sort of daze to the point where she didn't hear him come in. It was like talking to a ghost or a wall. Physically, Gianna was there, but mentally, she was somewhere far away. He had never seen anyone in that state before. Sure, he had seen breakdowns and people crying before, but that night—that panic attack, as she liked to label it—that was something else. That was a breaking point.

And it fucking terrified him.

"Have you had one of those since?" he asked, completely ignoring her question.

She shook her head. "No, I haven't."

"Good. If you ever feel like you might be getting one, you call me right away. Understood?"

"Okay," Gianna said. "I'll call you if I ever feel one coming on again."

"Good." He was satisfied with that answer. He would pray that it never happened to her again, but at least he could trust that if it did, he could be there.

"You never answered my question, by the way."

This put a smirk on his face. "You really want to know what I thought about you even when you were on the floor, nearly suffocating?"

She turned to face him fully this time, putting whatever makeup product she had in her hand down on the counter. "Yes."

Finn stood, stalking towards her until their chests were touching. He picked up a piece of her blonde hair, twirling it in between her fingers. She smelled like strawberries—like fucking heaven. He leaned down until their lips were only inches apart.

"I was fucking terrified seeing you like that, but when you looked up at me with those big blue eyes covered in tears, something sick and fucking twisted entered my head, princess. Once you were okay, once I knew you were safe, I couldn't help but think about how fucking perfect you would look down on your knees with those blue eyes full of tears again. Only this time, it would be because you were choking on my cock." His voice was deeper, rougher than it was before. The darkening of her eyes caused his dick to swell up in his sweats. She liked what he was saying.

His thumb swiped over her lips, feeling the plumpness of them before he pushed his thumb inside her mouth. Immediately, she sucked on his thumb, twirling her tongue around it like the fucking devil she was.

"That's what I thought about you, princess. Fucking perfection."

He pulled his thumb out of her mouth, fighting the urge to replace it with something else. Instead, he settled with pulling her lips onto his, giving her a devastatingly quick kiss before pulling back.

"That's it?" she asked.

"We have dinner plans," Finn said. "And you now have forty minutes to finish getting ready."

"Fuck the dinner." Gianna grinned, pulling him back in for another kiss. "Order room service."

"I'm taking you out for our first date. Room service can be saved for the next one." He gave her one more chaste kiss before pulling away, adjusting himself in front of her. "I need to get out of here, you're addicting."

"Seems like your problem," she said, closing the door to the bathroom.

He leaned his head against it, taking in a deep breath. Horrible thoughts. That's what he needed. Horrible, disgusting thoughts to help him get rid of the boner that was begging for Gianna almost as much as he was.

He walked to the kitchen, grabbing a bottle of water from the fridge. His phone was on the counter, a text from Augustus on the screen. He opened it, shaking his head when he saw the picture of a sleeping Cecilia and Augustus right beside her.

Augustus

I owe you my fucking firstborn.

I think I'm okay without it. I hope she's alive.

She decided to take a nap after hours of screaming at me.

Seems fitting. Enjoy your night.

There was no explanation for his best friend. None.

He made his way back into the guest bedroom, finally getting dressed in the charcoal suit he had purchased for the occasion. Surprisingly, he didn't have a suit just sitting around in his closet like the other assholes he knew. He threw on his shoes and sprayed himself with his signature cologne.

Gianna seemed to enjoy it because she was always taking whiffs of it when she thought he wasn't paying attention. He always caught it, though. That was why he'd repurchased it.

He pushed back his hair, keeping it messy but controlled. He wasn't the type to do the slick back look. It never looked right on him. The untamed look was always what had suited him the best.

He passed by the full body mirror, stopping abruptly when he saw himself completely. Finn looked every bit like what he had always wanted to be: the Kingsley Don. He looked confident, strong, and menacing. The man staring back at him was the person that his father had wanted him to become. Hell, the person in the mirror looked more like his father than he ever had in his life.

One part of him so badly wanted to embrace it, to accept that this was what he was meant to be. This was his calling. He was the name and the legacy.

But the other part of him wanted to run from it as far and as fast as he could. To end the Kingsley empire and let it burn with the tarnished memory of his father. And to think it used to be about family, but the family didn't exist. Not how they had once understood it. Luna was now a Vitali, his mother was somewhere in Europe, his father was dead, and he was the only one who could continue the name or end it.

And yet, his entire life, what he wanted was right there waiting for him to take, but he hesitated like a fucking coward. Like the unworthy bastard his father always knew he was.

He wasn't that child; that controlled being unable to fight back. He was changing, becoming a different man. And that ended with the self-hesitation, the wondering of what he was made to do. He would follow his own path, he just didn't know what the fuck that was yet.

TWENTY-EIGHT

GIANNA

ONCE GIANNA'S outfit was on and her hair was curled, she walked out into the living room where Finn was waiting. Her breath caught in her throat seeing him adorning a suit for the first time in so long. He looked damn good in it too. It was a stark contrast to the typical jeans and T-shirt look he usually wore. To be honest, she couldn't decide on which one she preferred more —the effortlessly careless look or the impeccably handsome businessman one.

Finn walked over to her in an instant, like a moth to a flame. His eyes trailed over her body covering every inch in his heated gaze. She felt feverish being around him and it only got worse when his arms wrapped around her waist, pulling her closer to him.

"You look like a fucking Goddess," he said, his voice laced with devotion. "Perfect enough to worship."

Her breath hitched in her throat, while her brain was unable to form any real words. She remembered him mentioning that word before—worship. Finn had mentioned on the night of her breakdown that she would know when someone worshipped the ground she walked on.

"You would worship me?" she asked.

"On my knees with my whole being, princess."

Gianna couldn't resist wrapping her arms around him, pulling him in for a kiss that showed him just how much she wanted that devotion, that worship. She was lost in the wave that was Finn Kingsley, the push and pull of his force that had made the largest indent in her life.

She pulled away when she felt herself needing air, lightheaded and dizzy. He leaned his forehead against hers, taking in a deep breath.

"We need to get out of this fucking room before I rip this dress off of you," he said, his lips tilting up in a smirk.

"This dress is too nice to be manhandled like that," she said, grinning when he growled and pinched her ass.

"You could be wearing pure gold or a sheet of crystals, and I would still tear it apart to get to you."

"So archaic."

"Yet you seem to love it."

With one last kiss, he was pulling her out the door, but the words were stuck in her head. Shit, did she love it? The side of him that lost control. She enjoyed it, of course. Loving it though? That seemed *intense*. Like perhaps another level she wasn't yet prepared to enter.

She desperately tried to clear her mind, trying to stay in the moment instead of letting her mind wander to other places that would ultimately only stress her out. When they got down to the lobby, she was able to ground herself in the moment.

Finn's hand squeezing hers also helped.

They got into the car that had a driver this time, traveling a short distance to the restaurant. The sun was now setting, painting the city in a warm glow of bright oranges and yellows. There were even small specs of pink and purple in the sky that blended with the clouds, which put a smile on her face. It was a beautiful night, that was for sure.

They arrived at a modern Asian restaurant, one that Gianna had never been to before but heard amazing things about. Finn kept his hand on the small of her back the entire time, walking her in and allowing the hostess to lead them to the private room at the back of the establishment. The warm lighting from the flower-inspired chandelier created a romantic ambience that was only further enhanced by the red velvet chairs. The space was quiet from the rest of the restaurant's chatter, leaving them in their own world.

He pulled out the chair for her, letting her sit before he pushed it back in. Instead of taking the seat across from her, he pulled the chair up right beside her, scooting until his thigh touched hers and his arm brushed along hers every time he moved.

"Could you have gotten any closer?" she asked, stifling her laugh.

"Without you sitting on my lap, doubtful." Finn picked up the menu, scanning over it. "What would you recommend here?"

"You've never been here?" Gianna asked, confused. "You picked it out."

"I knew you liked Asian-inspired food, so I wanted to go somewhere you've never been," he said. "What do you think we should get?"

She looked at the menu herself, her mouth instantly watering. "They seem to do a variety of different East Asian popular dishes, so let's just order a little bit of everything."

"That's perfect."

As soon as the waiter came in, they ordered their drinks: a Mojito for Gianna and an Old Fashioned for Finn. Ordering the amount of food that they did felt ridiculous, but she was starving. She hadn't eaten since before practice, and she was used to having a meal afterwards.

"Are you going to tell me what you have planned for afterwards?" Gianna asked. "Or are you going to remain cryptic and pretend like you can't tell me?"

"Have you always been this complicated with surprises or is

this something new?" Finn asked, leaning back in his chair and throwing his arm around the back of hers.

"Don't answer my question with a question."

He groaned, throwing his head back dramatically. "I have plenty planned for tonight, but I don't want to reveal them."

The waiter came in with their drinks, leaving them at the table and promising that their food would be out soon before walking back out. Gianna took a sip of hers, relishing in the cold minty taste drifting down her throat.

"Can I get a hint?"

"Sure, your hint is that I'm not going to tell you anything."

She frowned. "Ass."

"My princess is turning into a brat. Don't make me have to punish you, Gianna. I think I would enjoy that too much."

A jolt of curiosity mixed with annoyance rushed through her. "Punish me? And tell me, what would that entail?" Her voice was full of sarcasm, but it stopped when his eyes turned darker.

Finn leaned in. "How about I lean you over my knee and spank that perfect ass of yours?"

Goosebumps erupted over her skin. Her tongue darted out to lick her suddenly very dry lips, and his eyes followed the movement like a hawk. "That's fucked up."

"Really? I think you might like it. I think you might be getting wet at the thought of it right now," Finn said.

Gianna clenched her jaw. He was right. She could feel the tightening in her core at the thought of his calloused hands running over her ass, spanking her repeatedly before he fucked her into oblivion.

She turned away from him, grabbing her drink and taking a long sip. "You're wrong."

Finn shrugged. "Maybe I am." His lips met her ear, licking it before whispering, "Or maybe that's one of your surprises tonight. Who knows?"

Before she could say anything else, the waiter was walking in with plates of food and Finn pulled away. Gianna was hot and bothered, fucking starving while the man next to her looked completely unbothered. She still couldn't understand how he managed to have this much of an effect on her. Without a second thought, she shoved a potsticker in her mouth.

————

"Where are we going now?" Gianna asked.

They were back in the car now, driving somewhere unknown. She was thoroughly stuffed and a little bit tipsy, but nothing extreme. They had managed to have a normal conversation after the whole spanking fiasco, which Gianna was thankful for, but now they were headed to a mystery place.

Finn gripped her thigh the entire way as he sat impossibly close to her. Honestly, she enjoyed having his warmth as the brisk dusk emerged.

"We're almost there," he said, looking out the window.

And sure enough, they were pulling up to a club. One that her brother and Dante always went to and had crazy stories from that they would giggle with each other about but would never let her or the girls go to. All Dante would say is, "*You couldn't handle it, Barbie.*"

And it pissed her off.

But now they were here, just like nothing. Gianna turned to Finn, her eyes wide. "Are we allowed to be here?" she asked.

"You know what this is?" he asked, surprised.

"I've heard of it, and me and the girls always wanted to go. Apparently, it's some really hot club or something, but we were never allowed to just come here," Gianna said.

He laughed, shaking his head. "Princess, this isn't just a club."

"What is it then?"

"It's exclusive. The people who come here are high rank rich assholes. They come here to hide away and do the shit they couldn't do in public."

"This is a sex club?"

"Some nights it is," he said. "Not tonight. There's a fight here tonight."

"So we're here to watch a fight?" she asked. "That's all?"

"My, my, does little Gianna want to go to a sex club?"

"I don't share," she said. She fluttered her eyelashes innocently. "Unless you do?"

His hand tightened on her thigh. "Not a fucking chance in hell."

He got out of the car, exiting and going to the other side to open her door for her.

"So, you're not fighting tonight?" she asked, walking into the building with him.

"Not tonight. I enjoy watching it too."

All he had to do was flash his ID and they were letting them inside, leading him up into some private suite upstairs that would be looking down at the ring. Gianna didn't recognize anyone downstairs, but she still preferred to be hidden upstairs. The suite came with a fully stocked bar and all sorts of snacks. There were couches inside where they could sit and watch the fight, but there was also a balcony area with chairs set out where they could hang on the railing and cheer with the others. A waiter was also assigned to them while they were there, all they had to do was press a button on the wall and they would appear.

The ring here was significantly bigger than the one at the arena where Fight Night usually took place. It was a pristine white and covered a larger portion of the building. Nearly every seat in the room was filled, and from the balcony, Gianna could see that the other suites also held groups of guests. All were dressed in suits and fancy dresses, despite how violent the event was.

"Have you ever fought here?" Gianna asked, taking a seat on the couch.

Finn nodded his head, walking over to the fully stocked bar and picking up a bottle. "I have. Not my favorite place to fight though. I prefer something less sterile and stuck up. But this was the only place with a fight happening and I know you love to watch them."

Her mouth dropped open. "I do not love to watch fights."

He placed two glasses on the table and took a seat beside her. "You're a terrible liar."

"I show up to Fight Night because it's a part of the festivities and all the girls go," she said.

She hated the way his eyes could read right through every word that was escaping her lips. She swallowed harshly but kept her eyes locked on his.

He opened the bottle, shaking his head in amusement. "Even though I'm usually up in that ring, I see what happens in the stands before my fight. Hell, a lot of the time I see what happens during my fight too. I see you, princess, every single time."

"How?"

"Well, you're usually wearing pink so naturally you catch my gaze every single time."

Gianna huffed, rolling her eyes. "It's my favorite color. Kill me."

"But you're always up front too, watching the fights with this admiration in your eyes. Even when they get gruesome, you keep your eyes locked on them in awe like you can't look away. At my fight, fuck, at every one of my fights, you always looked at me that way." Finn shook his head, pouring the liquid into the glasses for both of them. "I know you like the fights, and I know you bet on me every single time. I just don't know why you do."

She licked her lips, grabbing one of the glasses and swallowing it down in one gulp. Fuck, did he have to ask these types of questions now of all times? He was so much more inquisitive than people gave him credit for, that was for sure.

"How did you know about the betting?" That was her first question.

"I have access to the records." He drank his own drink, pouring both of them another one.

"I don't like all fights, you're wrong about that," she said. "I like yours."

Finn stopped what he was doing. "Why?"

"Can I lie?" she asked.

He shook his head with a grin. "I would prefer you didn't."

A sigh left her lips. "When you fight, it's like art. Just like with my dancing, you move with grace, with a method. It's not just fighting for you like it is for other people; it's more. Because of that, betting against you would be stupid."

He set the bottle on the table, instead wrapping his hands in her hair and pulling his lips to hers. It was unexpected, but she accepted it all the same. She had expected him to say something, but in her experience, sometimes there weren't enough words, or at the very least good enough words, to fully encapsulate exactly what that feeling was.

Hell, he had made her feel it far too many times so now she recognized it.

Finn pulled back, a look akin to obsession in his eyes. It sent a shiver down her spine, heat tightening in her core.

"You probably should have lied to me, Gianna," he said, pushing a strand of her hair behind her ear.

"Why?" Her voice was small and unsure.

"Because I'm afraid I'm never going to let you go now. Not in this lifetime, not even the next. You're mine, princess."

She opened her mouth to say something. What? She didn't even know what she would have said. It didn't matter anyway. His mouth was on hers again, pulling her body onto his lap while he devoured her with every single fiber of his being he had to offer.

The lights dimmed and the announcers began to call out the fighters for the first round. Gianna pulled away this time, completely breathless. "The fight is starting."

"I don't give a shit," he growled. His mouth latched onto her neck, licking and sucking on the skin in a heated frenzy. Her eyes closed in pleasure, the moisture between her legs only growing worse with every touch.

"I thought you wanted to watch it."

"I have something so much more fucking entertaining right here, princess."

He ground his hips against hers, allowing her to feel the cock that strained against his slacks. It swiped against her slit, eliciting a loud moan from her mouth that she quickly tried to cover up.

"We're in public, we can't do that here." Her mind seemed to be logical, but with every single movement of his hips, his mouth, his hands, her body was about to scream, *Forget it.*

"We won't fuck then." He stopped everything, turning her around on his lap so she was now sitting with her back against his chest.

It was dark enough in both the suite and the arena that no one would be able to see inside, but still the thought of anyone looking in and seeing them in this position caused butterflies in her belly.

"What are you doing?" she asked as his hands settled on her thighs, rubbing the skin.

"Watching the fight like you wanted." His voice was deep and rough. Lips found her ear, biting on the skin before he whispered, "Just don't make a sound."

She swallowed harshly, biting her lip. His right hand moved up her thigh, disappearing under her dress. Gianna tried to focus on the fight happening down below. She had no idea who the fighters were or who she was supposed to be rooting for. So far, there was no blood on the ring and neither seemed to be in any serious pain.

She gasped when she felt his fingers through her underwear, rubbing along her pussy slowly. It was barely a touch, but her body was already melting.

"Not a peep, princess," Finn said, adding more pressure. "Wouldn't want anyone to know I'm playing with your pussy in here or we'll have to stop."

"Don't stop. Please," she begged.

She could feel his smile against her cheek. "Needy."

His movements stopped for a moment, but it was only so he could push her underwear to the side and feel her without any fabric in the way. Gianna closed her eyes, desperately trying to not make a sound.

"You're so wet," he groaned while rubbing circles on her clit. "Fuck, I missed this pussy."

He kept up the tortuous pleasure. Gianna leaned her head back on his shoulder, letting herself get lost in every single wave of pleasure that swept through her.

"Eyes open, princess. You need to be watching the fight," Finn said, stopping again. "Or are we done here?"

"No," she nearly shouted. "Don't stop."

She looked down at the ring again, noticing that both fighters were exchanging blows with each other. Blood was now smeared on the floor of the ring, coating their bodies as well. She thought about Finn the night of his fight, when he was covered in blood and sweat. A rush of pleasure shot through her.

It didn't help that one hand was still on her clit while the other one was now thrusting a finger inside of her, curling up to hit that spot inside that he had made his mission to find every single time. Gianna clenched her jaw, desperately trying to stay quiet. Her nails dug their way into his arm, the stimulation pushing her further and further to an orgasm.

"You're almost there," Finn said, moving his hands quicker. The sounds of his hands moving inside of her slick cunt filled the suite and it made her feel unbelievably dirty. "Don't come yet."

"What?" she asked, nearly delirious.

"You'll come when I say you can."

"Please," she begged. "Finn."

"I love when you beg, princess," he said, looking at her with dark eyes. "But don't be a brat and hold on for me."

She tried—fuck, she did. But everything was becoming too much. She looked down at the ring, seeing that one opponent was knocked out and the other one was standing above him in victory.

Gianna could feel her orgasm approaching. She couldn't hold on. Fuck, there was no way.

She turned towards him, pressing her lips to his to help silence herself as the orgasm ripped through her. Finn kept fucking her with his fingers, letting her ride out her orgasm until she was completely spent. Gianna pulled away, breathless and undeniably happy.

He slipped his hands out of her dress just as the lights were coming back on, licking the moisture from her off them. He grabbed a napkin from the table, wiping the rest of it off.

"Is there another fight?" Gianna asked, leaning on him. "Or what's the plan now?"

Finn gave her a look that she couldn't quite pinpoint. Something that looked wicked. "Now, we're going back to the hotel so you can experience your punishment."

"Punishment? What the hell for?"

He leaned in close. "You came before I said you could."

Her mouth dropped open and she thought back to it. He hadn't said it—in fact, he hadn't said anything. He pushed her and knew she was coming, but he didn't give permission. Not that she needed it; she was a grown ass woman.

Gianna's eyes narrowed. "You did that on purpose. You wanted me to do that so you would have a reason to spank me. Fuck, you wanted to since the restaurant."

Finn shrugged. "I guess we'll never know for sure."

He stood up, adjusting himself right in front of her eyes. She frowned, crossing her arms, ignoring the hand he stuck out for her as she stood by herself.

"If you wanted a brat, you're about to get her."

She walked out first, knowing he was following right behind her. Her skin was hot the entire time. All she could think about was what the hell she had gotten herself into.

TWENTY-NINE

FINN

IT WAS a silent car ride back to the hotel because Gianna refused to speak to Finn. He hated to admit that it only made his dick harder when she leaned into the bratty nature of her personality. Fuck, he lived for it.

He also lived for when she called him out on his bullshit. He knew she was coming, and he hadn't told her to come on purpose. He wanted a reason to spank her. The image getting put into his head during dinner fucking rotted his mind to the point where he couldn't think of anything else but seeing her ass red. He had never done the punishment shit before or the withholding of orgasms or even the spanking really, but with Gianna, he loved to play with her. It came so naturally to test her control and patience just like she did with him all the fucking time.

She didn't even talk to him in the lobby or in the elevator and he gave it to her. It was probably better to save it for the hotel room anyway. She walked ahead of him to the penthouse door, giving him a perfect view of her perky ass that he was sure she was moving more than usual just to torture him.

He swiped them into the room, immediately letting her in first and then locking it behind him. The room was dimmed, but the lights from the city shone through the open windows, providing more than enough light to see everything inside. Finn slid off his jacket, setting it on the couch in the living room before pulling the tie off as well.

Gianna stomped to the master bedroom, muttering something under her breath the entire time. He followed behind her, entering the room to see her heels thrown on the floor. He took his shoes off as well, setting them by the door.

"Gianna?" he called out, taking a seat on the bed.

He rolled up the sleeves of his button up, loosening the suffocating shirt. He hated wearing shit like this for that reason; it was always so uncomfortable.

The lights in the bathroom were on. The toilet flushed and he heard the sink turn on for a minute before it was turned back off, revealing Gianna once again. She glared at him, still wearing her dress.

"Can I help you with something?" she asked, crossing her arms.

He patted his lap, unable to keep the grin off his face. "You know what time it is."

Her cheeks turned red. "This is really dumb. I'm not into these types of fetishes."

His brow lifted. "Oh, and which ones are you into?"

She let out a frustrated sound, standing before him now. "One time. We're doing this one time and that's it."

"If you hate it that much, just say stop and we'll stop." He wasn't going to force her into anything, hell no. But he could tell she was curious, at least a little bit.

"We need a better word than stop," she said. Gianna thought for a second, biting on the skin of her nail. "Pink will be the word. If either one says pink, then we stop immediately."

"Deal."

She nodded. "Okay."

He leaned back, looking her over. "Take off your dress."

Gianna pulled it over her body, letting it fall to the floor. All she stood in was a pair of underwear that still had a wet stain on them from earlier, but there was no bra, meaning she hadn't been wearing one all night. The same ache returned from between his legs, reminding him of how long it had been since he had come.

She was confident in her body, not bothering to hide it. She didn't need to. She was absolute perfection, and he would always think so.

"Come here," he said, beckoning her closer. He pressed a kiss to her lips, slipping his tongue into her mouth. She responded immediately, wrapping her hands into his hair. He slipped her underwear down her legs, helping her step out of them so she was now fully naked.

He pulled away. "Lay over my thighs."

She looked hesitant but did so anyway. She laid her full body weight on him, exposing her ass to him. With her head angled towards the floor and her ass in his face, he was quite enjoying the view. Her pussy glistened in the light, clearly enjoying everything much more than she said she would.

"What are you waiting for?" she asked, her impatience peeking through.

He smiled, rubbing her ass with his hand. "Thinking about how many times I should spank you. What do you think? You promised to be a brat, so what do you think a brat deserves?"

"Maybe I can be your princess again and only get one?" she asked.

He laughed, squeezing her ass cheek. "I don't think so. What about twenty?"

"Hell no!"

"Fine, what about ten?"

"Five."

"Nine."

"Six."

"Seven."

"Fine," she groaned. "Seven."

Finn lifted his hand, letting the first slap come unexpectedly. The impact with her skin made her gasp.

"I thought you were going to warn me," Gianna said.

"You forgot to count," he said. "Should I start again?"

She shook her head immediately. "One."

He lifted his hand again, slapping the other one this time. Her thighs tensed and she gasped, but not from surprise this time.

"Two."

He did it again, and again, both slaps sending bolts of pleasure straight to his dick. He could see the moisture gathering between her legs and slowly the gasps became less out of surprise and started to sound more breathless.

"Three. Four."

"Is this your pussy getting wet?" Finn asked, running his hand through her slick cunt. Sure enough, it was soaked. "Are you enjoying this, princess?"

"Shut up," she muttered. "Just finish it."

"You can use your safe word, make this all end."

Gianna was quiet, but he didn't miss the slight shake of her head.

He raised his hand up again, striking her ass. This time a moan did leave her. "Five."

Finn gave her the next one, putting more pressure behind it. She arched her back, raising her ass more.

"Six."

He ran his hand over her ass, letting it drift over her pussy briefly. "Last one," he told her.

With one last lift of his hand, he let it meet her ass, the impact harsher than the others. She moaned, grabbing onto his leg.

"Seven."

"So perfect," he told her. He rubbed her ass cheeks, relishing in the red marks that now coated the once clear skin. "You did so good, princess."

Finn let his hand drift to her pussy, rubbing her clit before trailing up and over her asshole. She gasped, but he held her back down, rubbing the hole back there.

"Has anyone ever fucked you here, princess?" he asked, using his thumb to rub circles on it.

She shook her head. "No."

He nodded. "I won't do it tonight, but I'll be the only one to fuck you here."

Gianna seemed relieved, but that didn't mean he wasn't going to play with it. He leaned down, letting his tongue run over the back hole. A surprised noise left her lips, one of pleasure and shock.

He let his fingers find her clit while he continued licking her hole, letting moan after moan escape her lips freely now. He hated when she had to mute herself. Finn wanted to hear her loudly, to listen to everything he was doing to her.

Too bad his punishment wasn't over, though.

He bit her ass cheek before moving away from her. Finn grabbed her hips, sitting her up on his lap now. Her cheeks were flushed, and her pupils were blown wide, a careless smile on her face.

"How do you feel?" he asked, brushing his thumbs against her cheeks.

"Good," she said. "My ass is a little sore, but nothing I can't handle."

"Perfect. Now, get on your knees, princess."

This time, she didn't fight it. She slid onto the floor, undoing his buckle. Her hands made quick work of unzipping the slacks. Finn sat up, so she could pull them down his legs along with his underwear, letting them hang by his ankles.

Immediately, his cock slapped against his stomach. Pre-cum leaked out the tip, the need to come overwhelming. Gianna wasted no time grabbing the base of his dick and running her hand up and down, stroking it with a tight grip.

Finn could only watch her in awe, especially when she finally leaned down to innocently lick his tip. She rounded it with her tongue, looking up at him through hooded eyes. He groaned, desperately trying to stay in control.

So much for a fucking punishment. Gianna looked like she was enjoying how much power she had over him. He gave it over to her, fuck it. He didn't need the control when her mouth was on his dick, sending him straight to Heaven.

When her mouth wrapped around him, swallowing him down, his hand got wrapped up in her hair. What she couldn't fit in her mouth, she covered with her hand. The combination of her hand and her mouth working simultaneously made him dizzy.

But he needed more.

He pulled out of her mouth, causing her to look up at him with furrowed brows.

"Why did you stop?" she asked.

"I'm going to fuck your mouth. Is that okay, baby?" he asked, gathering her hair in his hands.

"I don't even know what that means," she said.

He leaned down, giving her a sloppy kiss, tasting himself on her. "I promise I'll be gentle."

Gianna nodded, her eyes filled with uncertainty as she settled her hands on his thighs. With one last peck, he was thrusting himself inside of her mouth, forcing his dick to the back of her throat.

She gagged but managed to take every single thrust perfectly.

"That's right, princess. Take it all." The moans escaped Finn's lips at an embarrassing speed, but fuck if it wasn't perfect seeing her on her knees choking on his dick.

Small tears slipped from the corners of her eyes, and he could feel his dick get harder. "Look at you crying on my cock. So pretty."

And fuck, she was. Absolutely the image of an angel. And just like that, he could feel the tightening at the base of his spine, traveling straight into his balls. Fuck, he was going to come, and he needed her to take all of it.

With one last thrust, he held himself at the back of her throat, suffocating her while he came. Her nails dug into his thighs, tears slipped out of her eyes, and he swore she never looked more beautiful in her life.

Finally, Finn pulled out, letting her take a deep breath. She swallowed as much as she could, letting the rest drip out of her mouth and onto her lap.

"Are you okay, baby?" he asked, taking off his shirt and wiping her mouth with it.

She nodded, leaning her head on his thigh. "Perfect."

He couldn't help the grin that settled on his face, helping her stand. "I guess it's time for your reward now."

She groaned. "There's more?"

"I promise you'll like this," he said, kissing her shoulder. He fell back on the bed, letting his body bounce while he looked up at her. "Come here."

Gianna got on the bed, straddling his lap. Finn shook his head. He would fuck her pussy, but he needed a real taste of her first.

"You got the right idea, princess, but wrong location."

Her eyes lit up. She moved so she was now straddling his face instead. "You could have told me this was what you meant."

"Where's the fun in that?"

He wasted no time in pulling her down, so she was properly sat on his face. Holding her there, he began licking her cunt and teasing her clit with his tongue. She bucked against his face, holding onto the bed frame with a tight grip.

His tongue snaked its way inside her slit, thrusting in and out of her. He could feel her tightening against him, pulsing with every movement he gave her. She gasped and moaned, begging him for something that he was sure she didn't even know what it was.

His hands moved up her body, pulling at her nipples that stood erect. It was hard to breathe between her thighs, but he would die a happy man as long as she came blissfully on his tongue. Knowing Gianna's pussy though, she needed the stimulation on her clit. It drove her crazy.

With that, he moved his mouth to it, sucking on her clit gently at first before increasing pressure. She ground her hips hard against him, riding his face and using him to chase her own pleasure.

"Finn," she whimpered, calling out for him like she was calling out to her God.

And finally, she came, her body shuttering. Heavy breaths left her lips; her eyes closed in bliss. She got off his face, lying next to him on the bed.

But his dick was back to being hard, and he was ready to finally fuck her.

He didn't give her a chance to recover before he was putting her on her stomach, lifting her ass in the air. He spit on his hand, stroking his cock before he entered her warmth, suffocating himself around her.

He would never get used to the feeling of being inside her, of how much it felt like he was returning home every single time they met up like that. It was an explosion that he had never been able to understand, and he wouldn't ever be able to. All he knew was that there was nothing more perfect, more pure, more fucking right in the world than what he had with Gianna, and he would never let anyone or anything take it away from him.

He thrusted like a madman, holding her waist while he fucked her from behind. She looked back at him, her makeup smeared and a look of pure admiration and lust on her face. There was something else there, something that rocked him to his core that he knew he matched. Something that he was fucking terrified of, and yet equally enthralled to have.

He lifted her head, kissing her passionately. It was messy and raw, but it was everything he fucking needed. Covered in sweat and dizzy with obsession, he gave her everything he could. She deserved it all. Not a coward, not a fucking insecure asshole; she deserved the person he was meant to be. The one that she believed in.

Finn reached down, rubbing her clit and matching every

thrust while she pushed her hips against his. This time, he didn't have to tell her to wait to come; they came together. Completely breathless and exhausted, they slumped on the bed, a mess of limbs, unsure of where the first one ended and the second one began.

Gianna looked up at him, a bright smile on her face.

He looked at her in question. "What?"

"Are you still my boyfriend?" she asked.

"Have I ever stopped being it?" He grabbed her hand, pressing a kiss to it. "Because as I recall, I always was. You just refused to accept it."

"Well, then that answers my question."

"Is this you accepting it?" he asked.

She shrugged. "Let's just say it's me not fighting it."

Finn shook his head. "Fucking brat."

But he still accepted it. Of course he did. He would accept it all, anything she gave him. Why?

Because Finn Kingsley was in love with Gianna Moretti.

THIRTY

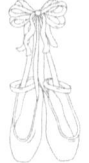

GIANNA

BLISS. That was Gianna's new favorite word. It was all she had been experiencing since they came back from their date and continued their secret little meet ups late at night or while they took the bike out. She was completely enthralled, constantly giggly like a schoolgirl with a new crush.

It sickened her.

But she loved it.

All she wanted to do was talk about it to everyone and anything, but that was the one downside. She couldn't. She could talk about it to Cecilia, but even then it wasn't the same because she wanted to be able to get all the girls in on it. She missed the group gossip and being able to talk about everything together.

While she was avoiding life with Finn, she was able to forget that so many people in her life didn't know about their relation-ship yet. The thought made her anxiety constantly flare, which caused her to push herself too much during practice, so then she was left messing up time and time again.

She let out a frustrated groan, pushing small bits of hair back that escaped from her bun. The studio was empty now, save for a couple of people who might have still lingered in the fitness room next door. Otherwise, she had the studio to herself, which she preferred. She hated messing up in front of her teacher, whose nose flared every single time Gianna's leg wasn't curled enough or when her face wasn't serene because she was concentrating instead on getting every move right.

When she was alone, she could let the music consume her without worrying about anyone's watchful eye.

"That wasn't a very elegant noise." Finn's voice came from behind her, forcing Gianna to turn around.

She snorted. "Yeah, well most things in life aren't."

He approached her, letting his hands settle on her waist. "What's got you so frustrated?"

"I can't get the move right and it's making me over think it. And when I overthink it, I just get more in my head about it when really I should be trying to get out of my head so I could just let my body move. Even now, I'm wasting time trying to explain it to you when I need to just figure it out," Gianna said with a huff, throwing her head onto his chest. "I'm so tired."

Finn pressed a kiss to her head, wrapping his arms around her. Surprisingly, the action did help her. It soothed her enough to make her think logically, even if only for a second.

"What do you usually do to get yourself out of ruts like this?" he asked.

She shrugged, pulling away to look at him. "Usually, I just dance until my feet bleed, then go home and eat while soaking them in ice water to forget about it all."

He rolled his eyes. "Yeah, that sounds healthy."

"Well, what do you recommend?"

"Why don't you go through the dance, and I can help you with the part you keep messing up on. You said it was some kind of jump or whatever, so I'll help you. Maybe I can see something you can't."

Gianna thought about it for a second. It wouldn't hurt to try. At this point, she really didn't have much to lose other than her dignity if she fell and completely embarrassed herself in front of him.

She nodded her head. "Fine. Sit against the wall."

She tried to walk away, but he held her in place for a moment longer. Before she could ask what was wrong, he leaned down and pressed a kiss to her lips, allowing it to linger there for a moment before he pulled away once again.

"You almost forgot that, by the way," he said, finally going to the wall.

"God forbid," she muttered, a small smile sneaking its way onto her lips.

He took her phone that was connected to the speaker, settling down on the floor while she faced away from him to look at herself in the mirror.

Finn shook his head. "No, try doing it without looking at yourself. Act like this is a performance. You wouldn't be able to stare at yourself if you were actually performing."

She turned around. "I also wouldn't have a crowd of only one person."

"Am I making you nervous?"

It did make her nervous. She was either comfortable performing for a group of people or for no one at all, not doing a one-on-one with someone like Finn who already made her stomach flutter uncontrollably.

Gianna took a deep breath. "I'll be okay. Start the music."

She got into her starting position, locking eyes with him as he clicked play on the music. The orchestral sound filled the room. The number began slowly, with her on pointe moving her arms rhythmically around her. She did several *chaines* turns as she moved across the floor, keeping her gaze locked on Finn's. His eyes didn't sway once.

Gianna bent over, allowing her arms to travel down her leg like a waterfall before she lifted her back leg, stretching it up behind her. She then let it drop, matching the crescendo of the music. The choreography called for quick *changements*, where she jumped in place, switching her legs and crisscrossing them each time. She kept her arms at fifth *en avant* before moving them out to *à la seconde*. As the tension in the music built, the moves became more frequent and dramatic.

She got into fourth *arabesque*, spinning quickly and using Finn's brown eyes as her spot with every turn. She stopped, landing in fifth position. Her legs were on fire, but the cellos and the violins in the music played more rapidly now. It was almost the end of the dance. Her thighs and feet were exhausted and aching, but she had to finish strong.

Gianna did the *pas de chat* until she was almost at the center of the floor now, transitioning into a *glissade*. This was the big moment. The one that she always choked on. The one she was never able to land.

Her arms stayed out beside her as she pushed off to leap into the air. With both legs extended on either side of her, she made sure to keep them taunt before she was back to landing on the ground. She dropped on her front leg first, never letting the one behind her touch the ground because she had another series of turns immediately after.

When the last one finished, she slowed down with the music, hearing the last of the violin with her as she did one last *glissade*. She dropped to the floor slowly, letting the music consume her as she did. Her legs burned, her heart beat rapidly.

And then the music stopped.

Finn clapped slowly, and when Gianna looked at him, he looked like he was in awe. She couldn't help the blush that settled on her face.

"That was fucking amazing," he said, standing up. "I swear I don't think I've ever seen anything more beautiful in my life."

She shook her head. "I messed up the jump. I always do."

"Princess, you nailed the jump and every turn after it. You didn't fall out of it today."

Her eyes widened as she thought about what he said. Gianna landed the move. She was so consumed with dancing and his presence that she hadn't even realized that she didn't fall or even tip over. She landed every single move.

She beamed as she jumped up, landing in his arms. "I landed it!"

"You did. You did so fucking amazing. I'm so proud of you." He pressed a kiss to her lips, one that she gladly deepened, feeling ready to celebrate in any way that she could.

"You might be my good luck charm."

"I don't mind coming and watching you practice," Finn said. "Hell, I'll be here every day."

She shook her head. "I hope you'll come to my show."

"I wouldn't miss it for the world." He leaned down, pressing his forehead against hers.

"What do you say to getting something to eat? I'm starving," Gianna said.

"Let's go. I know a great burger place not too far from here," Finn said.

"I have to change first."

"You know how I feel about the ballet uniform."

She rolled her eyes. "I know you would love for me to keep it on, but unfortunately this isn't for everyone's eyes."

"I can agree with that," he said.

She pulled away from him, pulling off the wrap skirt and top and replacing it with sweatpants and a T-shirt from her dance bag instead. She sat down on the floor, beginning to take off her pointe shoes.

"Fuck, Gianna, that looks painful," he said, kneeling in front of her. "Do your feet usually get all bloody like this?"

She shrugged. "It depends. I had a blister though, so the shoe was rubbing against it while I was dancing. It's not as bad as it looks."

He shook his head. "You need to take it easier on yourself." He pulled the gauze from her hands, helping with cleaning up the blood and locating the blister on the side of her pinkie toe.

"Once the show is done, I'll be able to. For now, I have to be strict with myself. Especially since this was the first time I finally nailed the jump. I have to start perfecting it." She handed him the antibiotic ointment she usually used, watching as he applied it to the blister on her foot. His movements were so gentle, so much so she could hardly feel him doing it at all.

"You scare me with your determination," he said with a small smile on his face.

"Well, if someone told you to stop fighting, would you?"

He shook his head immediately. "No, I don't think so."

"That's exactly the same case with me. It's my art. Without it, it would be like losing a piece of myself. In times like this, I have to see the pain as temporary."

Finn let out a small chuckle while he grabbed the bandage from her hands to place it on her foot. Gianna frowned. "What?" she asked.

"You're so fucking cute when you act just like me."

"Does that mean you act like a princess?"

He exhaled, sliding one of her boots onto her foot. "Probably."

"You know what, I would agree with that."

In a split second, Finn had her pinned with her back against the wooden floor. His hands rested under her head, providing a cushion for her. He had a smirk on his face. "If I'm such a princess now, that means you have to give me the princess treatment."

His lips found her neck, kissing the soft skin and moving to the space under her jaw. Gianna closed her eyes.

"Oh please, what sort of princess treatment do I get?" She snorted, frowning once again when he pulled away. She opened her eyes, crossing her arms. "What a tease."

"Princess treatment includes finishing, among other things," Finn said, grinning wickedly when her eyes narrowed on him. "But according to you, I don't give you the princess treatment, so I guess you don't need that anymore."

"Fine, you're not the princess, I am." She grinned, pulling him down to her. It was fun playing with him like this, riling him up so he would in return rile her up back. "Now, finish what you started."

"I thought you were hungry," he said, leaning down to kiss her. "And I'm not gonna let you starve."

"How about food first and then you finish me off?" Gianna suggested, wiggling her eyebrows.

"Best fucking deal."

THIRTY-ONE

FINN

THE BURGER SHOP was close to campus and was pretty busy considering it had just opened. Finn had already finished his food, but Gianna was such a slow eater that she was only halfway through hers. She kept stopping for her milkshake, using the straw to get the cookie chunks out of it instead of eating the actual food on the plate.

He would have gotten a milkshake of his own, but honestly watching Gianna dance had been a treat all on its own. He had never seen anyone move their body the way she had, in such a graceful manner. The way she transformed into her dancer-self, getting into the headspace the moment the music began was exactly what happened to him the moment he entered the ring.

It was like everything around him disappeared. It was just him and his body. That seemed to be what happened to her as well. She fell into her own.

He cleared his throat, catching her attention. Whenever her blue eyes locked on him, it made him nervous. Having her attention was like having the spotlight.

"After our date night, I've come to some realizations about my life," he said.

She raised her eyebrow. "Oh? Like what?"

"I think I want to take over the Kingsley empire," Finn told her. "I am the Kingsley heir and it's only right that I step up."

Gianna nodded, taking everything in. "What made you change your mind? I thought you were completely against it all."

He exhaled loudly. "I was. Shit, I'm still against how my father ran things. But something about that night and seeing myself, it gave me a sense of accomplishment. Our conversations too helped me realize that I don't have to follow what anyone thinks about me. This is something that feels right for me and I think I should give it a shot."

Her smile stretched across her cheeks. "Well, I think it's a great idea. As long as it's something you want to do, I know everyone will support you on it."

"Will you support me on it?"

Fuck. He sounded pathetic asking her, but truthfully, he craved her support. His stomach had been in knots since he decided to venture into the business side of the Kingsley family name, and he didn't think he could do it without her there. She had a way of calming him, of putting out the fire that threatened to destroy everything around him.

"Of course I will. One hundred percent I will be there every step of the way." She grabbed his hand, giving it a tight squeeze. "Speaking of, what is the first step?"

"I'm going to the office tomorrow with Valerio. He's going to get me caught up on all the investments and the business side of things." He ran his thumb over her knuckles. "And then I guess we'll go from there. I'm not anticipating that it'll take me long to catch up on all of it. I trained my whole life for all of it."

"Sounds like a good plan," Gianna said. "So, you'll be staying here for a while then?"

Finn couldn't help the smirk that settled onto his face. "Why? Were you betting on me leaving?"

She shook her head. "No, but I wasn't sure if settling down long term was in your plan."

Hell, he didn't think it was either. Until recently, he didn't know what the hell his plan was. He hadn't even had a plan. He just went wherever the world pulled him, like a leaf in the wind. Now, he was making plans for the future, taking charge of his life. New motivations did that to a man.

To be fair, not having a plan hadn't led him completely astray. He didn't have a plan when he met Gianna and that turned out to be one of the best things that had ever happened to him.

"I'm staying, princess," he told her, the certainty clear in his voice. "I guess that means I'll have to find a place to live."

"You're going to move out?" Her eyes were wide. "What the hell? I actually don't like this plan at all."

"Why don't you move in with me?"

The shock on her face matched the feeling he felt inside. He couldn't believe that he had dropped the question too. So casually, at that. The shock wasn't even from asking her to move in, but rather at how soon he was able to ask it and how comfortable he felt around her that he felt like they could live together no problem.

It should have terrified him how significant the relationship had become, how much Gianna meant to him. But it didn't. Instead, it felt like it was exactly what should have been happening.

"Move in with you?" she asked, stuttering over the words. "Like live together?"

"I know. What a wild concept. It's not like we've ever done that before," he said, sarcasm thick in his voice.

She frowned. "That's different. The way we live together now would be completely different to the way it would be if we really lived together. We would be alone and share a bedroom. I barely have space in my room for all my clothes now, where would I put everything?"

"I'd give you a whole room for your clothes, another for your studio. Hell, decorate it to your heart's desires in whatever way you want. As long as you're there, I would love it."

"Well, now I'm dreaming about this home," she said, her eyes glossed over.

Finn let out a hefty laugh, shaking his head. "Dream all you want, just make it a reality. Luckily for you, I don't need an answer yet, princess."

Gianna nodded her head, keeping her smile on her face. "What time are you joining Valerio tomorrow?"

"Too fucking early. I think the asshole is purposely making the time earlier just to fuck with me," Finn said.

"Knowing Valerio, he probably is."

"What are your plans for tomorrow?"

Gianna shrugged. "I'm not sure yet. I have class and then I'll probably try to hang out with the girls. It's been a while since we've had a girls' night."

"And tomorrow night?"

She rolled her eyes. "I just said girls' night, you ogre."

"You're going to leave me without my fix of you?" Finn asked.

"You have me right now."

"Not enough."

"Has anyone ever told you you're clingy?" she asked, raising her eyebrow.

He snorted. "Clingy? Is that how I've been?"

"Mhmm. Totally clingy."

"Huh, I didn't know. I've never had anyone to be clingy with."

Gianna shook her head with a smile. "You're ridiculous."

"Only for you, princess."

Fucking hell, it was only for her.

He paid the bill when it came. They got out of the booth, walking towards the exit. Finn held her hand the entire way, being the clingy man that she now labeled him as. From the corner of his eye, he saw someone staring with wide eyes and an open mouth. He probably should have looked closer, but his girlfriend had a way of keeping his attention always. Still, he could have sworn that he recognized the caramel hair that sat with the pretentious pre-law students, thinking it looked a lot like Blair Adler herself.

It all slipped his mind the moment Gianna gave him a kiss, though. She got onto the bike with her helmet on and he did the same before revving the engine and taking off.

Finn shook his head, letting himself relax with her arms around him. He would hold onto that peace for as long as he could.

THIRTY-TWO

FINN

FINN WASN'T one to enjoy early mornings. He had always preferred the potential for trouble late at night much more than the ambition of the early morning, but Valerio seemed to be an early riser, so he was forced to adapt.

He showered and threw on a nice suit, making sure he looked every bit the part he was meant to be playing. Fuck, he really wished it would eventually stop feeling like he was pretending and instead feel natural, like he was meant to be in the role.

Finn headed out of his room, wanting to go to Gianna's to say goodbye before he left, but was met with an overly cheerful Dante instead.

"What are you doing here?" Finn asked, confused.

"Thought we could carpool." Dante wrapped an arm around his shoulders as they walked. "I go down to the office on certain occasions to help Valerio out, so does Allister."

"And you're both going today?"

"Yep. It seemed necessary to help welcome you to your new life."

Finn rolled his eyes. "This isn't new. You're forgetting that I grew up an heir too. I know my way around this business bullshit."

Dante threw his hands up in surrender. "Hey, I'm sure you do. But now that we're family, you've got to realize that we all support each other. I know that's a foreign word for you, so I'll spell it out. S-U—"

They had reached the kitchen when he was interrupted by Allister who was already awake and typing away on his laptop.

"Finally. Let's go before we're late. There's coffee at the office," he said, closing the laptop and standing.

Finn looked at the clock. "It's not even seven yet."

"Allister is a little anal about time management," Dante said.

"Dante just likes anal," Allister snapped back.

"If I was drinking anything, I would have choked."

Finn could already feel a headache coming on and they hadn't even made it out of the house yet. They walked to the garage, and there seemed to be no argument about who was sitting where. Dante was driving, Allister was in the passenger, and that left Finn in the back seat. It made him stop to consider if he would ever be a part of this routine where things fell into a natural order like this. Hell, normalcy and routine hadn't been a thing in his life since before his father died. Even then, the days were always so unpredictable because of his father's attitude. In a split second, the way he felt would change the projection of Finn's day from being the best to being the worst.

It was hard not to think about such things while they drove, and no one made any conversation. Dante played music and Allister typed away on his phone. Finn was bored. He pulled out his phone, sending a text to Gianna to wish her a good morning whenever she woke up. Knowing her, she would probably be sleeping for another couple of hours.

He wished he had the ability to sleep as much as she did.

They pulled up to a skyscraper of a building. The letters at the very top and on the entrance spelt out 'Vitali,' letting everyone in the city know exactly who owned it. Finn wouldn't have expected anything humbler from Valerio, but who was he to judge?

The valet grabbed the keys from Dante and soon the three

were walking through the front doors. Despite how early it still was, the building was bustling with people moving around, talking on their phones or with other colleagues, cups of coffee in their hands. This looked like a legit business and less like the illegitimate shit their fathers had been running for so many years.

Finn followed Dante and Allister into the elevator. The button for the top floor had been pressed. The elevator was surrounded with tinted glass, meaning that as they rose up the many floors of the building, the skyline of the city with the rising sun came into view. It was breathtaking to see and felt oddly motivational early in the morning like that. Maybe there was some psychology between hope and sunlight.

The doors opened and they exited, grabbing coffees that were waiting at the receptionist's desk for them. Everything was so organized and pristine; it kind of freaked Finn out. He knew that Valerio was set in his fucking ways, but this level of control was over the top.

Or was it because he had no structure in his own life? Fuck, how was he supposed to know?

The bitterness of the coffee immediately hijacked his senses. It was plain black, no sugar or milk anywhere near it. God, Valerio seriously was as bland as they came.

The three of them walked past a couple of cubicles that were lined on the sides of the walkway.

Finn cleared his throat. "Do either of you have offices here?"

"We both do. They're next to Valerio's though for obvious reasons. Up here are the more important staff members that work with him directly, and then those people usually delegate the work down to the floors below," Allister said. "He has a very organized way of doing things."

"I think that's pretty obvious." Finn snorted.

"I wish I could have gotten some of his organizational genes. My life is a fucking mess," Dante said, huffing.

Finn couldn't have felt that on a more personal level.

They reached his office finally and Allister knocked on it,

waiting for the voice on the other side to let him in. Immediately, Finn could tell that Luna had a lot of influence on the space. The entire room felt like an old librarian's office with the mahogany desk, the floor to ceiling bookshelves filled with law and business books, and even the dark brown leather couch that had a white throw blanket on it. It all felt so homey and unlike the rest of the building, which was what immediately gave it away.

"Finally, you're here," Valerio said, looking up from his stack of papers. "I thought that when we had agreed on a time, you would have had the decency to make it at that time."

Finn rolled his eyes. "It's still early as fuck. You're fine."

"What's on the agenda today, boss?" Dante asked, immune to any of the tension in the room. He plopped himself down in one of the chairs in front of Valerio's desk, leaning back in it. "Is it a boring day or a fun one?"

"I never know how to answer that question for you."

"So it's a surprise?"

Allister shook his head. "Some of the contracts from the Irish came through last night. I was looking over them this morning, but I didn't have a chance to finish them."

"Get that done as soon as you can. I want to have a look and send back my feedback before anything is signed and confirmed," Valerio said.

Finn stood there, confused about what any of them were talking about. "This isn't Bring Your Child to Work Day. I'm here so you can show me what you've been doing with the Kingsley businesses. I'm not going to fuck off and twiddle my thumbs all day."

"Of course not. Why would you make my life easier?" Valerio said, rolling his eyes. "Dante, help Allister with the contracts."

Dante opened his mouth to argue but quickly shut it when a look passed between the brothers. Some sort of understanding or something. Him and Allister left the room, leaving Valerio and Finn. Valerio motioned for him to take the seat that Dante had been in, and Finn did. It was silent and awkward once again, the tension rising as neither one spoke for a good minute.

"What do you know about the Kingsley accounts?" Valerio asked, finally breaking the silence.

"What? Like right now?" Finn asked. "Jack shit."

He let out a deep breath. "What did you know about them? Or how involved in them were you when your father was alive?"

"I wasn't allowed to touch the accounts or move any money around ever. The most I ever did was any pickups, but that was in cash, and I immediately had to drop the money off to him." Finn cleared his throat. "I sat in on meetings and met with his men, but he dealt with the money side of things on his own for the most part."

"Did you ever ask for more involvement?"

He snorted. "Of course I did. I would have fucking killed to know more about the family business, but he hesitated and waited."

Really, his father had always said that Finn wasn't ready. The one fucking thing Finn had never believed in his life, but his father refused to backtrack on.

Valerio opened one of the drawers in his desk, pulling out a large folder and set it in front of him.

"What is this?" Finn asked.

"This is everything we had to do when we took over the accounts, the properties, everything."

He placed his hand on top of it, hesitating to open it. There was something Finn was missing; something Valerio wasn't telling him.

"What are you leaving out?"

Valerio huffed, leaning back in his chair. "When we took over the accounts, there was close to nothing in them. Your father had been reckless and drained everything. Multiple accounts were closed, several properties were being foreclosed on, and I had to pour money into it to save them."

Finn felt his heart drop. "What?"

"Looking back at it, that's probably why he wanted to sell Luna off to the highest bidder, and honestly, it doesn't look like you would have been safe from it either. He was running out of money, becoming careless."

He shook his head, running a hand through his hair. There was no way. Their entire lives they had lived in a curtain of wealth with parties and galas and the nicest houses. Reece Kingsley had thrown money around like he had it to spare. He hadn't allowed Finn to see or touch any of it as if he had something to protect.

Maybe this was his dark secret. The fact that he had run a multi-generational crime family into the fucking ground. Luna, Finn, their mother—they all had poured their trust into him, and he would have left them to starve, to die.

"The money I got when he died, where did that come from?" Finn asked.

"There was still some left over, so that was what you received. But there's more to the story."

"What? What could it possibly be?"

The look on Valerio's face sent a chill down his spine. It was a look of pity, one that Finn didn't want from anyone.

"Read the will," was all Valerio said.

Finn threw open the folder, immediately finding the will sitting on top. His eyes traced every word, every line and he had to force himself to slow down so he could actually comprehend what he was reading.

All estates, accounts, money, investments, and life insurance will be left to the heir of the Kingsley family name. In the case of Reece Kingsley, this will be the husband of his daughter, Luna Kingsley, or whoever Reece Kingsley appoints otherwise, who will act in his stead after his death.

Finn let out a strangled gasp, nearly throwing the entire folder on the floor. He looked up at Valerio, feeling the boiling of his blood consuming every inch of his body.

"You? He left everything to you?" Finn screamed.

Valerio shook his head, refusing to get up. "No, he didn't want me to marry her, remember. He's probably in Hell right now cursing me for it. But either way, if I didn't marry her, it wouldn't have been yours. It would have belonged to whichever fucking freak your father had appointed or was going to get her to marry. Luckily he didn't have anyone appointed either, a mistake on his part it seems because everything was given to me."

Finn shook his head, a blinding madness settling into him. For years he had stood by his father with loyalty and love. He took the beatings, he took the screams, he took everything for the sake of becoming heir. He killed for Reece Kingsley. He lost himself for Reece Kingsley. He destroyed his fucking life and grieved everything for Reece Kingsley.

Heir was supposed to be his, not given to whatever asshole his father selected.

Finn had been born for it. He was destined for it. He shaped his entire fucking life for it.

For nothing!

The irony was so strong that even from the grave his father was still finding ways to attack him. He had to admit that this betrayal hurt worse than any beating ever had. Hell, he would take a broken rib, a broken femur, even a fucking broken spine over this.

Finn couldn't control the rage that shook his body. He got up without another word, grabbing the folder with him and walking out of the office. He didn't know where he was going, all he knew was that he was expelling himself of the Kingsley name.

The one that he no longer deserved.

THIRTY-THREE

GIANNA

A GOOD MORNING text from Finn first thing in the morning was the perfect way for Gianna to wake up. Actually, she might have preferred for him to have been in bed with her, but the text had been a close second.

He was at the office being some kind of businessman, and honestly, she was digging his new drive to change. Still, she didn't want him to change drastically. She was falling for the Finn that he was already, not any other version she was sure others wanted to see.

Gianna got ready for the day, throwing on a pair of jeans and a pink sweater. She had her theory class today and it was always freezing in there. She opened the door to her room but screamed when she saw that two people already stood there.

Blair had her arms crossed, a look of disappointment on her face and Cecilia stood behind her with wide, scared eyes.

"What's going on?" Gianna asked, opening the door wider. "I'm trying to go eat."

Blair pushed through, letting herself in while Cecilia followed meekly behind. Gianna desperately tried to look at her, to see if she had accidentally mentioned anything, but she refused to make eye contact.

Anxiety settled into her gut like a boulder. Gianna closed the door, swallowing harshly. "Are you going to say anything or are you just going to be silent the entire time?"

"What the hell were you doing last night at a diner on campus holding hands with Finn?" Blair finally asked, breaking the silence.

Gianna's eyes widened. The urge to throw up swept through her entire being. "How do you know about that?" she whispered.

"I was there with the pre-law society," Blair answered. "The one that your brother also happens to be a part of."

"Was he—"

"No, he wasn't there last night. I don't think he would have waited until morning to confront you if he was," she said. "What the fuck are you thinking, Gianna? And telling Cecilia of all people? Have you lost your mind? Did you forget who Finn is or do you need a reminder?"

The questions overwhelmed Gianna. She took a seat on the bed, running her hands through her hair before she settled on biting on her fingers. "Cecilia found out accidently. As for how it happened, I honestly couldn't tell you. It just kind of did." She let out a long exhale. "I know who he is, and I get all of that, but he's grown on me."

"Want to know what else grows on people and is bad? Diseases," Blair hissed.

"Come on, Blair. Don't be so harsh," Cecilia said, speaking up. "She knows all of this. Just let her live a little."

"Living a little is going on a trip. Living a little is buying a nice bag or a treat for yourself. It is not fucking your best friend's brother." She sighed, pacing the room. "What the hell are we going to do because all three of us are now lying to Luna?"

Guilt rattled through her core with a power she had never felt before. Gianna's hands shook as she raised them to her mouth, the nerves finally hitting her all at once. She shook her head. "I never wanted any of you to get involved for this very reason."

"Well, it's a little too late for that now."

Blair's words only dug the knife deeper. Gianna had let herself believe that what she was doing was okay, perhaps even right, because it felt good. But everything about it now felt wrong, horribly wrong. The guilt, the betrayal, the lying, the disappointment—this was what a relationship with Finn really was. Maybe there would never be any good to it.

But then what were all those feelings while she was with him? The lightness, the warmth, the fun, the *understanding*. That couldn't have been something she made up in her head. No, it couldn't have been. Not when she had tried to push him away over and over again and he held on. That was real. All those feelings were real.

"I'm sorry you're in this position now," Gianna said, setting her hands on her lap. "But I'll tell Luna myself about it. I'll keep you both out of it, so she doesn't get upset with either of you. If you choose to take her side, I won't blame you. Hell, I'd probably take her side too."

"What are you talking about?" Cecilia said, shaking her head. "There aren't any sides to this. We're all best friends. This is something that needs to be worked out because we're not throwing away our friendships just because you fell in love with Finn."

Gianna's eyes nearly bugged out of her head. "What?"

"That's what this is, right? That's why this all matters so much?" Cecilia asked. "If it didn't, we wouldn't even be having the conversation. Hell, you wouldn't be considering going to Luna yourself if it didn't mean something."

Blair ran her hands through her hair. "Is that true?"

She swallowed harshly. Was it true? How the hell was she supposed to know? It was too early to tell. Gianna had only really accepted the relationship a few weeks ago, and to be honest, the thought of moving that quickly terrified her immensely.

They must have seen the look of pure confusion and shock on her face because they both nodded their heads. Well, Cecilia did. Blair huffed again, muttering something under her breath.

"Take your time to figure out whatever you need to," Cecilia said, grabbing her hand. "I'm not rushing to tell anyone and neither will Blair."

Said girl rolled her eyes. "I'm not going to run off and scream it at the top of my lungs, but I'm not accepting it either. Think about it long and hard before you make any final decisions on the matter."

Gianna nodded her head. "Thank you."

Blair opened her mouth to say something when her phone began buzzing in her hand. "Speak of the devil," she said, answering right away.

Gianna tried to listen to what was being said, especially when Blair's face contorted from one of confusion to one of worry. Blair shook her head. "No, I haven't seen him, but I'll let you know if I do. The same goes for Cecilia and Gianna. Keep me updated."

Blair ended the call, looking directly at Gianna. "That was Luna. When was the last you heard from Finn?"

"He texted me this morning before he went to the office with Allister and Dante. Why? What's going on?" Gianna asked. The tightness in her abdomen only got worse when she realized that Finn hadn't answered her in a couple of hours. He hadn't even read her text. "Blair? What's wrong?"

"Something happened at the office, and he disappeared. The boys can't find him anywhere and his phone is turned off."

"What happened?" Cecilia asked. "Did Luna mention anything?"

Blair shook her head. "All she said was that he finally found out the truth about his father."

Gianna pulled out her phone, immediately trying to call him but it went to voicemail. She tried again, but still no answer. She sent him a text asking if he was okay, to at least give her some response to let her know she didn't have to worry, but nothing.

She stood up, grabbing her purse and opening her bedroom door. There was no way she was going to be able to sit there and wait for him to answer her, not when he was clearly in a bad headspace. She needed to make sure Finn was okay, or at the very least, alive. God, the thought sent a stab of pain through her heart.

"Where are you going?" Blair asked.

"I'm going to go look for him."

"What happened to taking time to think things through?"

Gianna shook her head. "I don't care. He's out there alone somewhere and I'm going to at least try to find him. He would do the same for me, so I'm not leaving him alone."

Cecilia grabbed her arm. "Do you want us to come with you?"

"No. It'll be better if I'm alone. If you guys stay here, please text me if he comes home."

Blair sighed. "Take my car at least. It'll be easier to drive."

"Thank you."

"Just keep us updated and please be careful." She squeezed her hand tightly. "If your brother comes home, we'll tell him you went to practice."

"And here I thought you were above telling lies," Cecilia said, cracking a smile.

"Never for my best friends," Blair said.

Gianna gave them a quick hug before pulling away. "I love you both."

She rushed down the stairs to the garage where Blair's bright red convertible sat. Grabbing the keys, she walked to the car and got in. The top was up, and she decided to leave it like that. The wind blowing through her hair in the middle of her worrying would only send her over the edge.

Luckily, Gianna actually knew how to drive. She wasn't an expert driver by any means, but when she turned sixteen, her father made her take driving classes and get her license. She rarely had to use it because they were always being driven around and they lived in such a walkable neighborhood, but at times like this, it seriously came in handy.

She turned on the car, and it purred to life. Once the garage was open, she carefully pulled out, testing the brakes and the gas to get comfortable. Only when she was past the gate and on the road did she feel comfortable enough to drive with more haste, thinking about every single place Finn could be.

It was a long list, but she needed to check every one of them. Gianna only prayed that he hadn't left New York completely. Considering his bike was still at home though, she doubted it. Or at least she hoped he would need it if he was deciding to leave.

She sighed, pressing on the gas. Regardless of everything, she was going to find her Finn. She would be there for him the way he had been there for her. Gianna just hoped he was open to company.

THIRTY-FOUR

GIANNA

SO FAR GIANNA had driven to the arena where Fight Night usually took place, the lake where they had gone to a couple of times, and even the hotel they stayed the night at. He was at none of those places.

She was losing time which only added to her stress. Cecilia had texted saying that he hadn't made it home yet and that Luna and the boys still couldn't pinpoint his location either. He was sending everyone on a wild chase at that point, and it was maddening.

The only place Gianna considered going but hesitated was the old Kinglsey house that had been burnt to the ground by Finn himself. From what Luna had told them, there was nothing left. Even the ashes had been blown away. That was why Gianna had been resistant to even make the drive out knowing it would take a good hour to get there, but when desperation called, she answered.

The only memories Gianna really had of Luna's family home were from their younger years and usually they were tainted with a dark shadow. That shadow had been their father, Reece Kingsley. While the girls were growing up, there were so many times where the sleepovers at Luna's house felt more like a prison than it did anything else. Luna and Finn had always seemed so desensitized to the way they lived with the constant surveillance and the control their father had on every aspect of their lives. Gianna hated going over, but sometimes it was the only way to see Luna. College had been a saving grace for both of the Kingsley kids and burning that house to the ground was the best choice for it.

The neighborhood was empty now, whereas once before it had been filled with guards and other employees. The once ornate gate was now covered in rust and blown wide open. It was so odd to see an entire fence enclosing around a space that was now completely empty, but a grandiose home had stood there once upon a time.

Cecilia saw a black SUV parked towards the side. She stopped the car and placed it in park, turning it off before getting out. The whole scene in front of her looked like something out of a war movie. Burnt pieces of wood still lingered on the ground along with some ash, but otherwise it was all gone.

That was when she finally saw Finn. He was hunched over on the ground in the center of the large space.

She was careful walking over, not wanting to scare him. But it didn't seem to matter because the moment she stepped on a twig and it cracked under her weight, he was turning around with a gun in his hands. Gianna threw her hands up, a gasp escaping her lips. Finn's eyes were red, as was his nose. He looked completely broken sitting on the floor in front of her.

She swallowed harshly, trying to calm her nerves. "Finn? Are you okay?"

"What are you doing here?" he asked, his voice filled with venom. He didn't move the gun either. It stayed on her the entire time.

"I came to check on you. I wanted to make sure you were okay," Gianna said.

"You shouldn't give a shit," Finn spit out. "No one should. I'm a fucking joke."

She shook her head. "I don't think of you that way."

"But you did. A couple of fucking weeks ago, you wanted nothing to do with me. No one wants anything to do with me. I'm fucking useless."

"You're not useless. Why are you saying all these things about yourself? What happened?" Gianna asked, trying to step forward. "Please, Finn. Talk to me."

He stared at her for a long moment, almost like he was weighing out whether or not he could trust her. She really didn't understand what could have happened that would have drastically shifted him this much, but whatever it was had to have been extreme.

"Come here," he muttered, finally moving the gun.

Gianna ran over to him, sitting right beside him on the ground. She waited for him to start talking first. She wanted to grab his hand, to reach for him, but instead she gave him space. She would do things on his time. It seemed like the safest way to play it.

"My asshole of a father left everything in his will to Valerio," Finn spat out. "Well, more specifically, to whoever Luna was going to marry or to whoever he appointed. He had no intentions of me becoming his heir or of me taking over the Kingsley name."

Gianna's eyes widened. She opened her mouth to say something, but she had no idea what to say. The betrayal, there was no way to understand that. Hell, there was no way to justify it.

"This whole fucking time, I grieved him. Hell, I was wondering if there was another way things could have ended. If maybe my mother needed a punishment for killing him." The words escaped his mouth like fire, threatening to burn anything in his way. "I couldn't fucking kill him myself. And for what? Because I thought I was the heir? Because I thought every fucking hit was training, was teaching me how to fucking run an empire!? I let him whip me when I could have thrown him to the ground and killed him. And he didn't want me as his heir. He doesn't want me as the Don. The fucking asshole died without even telling me any of this. He put it in his fucking will to make sure I wouldn't get anything. He's still making my life miserable from Hell! And I wasted so much time, so much energy for nothing. Every fucking thing I did was for nothing!"

The more he went on, the louder he became. He was screaming by the time he was done. She could feel the frustration in his voice, the hurt, the brokenness. It was all hitting him at once and he needed to let it out before it consumed him.

"Why couldn't he have fucking loved me? Why me? Why did he do this to me, Gianna?" Finn asked, the words raw in his throat.

Gianna shook her head, begging for her own tears not to fall. "He didn't deserve you, Finn. Your love, your drive, your intelligence, everything you are, didn't deserve to be used and wasted by him. You are the Kingsley heir regardless of what your father tries to claim. You were born for it; you were made for it. There is no one out there who could do it better than you. And a real heir would take what is his and prove everyone wrong, especially Reece Kingsley."

"What if you're wrong?"

She finally grabbed his face, not caring if he still held the gun. Fresh tears slipped out of his eyes, and she finally let hers fall as well. She could see the little boy in him who throughout his life was subject to such abuse and hurt. He tried to justify the pain and violence by thinking there was an end goal or purpose for it, but now that there wasn't, he was forced to realize that the abuse was just abuse.

"If I'm wrong, then that would have been the first time I ever was," Gianna said, letting out a small laugh. It seemed to do the trick, even as ridiculous as it was, because Finn managed to crack a small smile. "Prove me right, though. Prove to me that you can do this if this is what you want. And if this isn't what you want, we'll find something else. Whatever path you want to take is the one we'll go with, and I'll be there with you every step of the way."

"You don't deserve to have to deal with this fucked up shit," he muttered, shaking his head. "I can't force that on you."

"You're not forcing anything on me. I'm choosing it. I'm choosing you."

When he pulled her into his arms to hold her in his lap, she was startled at the sudden movement but settled into it within seconds. She let him hold her and in return she held him back, afraid that he would slip out of her arms without a moment's hesitation.

Gianna wasn't sure how much time slipped away between them while they sat in silence, but eventually it was broken by Finn speaking up.

"Do you think we grow up to become our parents?"

The question hit Gianna hard. She felt the air get ripped from her chest just thinking about becoming someone like her mother: selfish and narcissistic. Every day, she feared that she was becoming like that the more she did whatever she wanted to for herself rather than what might have been the better option, like in her current predicament.

"I really hope we don't," she said. "Otherwise, I'm screwed."

"Why do you say that?" he asked.

Gianna sighed. "Because my mother isn't someone I ever want to become. She left when I was a baby and only comes back to visit once a year as a cruel reminder that she exists, but not with us. Not with the family that she helped create."

"Why does she come back to visit?"

"Probably to try to fill the guilt in her conscience."

Finn only nodded his head as if he was taking everything in. "Well, for what it matters, I don't think you'll ever become like her."

"Why?"

"Because you have too kind of a soul to ever want to inflict that type of hurt onto anyone the way you've had to deal with it throughout your life." He moved back until he was able to look at her face and it made Gianna swallow harshly. "I've never met your mother, but I think she missed out on knowing a wonderful woman. The fact that you keep yourself open to those visits with her every year shows that you are every bit as wonderful and fantastic and breathtaking and enthralling as I know you are."

Her heart felt like it could erupt out of her chest at any moment. One more word from Finn's mouth and she was done for. The way he viewed her was the way she wished everyone would. Hell, it was the way she wished she could view herself. Maybe one day she would and maybe it would be Finn showing her the way to do so.

"I never know how to reply to you," she admitted. "Words don't seem enough."

"I don't need anything in return," he said. "Ever."

She wrapped her arms around his neck. "Well, this isn't in return, this is answering your question from before. I don't think you'll ever become like either of your parents either."

His lips pulled up into a small smile. "And why do you think that?"

"Because as hard as you've tried to fight it, there's a heart inside of you. One that demands to be let out, that wants to feel and love. And despite what everyone may say about your quick impulses, you weigh out all your options before you make a decision. Not to mention that you have such a strong sense of loyalty. It's the type that once you have it, you never want to lose it. One that makes you worth following and trusting. All of that makes you a better man, hell, a better person than either of them ever was." The words slipped from her mouth without having to put much thought into it. She had always thought this; it was like muscle memory to say it at that point.

His eyes gleamed with something Gianna couldn't make out fully, but it sent butterflies hurling throughout her stomach. "Careful, princess. I'm starting to think you might actually like me." He leaned in closer until his lips were only a few inches away from hers. "Or maybe you're finally starting to feel more."

Her eyes widened, but his kiss served as a distraction from what he'd said. His insinuation that she was starting to *love* him made her nervous. That was the next step after like, wasn't it? Love. The four letters that terrified her to the core.

She kissed him back passionately, desperately trying to forget about what he'd said. But then she started to think about whether *he* felt it or not. His 'finally' made her think that maybe he was waiting for her to catch up.

Did Finn love her?

The thought that he could sent a rush of warmth throughout her body. She was jumping ahead and needed to slow down. He hadn't even used the word, so for all she knew that could be the last thing he was referencing. When that thought crossed her mind, she expected to feel relieved, not disappointed.

Finn pulled back, pushing her hair back. "Are you ready to go home now?"

She nodded her head. Sleep was definitely what she needed. She'd missed her classes for the day, she'd missed lunch, and now it was almost dinner time. "Are you sure you're ready to go back?"

"I am. I'm going to take what's mine and go from there. Everything else can follow along afterwards."

She grabbed his hand, holding him on that promise that she would be there right beside him the entire time. For the first time in her life, it wasn't a question of whether she would or wouldn't. It was a clear answer.

She was choosing Finn.

THIRTY-FIVE

FINN

WHEN FINN finally stood from the hard ground, he realized just how much time had passed. His mind felt clear, but there was still something there that was almost nagging him. He had finally made the decision that he was going to be the Kingsley Don, but it was almost as if there was one last thing he had to do.

She stood beside him, her hand soft in his as they looked out into the empty lot of land. "What about this area? Do you know what you're going to do with it?"

He shook his head. "I have no clue. I'll probably keep it under the Kingsley estates for now until I decide to get rid of it. I doubt I'll be back down here for a long time though."

"Well, is there anything else you want to say to him while you're here?"

Finn raised his brow, turning to look at her. "What do you mean?"

"Reece Kingsley died here, his soul probably still lingers in some part of this area. If you want to say something to him to close that part of your life, maybe now is a good time to do it."

He wanted to laugh at the ridiculous idea to talk to the dead. Finn didn't believe in ghosts. He wasn't even sure he fully believed in Heaven and Hell, but still if his father's soul was going anywhere, it was going straight down south. But the sincerity in Gianna's voice made him realize that maybe there was something more to it than he thought.

He wasn't actually supposed to talk to his father, but instead maybe he was supposed to use the chance to get out anything he ever wanted to say but never had the chance to. The day his father died, he was gone long before Finn and Luna even showed up. They had no chance to ask about their lives and everything he ever did to them. Reece Kingsley had no chance to attempt to atone for his sins before he met death cruelly.

Finn nodded his head. "I guess I could try it."

"Do you want me to go to the car? Give you a minute alone?" she asked.

He shook his head. "No, I want you here."

In case he fell apart all over again, he meant to say but left it out. The nerves sat in his stomach like lead. Gianna squeezed his hand tightly one last time before she let go, moving back a few steps but still staying close.

He took a deep breath. "I don't know where to start. Truthfully, life with you had been hell. You were a man who couldn't ever be pleased. No matter how hard I tried throughout my life to be the perfect son, it was never enough. I was never enough. I stood by your side for so long, defending and turning on my own beliefs and morals because I thought it was the honorable thing to do, but nothing with you was honorable. You don't know that word. Loyal, powerful, brave—all words that I thought you were until I realized what you really were: a fucking coward. You're a coward. A coward who tried to sell off his daughter, a coward who tried to buy himself the perfect heir and son, and a fucking coward who beat his children relentlessly! Did that make you feel like a man? Hitting a fucking child? Every scar on my body will fade and I might not ever forget them, but I get to say that I'm still here. I'm alive and I have a family, and you have nothing.

Everything you never wanted for me is going to be mine. The name, the estates, the money, the loyalty, it's all mine. I know you hate it, and you can continue hating it, but you're powerless, you fucking coward! There's nothing you can do anymore. I burnt your body to a crisp and I would do it all over again to make sure there wasn't a single piece of you lingering anymore. Goodbye, Father. Maybe I'll see you again one day, though I doubt it."

His chest was heaving when the last sound left his lips. All the tension, the frustration, the built-up hatred left with every word he spat out. He knew he had been screaming the whole time, but the emotion became too much for him to pay it any mind. Now, his throat felt raw.

But for the first time in so long, he felt a sense of peace he hadn't felt in years. Honestly, probably ever in his life. It was like he had finally expelled his demons, letting them out of him once and for all. Reece Kingsley could no longer control him and that was a relief he had been chasing for too long.

"Finn?" Gianna called from behind him.

He turned around. "Yeah, princess?"

"Are you okay?"

He nodded his head, walking up to her. Grabbing her hand, he pressed a kiss to her forehead. A wave of comfort and calm rushed over him once again being in her presence. "I'm okay."

And that might have been the first time he actually meant it.

———

They decided to take Blair's car back and leave the other SUV to get picked up. Valerio could live without one of his office's cars, but Blair deserved to get hers back. After Gianna spilled about how she found out about the relationship, he knew it was a matter of time before everyone found out. He wasn't the one who cared though. Blondie in the passenger seat was the one with the problem.

He was touched hearing about her search for him. When he left Valerio's office, he wasn't even sure where he was going. All he did was drive and before he knew it, he was at his old family home. Or at least where it once stood. Looking back, it was fitting that his subconscious decided to bring him there rather than anywhere else. He had issues to solve and that was the only way he could do it.

They stopped for dinner at some drive through at one of the exits on the way home, and now they were almost back. Gianna had nearly fallen asleep, but kept fighting to keep her eyes open, which was honestly quite hilarious. She kept saying she didn't want to fall asleep because waking up so soon after was going to suck, but the way her head kept falling forward was too much to watch.

Luckily, they had just pulled into the house when she stretched across the seat, nearly hitting him in the face.

"Thank God, we're here."

"We are," he said, turning off the car after parking it in the garage. She went to open her door, but he stopped her, closing it.

"What's wrong?"

"Before you go inside and we have to pretend nothing happened tonight, I just want to say thank you for everything. I really needed someone today and you being there meant the world to me." He cleared his throat, nodding his head. "Thank you, princess."

Gianna beamed, grabbing his hand. "Always, Finn."

"Let's go inside now. I'm sure everyone is sleeping, but I should probably call Luna and let her know that I'm okay."

"That's probably a good idea," she said. "I should have texted the girls too, but I'll stop by their rooms before I turn in."

They both got out of the car and entered the house. Finn had expected it to be empty or at least quiet like it usually was during the weeknights, but instead there was a gathering in the living room. Luna, Valerio, Dante, Allister, Blair, Cecilia, and Augustus all sat there, and the moment they saw him and Gianna enter, they stopped everything they were doing.

Well, almost everyone did.

Allister marched up to Finn, knocking a cold-hearted punch directly into his nose. Gasps and screams were heard from around the room, but he couldn't focus on any of it. The confusion had barely washed away when Allister was hitting him again, this time sending the punch directly into his stomach.

"What the fuck was that for?" Finn wheezed, wiping away the blood that oozed out of his nose.

"What was that for? How about you tell me why the fuck my sister knew to come look for you? Why she ditched her fucking classes today to come find your scum ass?" Allister hissed. He sent out another punch, but this time Finn blocked it.

"Allister, stop," Gianna screamed, trying to jump between them but Dante grabbed her before she could. "Let go of me. You're overreacting for no reason."

"Am I? Then why did you go look for him? How did you know where he would be?" Allister asked, this time turning to face her.

The opening was the perfect chance to pounce on him, but Valerio held his gun up, keeping it trained on Finn. "Not one step," Valerio said.

"What? You're just letting this happen?" Finn asked, but this time he directed the question to his sister who sat there with wide eyes.

"I'm trying to understand what's going on," she said.

"We're friendly, okay? After Luna called Blair and mentioned he was missing, I went out to look because he mentioned some places to me. Why? Because we're friends. We live in the same house. Nothing has ever happened between us," Gianna said. The lies fell out of her mouth effortlessly, but still Allister didn't believe her.

Annoyance swept through Finn. Why the fuck was she lying? Now was the perfect chance for her to admit the truth. She cared about him, he cared about her, who gave a fuck about these idiots and what they thought about the relationship? He sure as hell didn't.

"And I'm just supposed to believe that?" Allister asked, stalking closer to her. His eyes searched for the lie, but it seemed like Gianna had perfected it with the way her eyes hardened.

"It's the truth. Ask the girls. I would never be with someone like him," Gianna said.

She didn't bother looking over at him when the words left her mouth. It was probably better she didn't. The anger and the betrayal that swept through him was clear on his face. She was allowed to be scared, she was allowed to have reservations, but what she did was something Finn would never have done to her.

After everything he went through today, he couldn't believe it. Maybe it was the worst day of his life.

That answer seemed to appease everyone in the room. Allister's shoulders fell back, Dante let go of Gianna, Valerio put down his gun, and even Luna seemed somewhat relieved. They all were happy to know that the fuck up known as Finn Kingsley hadn't gotten his hands anywhere near the perfect Gianna Moretti.

Everyone except Cecilia and Augustus did, at least. They seemed to be the only ones who knew about the relationship, how good it was, how fucking pure and perfect it was. Now it was being tarnished in the blink of an eye to protect her reputation.

To protect her brother's feelings.

To protect her best friend's feelings.

Well, fuck that.

"Nice job, Gianna. You're such a good liar you almost had me convinced. Too bad I still remember the taste of your sweet pussy, or let's not forget how hard you rode me when you got jealous at the thought of me being with someone else, princess," Finn said with a sick grin.

Every word cleared through the room, leaving behind a clean silence. Gianna's mouth dropped open in horror, and satisfaction filled him.

"You weren't just with someone like me—you let me claim you as mine, over and over and over again," he said, making sure she heard every single word. "I don't blame you. I loved it, just like you did. Isn't that right, princess?"

Gianna's eyes widening was the last thing Finn saw before a sharp hit came from the back of his head, and all he saw was black.

THIRTY-SIX

GIANNA

ONCE FINN FELL unconscious from Valerio's hit to the head with his gun, the tension was unbearable in the room. Gianna wanted it to swallow her whole. She was sick to her stomach seeing him lying on the ground and for betraying him the way she had. Now, three people she cared about hated her. She had ruined everything.

Allister stared at the ground, and she was scared to know what he was thinking about. No doubt he was putting things together, getting to the bottom of whatever it was that he thought was going on. The cat was out of the bag now, and even if Gianna tried to lie her way out, there was no way anyone would believe her.

She could thank Finn for that.

"Allister?" she called out gently.

He raised his head, locking eyes with her. The usual warm blue of his eyes was now an icy shade of grey. He was the one that was logical and could see reason, but on the rare occasions when he lost it, he became someone completely unrecognizable.

"You lied to me," were the first words out of his mouth.

Gianna shook her head frantically. "I didn't want to lie. I wanted to tell you everything."

"I gave you the chance to tell me. You chose to continue lying."

"Allister, let me explain."

He turned around and stormed out of the room. Dante followed after him immediately. Augustus, who Gianna had forgotten was even there, walked towards Finn and picked him up, hoisting him with some difficulty over his shoulder.

"Where are you taking him?" Luna asked, standing.

"Um, I'm going to put him to bed. I don't think it's right for him to continue laying on the floor," he said, as if it were the most self-explanatory thing in the world.

"I'll come with you," Gianna said, wanting to leave the room and check on Finn. She could see the movements of his chest, but she wanted to be sure that he wouldn't suffer any permanent damage after what Valerio did.

"No, you're not going anywhere," Valerio cut in.

"That's not your decision to make," she said.

"We need to talk," Luna said. "And now is the perfect time to do so."

Fuck. Yet another hurdle Gianna was not trying to face, now or ever. But the confusion on Luna's face and the frown on her lips only added to the guilt that she was feeling. Now would be a perfect time for hell to freeze over, or for a meteor to strike Earth.

All she could do was nod her head and take a seat on the couch, crossing her legs before uncrossing them, wiggling around and trying to get comfortable. Her skin was itching from how awkward the whole situation felt.

"Would you give us a second?" Luna asked her husband. Her voice was disgustingly sweet, but he simply nodded and gave her a kiss on the forehead before leaving the room.

"Do you want us to leave too?" Cecilia asked, finally speaking up. "I really don't want to, but I also completely understand."

Gianna left it up to Luna. Cecilia seemed to support the relationship, so of course she wanted her there for moral support. Blair was no doubt playing moral police and would be arguing how terrible it was of Gianna to keep this from her best friend. As if she didn't know that already.

"Stay. It'll probably be better to have people here," Luna said.

Gianna's eyes widened. "If you're going to ask Valerio to dispose of me, that's fine. Just make it quick and don't let anyone touch my shoes even in the afterlife."

"What the fuck is wrong with you?" Blair muttered under her breath.

"I'm not going to do that," Luna said, shaking her head. "I just can't understand why you didn't tell me that you were dating Finn. I mean, you came to me telling me how much you hated him, begging me to take him back, and now this secret comes out? It's so hard to believe."

She ran a hand through her hair, letting out a deep exhale. "Tell me about it. I wasn't planning on anything happening. Believe me, I fought it until the very end. Hell, some might say I'm still fighting it. But he snuck up on me so quickly, Luna. I swear I was trying to figure out something, but I needed to get my head in order with everything before I could tell anyone."

"But you told Cecilia and Blair."

"I caught them out in public," Blair said. "And it was actually this morning that I confronted her."

"So then Cecilia knew the longest," Luna said, sending an accusatory look towards her.

Cecilia put her hands up. "She forced me to go shopping and I got it out of her. I paid the price for it, believe me."

"Finn wanted to tell you about it, but I didn't let him. I was so scared that you would end our friendship over this or that you would never talk to me again. I can't blame you if you still want to do that, but I just want to say that I can't lose any of you. I just can't," Gianna said, looking down at the ground. "But if you need to let go of this friendship, then I can find a way to live with that."

She heard footsteps and someone walking towards her. She expected to feel a hit, maybe someone pulling her hair, but instead, Luna got on her knees and grabbed Gianna's hands in hers.

"I'm not leaving you, especially over something like this," Luna whispered. "Do you care about Finn?"

Gianna nodded her head, biting her lip to stop the sudden flood of emotions that wanted to make their way down her face. "I do. Holy shit, I do."

The smile she gave her was big and bright, but most of all it was genuine. "Then who am I to get in the way of that? I thought you knew by now that I'm not in the business of controlling love stories."

"You're genuinely not mad?"

"Mad? No. A little grossed out? Yes. He could have been a little less vulgar with his comments before Valerio knocked him out," Luna said, scrunching her nose.

Gianna let out a real laugh, shaking her head. "Yeah, he could have. But I was an asshole."

"And now they're totally going to give him the full mafia tie-down lecture," Blair said. "It's kind of funny when you think about it. They think torturing him will get him to spill on the details of your relationship."

"Is that what they're planning on doing?" she asked, panic rushing through her.

"They're seriously the most dramatic people I've ever met in my life," Cecilia said. "Hate to break it to them, but her innocence is long gone if that's what they're trying to protect."

Gianna slapped her on the shoulder, eliciting an "ow" from her. Despite hearing what could have been happening to Finn, she felt a huge sense of relief lift off her shoulders knowing that her relationship with Luna was fine.

For a moment, she wondered if it was an act. If Luna was pretending that it was fine and then she would quickly turn it around and decide she wanted nothing to do with Gianna after all, but she had to let that type of thinking go. The people in her life loved her, despite the fear that pushed her to such extremes to believe otherwise.

"Is Finn okay, though?" Luna asked her. "After what happened this morning, I didn't know what kind of shape he would be in."

Gianna nodded. "It was a lot. He had an emotional day, but he'll be okay."

If she hadn't just completely destroyed everything by not standing up for him when she had a chance. God, she wanted to beat herself up. After everything, she was a coward. She was selfish and disgusting. He needed her and she completely let him down.

Luna's shoulders relaxed and a breath of relief escaped her. "I'm glad. Thank you for being there for him."

What did it matter when Finn would want nothing to do with her anymore?

Her brain was telling her that even if Luna and Allister stayed, she had lost Finn. Wasn't that what she had decided on so long ago? That she was willing to sacrifice her relationship with him to save the others? So then why did she feel like ripping out her heart at the thought of him leaving her?

She couldn't imagine a world without Finn in her life. She needed to talk to him, make sure he understood how sorry she was. She would prove it to him.

And she would hope he still chose her in the end.

THIRTY-SEVEN

FINN

WHEN FINN OPENED HIS EYES, the last thing he expected to be was tied up to a chair downstairs. Everything from earlier in the night came back to him, and suddenly Allister, Dante, and Valerio standing in front of him made complete sense. He just had no idea what Augustus was doing there, sitting on a chair in the corner nonchalantly.

Every movement of his head sent a rush of pressure through it, so he decided to continue staring straight forward, hoping everyone would stop their dramatics soon. Nothing was worse than a fucking concussion and a potentially broken nose after the day he'd had.

"Oh good, you're alive," Dante said, alerting the others. "None of us knew if you were going to pull through, Valerio's hit was a little too hard."

"What is all this?" Finn asked.

"This is how I'm going to learn about you, Finn Kingsley," Allister said this time. His eyes had returned to a normal shade of blue, but the bite in his voice was still present.

"Believe it or not, but there's actually not much to learn about me."

Augustus snorted. "Isn't that the truth."

"What the fuck are you doing here, by the way? Whose side are you on?"

"I'm here to make sure nothing goes too far, dumbass. Without me here, you probably would have already been missing fingers."

Finn let out a huff, attempting to roll out his shoulders. "Do I really have to be tied up for this?"

"I think we should end everyone's misery and bury him alive like I suggested," Valerio said. "You're not going to get anything out of him. At least, nothing useful."

"You're too kind, brother-in-law."

Allister stormed up to Finn and wrapped a hand around his neck, taking the joking vibe out of the room. He could feel his throat closing, the need for air building more and more the longer his hand stayed glued in place. The fire in his lungs was unbearable, but that was suffocation. It wasn't meant to be pleasant.

"What the fuck did you do to my sister?" Allister hissed.

Valerio was the only one who was able to rip him off, and thankfully Finn was able to take in mouthfuls of air just as his vision had begun turning blurry. The fucking asshole had nearly killed him, and for what? Because he thought Finn did something to Gianna? What the hell did she tell them?

"What are you talking about?" Finn muttered, still coughing.

Allister pushed Valerio off, but he didn't approach again. Instead, he stayed a few steps away, keeping his hands at his sides in tight fists. "I'm talking about how you managed to get her to lie to me, to everyone she fucking cares about. She would never date someone like you, and she would never fucking destroy the relationships she has with us for you either. So, what did you do to her to get her to this place? Did you threaten her? Bribe her?"

Finn's face contorted into one of disgust. He couldn't believe the accusations being thrown against him. For the first time in his life, he finally understood why Gianna had wanted to keep them a secret. Every single one of them was out of their fucking minds.

"Do you really think I would do something like that to her?" Finn asked.

"You tell me."

His jaw clenched in anger. The ropes that were keeping him tied up were the only thing stopping him from launching at Allister, at everyone in that room. For such a fucking smartass, he truly was the biggest idiot Finn had ever met.

"You want to know how I got her? I was there for her. I listened, I cared, I fucking took the time to make sure she was appreciated and understood. I wasn't the one that got her to lie to everyone; she was the one who got me to lie. I wanted to fucking scream it from the rooftops, but she commands every fiber of my being. She says walk, I walk. She says run, I run. Hell, if she says bark, I'll fucking bark. She wanted to keep it a secret and she didn't want anyone to know. Why? Because she was scared of your reaction." Finn shook his head, letting out a mocking laugh. "And how is that going, by the way? For a girl who struggles so much with her family already, how do you think it feels when she can't come to you, her own brother, with her own love life?"

Allister opened his mouth to say something, but Valerio cut him off. "You're in love with her, aren't you?"

The question was so direct it hit Finn square in the chest. It had been a question he was so sure he would never be asked, a question he was sure he would never answer. But as soon as it came, he knew his answer immediately, as if it were second nature.

"Yes. I am."

The silence in the room was suffocating, nearly worse than when Finn was getting choked out. At this point, he might have actually preferred that over the way Allister stared at him with that calculating look. It made his skin crawl, and as the moments ticked by, it only got worse.

"Did you all die?" Augustus asked, breaking the silence. "What the hell just happened?"

"Way to kill the moment," Dante muttered, rolling his eyes.

"Do you actually love her?" Allister asked this time, testing out the words as if he couldn't believe them himself.

"I do." And it was the honest truth.

"Fucking hell." Valerio huffed, running a hand through his hair.

"Does she feel the same way towards you?" Allister asked.

Finn exhaled loudly. "I think she does. That's something you'll have to ask her yourself. She's too stubborn to come out and admit it to me."

There was a small pull at the corner of Allister's lips, almost as if he wanted to smile. But as soon as it was there, it was swiped away. Gone without a trace.

"Well, this is just great. They're in love. Good luck trying to break that up now and remaining the best brother in the world," Dante said, shaking his head.

"It doesn't fucking work. You can hate the asshole all you want, but as long as she loves him, seeing her happy is what matters," Finn said, looking at Valerio. "Believe me, I tried."

"And failed," Valerio said.

He rolled his eyes. It was true. No matter how much he could have hated Valerio and wanted Luna with anyone else in the world, there was nothing he could have done. It wasn't his say to play in her love life that way. Not back then, not now either. He just kept the thoughts of destroying Valerio inside his head now instead of letting them out into the open.

"It's not for you to understand why anyone falls in love with anyone. Fuck, it was the last thing I thought would happen to me, but it did. Hate me all you want, but I'm not going anywhere. As long as Gianna wants me here, I'm hers," Finn said.

"I'll talk to her about it," Allister said, seeming to finally wrap his mind around it. "If she gives a shit about you, then I'll consider keeping you breathing. The minute you fuck up and hurt her, you're out. I'll make her think you ran away again, only you'll be buried six feet under a slab of concrete where I'll have a new gazebo set up. Understood?"

"I would never hurt her," he said. "Ever."

The threats didn't intimate Finn in the slightest, but he would play along only because it was her brother. He would never dream of hurting Gianna. Quite frankly, he was over the entire situation. He wanted a shower and his girl out in the open now.

A look of acceptance passed through Allister's eyes, and for a second, Finn swore he saw his body relax if even for a moment.

When the three of them finally left the room, it was Augustus who came over and cut the ropes off him. His arms were numb, and the tingling was a bitch when the blood started rushing back into them.

"See, that wasn't so bad. Was it?" Augustus had a grin on his face, having enjoyed the show.

"It was fucking pointless. They couldn't demand me away from her even if they tried," Finn said, finally standing. "She's mine, regardless of what her dumbass brother thinks of me."

"But now you don't have to worry about that. They know your intentions with her are good and the relationship could prosper or whatever the fuck happens now."

They walked up the stairs, back into the main living room where everyone once was. It was empty now, seeming like everyone had gone home for the night or retired to their rooms once the drama had died down. It was late, Finn was fucking exhausted, and it had been an overly emotional day for him.

"I'm going to shower. Are you hanging around here?" he asked.

Augustus shrugged. "I have someone I could go bother."

With that, he left Finn standing alone again. His legs felt like lead as he crawled up the stairs making his way into his room, and then finally into the bathroom. He turned the shower on and got in, letting the warm water relax his muscles. Bruises covered several parts of his body already, but they would fade in no time. When he turned his face, he let the water wash away the blood from his nose. It was dried up, but scrubbing slightly managed to get it off.

After the shower, he managed to dry off with a towel and secure it at his hips before he walked to the bed. He fell back on it, closing his eyes for a moment as everything rushed over him.

What a fucking shitshow.

THIRTY-EIGHT

GIANNA

IT WAS LATER into the evening, and Gianna had finally changed into her pajamas and managed to relax somewhat when a knock came at her door. She hoped it was Finn, but instead it was Allister. He wasn't bloody or bruised, so she could assume that at least nothing graphic happened.

He gave a small smile. "Can I come in?"

She nodded immediately. "Of course."

He did just that, walking over to her bed and taking a seat on the edge of it. She sat on her vanity chair, turning to face him. It was hard to look at him, to know that he was disappointed in her. Maybe that was what she hated more than anything. The fact that his approval meant everything, more so than her father's because Allister had always been there for her. If he didn't approve or if he was disappointed in her, it destroyed her. But if he didn't like Finn, what did that leave? She didn't want to choose between them. That was something she just couldn't do.

"Why didn't you tell me about the relationship?" he asked, immediately jumping into it.

"Would you have understood it more if I told you a week ago, or two weeks ago, or when it first started?" She shook her head. "I kept it a secret because I had to figure out if this was something I actually wanted, if it was worth my life and all these dynamics changing."

"And can you say it is?"

Gianna couldn't help the small smile that found her lips. When she thought about the moments she shared with Finn, there was no way they weren't worth it. Every moment with him was absolutely worth it. Maybe she hadn't realized it at first, but now, she knew it without a doubt.

"Yes, it is. There's no doubt in my mind that I want to be with him," she said.

Allister let out a loud exhale, running a hand down his face. "Fuck my life."

"Come on, Alli. Don't be so dramatic. Remember when you guys went to the club and you admitted that you actually enjoyed his company? He's still that guy," Gianna said.

"No, he's not. This time I know he's dating my sister."

"He's a great guy and he makes me happy. You should want me to be happy. I want you to find a nice girl who would make you happy."

"Of course I want you happy, dummy. I just didn't think it was Finn Kingsley of all people that would be the person to provide some of that happiness." He shook his head. "It's going to take me some time to understand all of *this*."

She nodded her head. That was understandable. Honestly, she hadn't expected him to be so approving of it right away. It would take time, but she knew that Finn and Allister would be able to have a great relationship. One day, at least.

"Are we okay?" she asked.

"We always are, Gianna." He gave her a gentle smile, grabbing her hand and squeezing tightly for a moment. "I just want you to remember you can always come to me. I will never turn you away or make you feel judged. If I have in the past, I sincerely apologize for it. From now on, I'll do better about being more open so you can come to me."

This time, she gave him a beaming smile. "It wasn't about

that. It was about not wanting to upset you or disappoint you. You're the best brother I could have asked for, Allister."

"And you're the best sister, even though you cause most of the gray hairs on my head," he said, standing. "I'm going to bed; it's been a long day. I suggest you do the same."

"Yeah, I will."

Allister nodded, walking towards the door. "Goodnight, Gianna. I love you."

"I love you too," she said, watching as he closed the door behind him.

Finally, it felt like all the weight she had been carrying the past couple of weeks had lifted off her shoulders. She felt lighter, freer. Hell, she felt like she could fly. She'd had a long day that was overly emotional and had seriously done a number on her, but still, she was restless.

With careful steps, she walked towards the door and opened it quietly. The hallway was empty and dark, meaning everyone else was in their rooms or already sleeping. She closed the door behind her and tiptoed down to Finn's door, knocking once quietly. He didn't respond. It was possible he didn't want to see her, but she needed to make sure he was alright at the very least. She entered his room, submerging herself in the warm glow that came from the lamp on his nightstand table.

It felt like she was sneaking around once again, only they didn't need to anymore. There was a certain thrill that came with the late-night meet ups that she didn't want to admit to liking.

Finn lay on his bed, barely raising his head when he realized who it was. He dropped back down, letting a groan escape his lips. "It's late. What are you doing here?"

Gianna walked with careful steps to the bed, sitting down beside him. Immediately the guilt returned in full force. Bruises covered his skin, his nose was slightly swollen, his lip was busted open, and on top of everything, she had been vile towards him earlier after the day they spent together.

"I came to make sure you were okay and to apologize."

"For what?"

"For saying I would never be with someone like you. Truthfully, I think I said it because it makes me think that in another world, you would never be with someone like me. That if you had never been forced back home, if you had never been forced to live here, if we didn't have our paths constantly crossing, you wouldn't be with someone like me. I'm a coward, a bitch, someone who acts tough but isn't." Gianna shook her head, letting the words slip out of her mouth. "Part of me wonders if that's why people have a hard time loving me. Because of who I am. Either way, seeing you like this, everything you went through today because of me—I'm so sorry, Finn. I told them all the truth. That I didn't want to reveal our relationship, that I wanted to keep it a secret, that I want to be with you. If this was all for nothing, I understand that too, you know."

Finn's hands reached out to grab her cheeks, pulling her down so she was only a couple inches away from his face. "You talk a lot."

"I know."

"I accept your apology. It's rare I get those," he said, a small smirk on his face. "But there's some things that I need to say."

She nodded, keeping her eyes locked with his.

"First, don't ever insult yourself in my presence again. You're not a coward, or a bitch, or someone who pretends to be tough. You're brave, courageous, and have a heart of gold. Second, don't think about what could have happened; think about what did happen. Something brought you into my life. Whether that was fate, God, some other being, I don't know, but you're mine. Now, and forever. Third, everything I went through today wasn't because of you or our relationship, it was your brother being a little bitch, trying to understand something that wasn't for him. What we have, this thing between us, is only for us. No one else deserves any part of it. Only we deserve the truth, and do you want to know what that truth is, princess?"

"What is it?" she whispered.

He brought her closer, lowering his voice. "I'm so fucking in love with you. There isn't a single thing I wouldn't do for you. There isn't a single place I wouldn't go to for you. I would take every single fucking hit again for you if that is what it takes for this relationship to work, for us to not have to keep it a secret anymore."

Gianna felt like her heart could leap out of her chest at any moment. It felt like time had stopped completely when the words, *those words*, escaped his perfectly plump lips. The words she had never heard from any man before, the words she had felt from him but wasn't sure about.

The words she knew she felt as well.

"You love me?" she whispered. Her eyes were glossed over with emotion and her hands shook, but she needed to know for sure.

Finn's lips lifted into a smile. A genuine one. The type that made him look younger and took the stress out of him.

"I love you, Gianna."

She gasped and connected their lips, pinning him against the bed. His tongue found its way into her mouth without any issue, taking control of the kiss within seconds. Gianna didn't care. She felt the very essence of her soul exploding with fireworks and bombs. She lavished in his kiss, tasting and taking what was hers.

Because Finn Kingsley was hers.

She pulled away out of breath, leaning her forehead against his.

"I love you too, Finn."

His eyes widened for a fraction of a moment as he heard what she said. The admittance felt freeing, vulnerable. She wasn't used to baring her soul for anyone in that way, but telling him exactly what she felt, it was perfect.

"Say it again," he muttered, pressing a kiss to her lips.

"I love you."

"Again."

"I love you."

"Again."

"Finn!"

"What? You can't blame me. Those are the best fucking words I've ever heard come out of anyone's lips before," he said, kissing her again. "I love you, princess. More than you could imagine."

Gianna leaned against his body, accidentally pressing against one of the bruises on his abdomen. He let out a groan, hissing in pain. She sat up immediately, looking at all the bruises and marks on him.

"What can I do to help with the pain?" she asked.

He reached for her again, attempting to pull her back down. "Don't move away from me for starters."

She rolled her eyes. "You're in pain. Let's get that solved first and then we can cuddle all night."

"Fine," Finn sighed. "In the bathroom cabinet I have some pain meds. There's a first aid kit under the sink too. Grab them and bring them out here."

Gianna did exactly that, coming out a minute later. She handed him the water on the nightstand and two pills, helping him sit up so he could take them before transitioning him against some pillows leaning on the bedframe.

She opened the first aid kit, staring at the contents in confusion. "So, what do I do now?"

He shook his head, letting out a small laugh. "There are some instant ice packs in there. You pop them and they freeze immediately. You can help ice the bad bruises."

She grabbed two of the ice packs, popping them like he instructed and placing one on his stomach and the other on his neck where a couple of bruises stood. She hadn't seen them earlier, but from what she could tell it was from wherever he had been with Allister. She gave him one more for the back of the head where he was hit with the gun.

Gianna frowned, grabbing his hand. "I'm really sorry Allister hurt you like this. Valerio too. They shouldn't have touched you."

"Not your fault, princess. You didn't do anything. Besides,

I'm sure I'll end up beating their asses eventually. That'll be my karma." Finn shrugged.

She nodded her head, accepting it. "Well, no one is going to put their hands on you ever again. Not without your permission. Your fights are a different thing."

He squeezed her hand, bringing it up to his lips. "Since when did you become so protective over me?"

"Why? You don't like it?"

"No, I fucking love it. It's sexy seeing you get all possessive and defensive over me."

Gianna couldn't help the blush on her face. She instead focused on closing the first aid kit, setting it beside the bed. "Well, you're mine and I'm not going to let anything happen to you."

"Oh fuck," he groaned, looking at her with dark eyes. "Say it again, princess."

"You can't get all worked up. You literally can't move without being in pain," she said.

"I don't give a shit," he said, throwing the ice packs off. "Say it again. Say what you just said."

She grinned, shaking her head. "I said that you're mine."

Within a split second he flipped her over on the bed, hovering over her with a wild look in his eyes. "Now, that is the second-best fucking thing that has ever come out of your mouth."

Her hands wrapped their way into his hair, getting lost in the soft brown curls that sat against his forehead. She wrapped her legs around his waist, just then noticing how the towel that was around his waist earlier had slipped off and he was left completely bare now.

"You're naked," she whispered.

Finn grinned, pulling on the straps of her tank top. "Am I? How convenient is that?"

"You should be resting, not doing any strenuous activity." Her argument fell on deaf ears as he began placing soft kisses against her neck, sucking and licking the skin under her jaw before moving down her clavicle.

"This is good for me," he muttered, lifting her shirt over her head. "I need to stretch my body out, and you just happen to be here, princess."

Gianna shook her head but immediately closed her eyes when his lips fell on her nipple. His tongue flicked at it, before his teeth grazed the sensitive skin, causing a breathy moan to escape her lips. One of his hands focused on the other breast, playing and pulling on the nipple like he had all the time in the world. She could feel the heat growing in her core, already soaked from his touches.

When he finally pulled her shorts off and the cold air hit her wet pussy, a little whimper left her lips. God, how had her body become so responsive and sensitive like this?

Slowly, one of his hands slipped down her body, finding its way between her legs like it belonged there. She opened her eyes for a moment to find Finn's heated stare already on her. He gave her a soft smile and a quick kiss before slipping his finger inside of her. The moan that left her lips was louder than the others. Immediately, she held her hand over her mouth.

"Careful, princess. We have a full house," he said. "We don't want everyone to hear us."

"Stop teasing me then."

He shook his head, continuing to thrust his fingers in and out of her. "You know I can't do that."

Gianna shrugged, losing it for a second when he brushed against the spot inside of her that drove her insane. "Then I don't know what to tell you."

"Maybe you need something in your mouth then?"

She frowned, confused by what he was talking about and then annoyed because he took his fingers out of her. Quickly, he replaced his fingers with his cock, aligning himself up and thrusting inside without a moment's hesitation.

Gianna gasped at the overwhelming fullness. The moans were on the tip of her tongue, waiting to slip out but Finn instead slipped two fingers inside her mouth, holding them there.

"Suck on them," he said, noticing the bizarre look on her face. "Focus on my fingers, princess, because I need to fuck you and I'm not in the mood to get interrupted by anyone."

It was weird having his fingers sitting in her mouth while he fucked her, but the more he thrusted, hitting every delicious spot inside of her repeatedly, the more she forgot about why she cared in the first place. She wrapped her mouth around his fingers, sucking on them like they were his dick instead.

His eyes turned a darker shade of brown, one that was almost black when he realized what she was doing.

Her tongue swirled around his fingers, tasting every bit of herself on them. He pushed them down deeper, letting them hit the back of her throat for a second before he pulled it back out.

"Do you like that, baby? You like the thought of having a cock in your mouth while you have one in your pussy?"

She wanted to scream, to moan, to reply in any way she could. His body against hers, leaning down so she could smell him, feel him—fuck, it was mind blowing. He shifted her body slightly, raising her hips so he was hitting that spot from a new angle, sending her to a newfound pleasure she hadn't been to in so long.

Finn leaned down closer, his lips against her cheek. "Too fucking bad I don't share and I never will. You're mine, Gianna. Only mine for the rest of our fucking lives."

She came without any warning. The orgasm ripped through her entire body so viciously, she bit down on his fingers to keep quiet.

Finn came immediately after, filling her with everything he had. He pulled his fingers out of her mouth, pulling her lips onto his instead. It was a mess of bodies, one that Gianna didn't care about as long as he held her.

"I love you," she whispered, feeling the contentment wash over her like waves on a beach.

"I love you too, princess."

And like that, they fell asleep.

THIRTY-NINE

FINN

FINN HAD a new outlook on life. He had come to realize that it wasn't as bleak and shitty as he had originally thought it was. He had also come to understand that love was fucking fantastic. Seriously, it was the best thing in the world. He couldn't understand why anyone would ever want to not be in love or have a soulmate in the first place.

Hell, he used to be like that, but having Gianna made him a new man. A man with a life that he actually woke up to in the morning not fully dreading.

For the past week, they had been in complete paradise. His bruises were still healing, but other than that, nothing was stopping them. With the relationship out in the open finally, Gianna wasn't so scared about hiding anymore. Instead, she sat with him on the couch, kissed him goodbye, and slept next to him at night. She still chose to not use such heavy PDA around Allister for obvious reasons, which Finn could understand for now.

Still, every time he grabbed her hand or pressed a kiss to her cheek in front of Allister and he did that weird face scrunch thing, it sent copious amounts of serotonin through his brain. Slowly he was getting his revenge.

The only thing that still remained was finally taking control of all the Kingsley businesses. He didn't dread it as much as he thought he would have, but it made him fucking nervous. This time, instead of going to the office, he was invited to Luna's and Valerio's home, probably so that if he ran, they could catch him quicker this time.

Finn wasn't running anymore. He was done with that part of his life.

He was let in by one of the many staff who worked there and led through the grand foyer to the sunroom where there was lunch being set up. Small hints of spring decorated the home, mostly through the addition of intricately assorted flowers in vases. After learning about how much Gianna loved the season, he had a different outlook on it than he had before.

Valerio and Luna sat in the sunroom, smiling and talking to each other in hushed voices. They didn't even notice when Finn walked in or sat down. It took him clearing his throat loudly for Valerio to roll his eyes and finally turn towards him.

"What?"

"It's great to see you both as well."

"Sorry, I didn't know you got here," Luna said, giving him a warm smile.

Finn looked around the table noticing that there were two other plates set up as well. "Are more people joining us?"

"Allister and Dante are. They're involved in all my business matters, so I need them involved with this as well," Valerio said. "They'll be here in a couple of minutes."

He could only nod, twirling his thumbs together at the awkward silence. When he looked up, he saw that Luna stared back at him with a hungry smile. One that almost scared him.

"Why are you looking at me like that?"

"Because you have a girlfriend now who just so happens to be my best friend and I want to know how that's going," she said, the excitement clear in her voice.

"It's going fine."

"Fine? That's all I get? Give me more. Like when did you

realize you were in love? Have you always been into her? Did you guys have something going on when you were younger? I need some details," she said.

"Yeah, Finn. Give her the details," Valerio said, smirking.

He rolled his eyes. "What details? We never had anything going on before, and it just kind of happened."

Her face fell. "You suck at this."

"How can I suck at not wanting to talk about my love life with you?"

"Because you're in love and it's special. I want to know how you feel, how you're experiencing it, how you're treating her."

"You might have to use extreme measures to get anything out of him, baby." Valerio grabbed her hand, pressing a kiss to it.

Finn let out a long exhale. "It feels amazing. She's the most amazing person I've ever met, and this feeling is like I'm flying on fucking clouds. It terrifies me how much I love her because if she ever leaves me, I'll be a disaster, so that's what I'm going through."

"Oh my God, you are in love," Luna said, holding a hand to her heart. "We all feel those things, especially at first. It's scary and vulnerable, but it's so magical and it's the best thing you'll ever feel. Lean into it and enjoy it. You both are perfect together."

Finn could only nod his head. He hadn't expected to get serious, but when he started spilling, it all kind of tumbled out of him. But there was a comfort in knowing that the feelings were mutual—the fear and the terrifying part were on the same coin as the blissful, heavenly part of it.

Luckily, his response wasn't needed because Allister and Dante were walking in, loud and obnoxious. They sat down at the table, immediately pulling the attention onto themselves.

"Sorry we're late, someone couldn't find an outfit," Allister said, rolling his eyes.

"I didn't know where my corduroy pants were and that was the vision for today," Dante said, shrugging nonchalantly.

"Let's just start," Valerio said.

They acted like it was a real meeting, snapping into it right away. A couple workers came out to bring drinks and food before leaving the room and closing the door behind them. Finn grabbed some sandwiches and salad, filling his plate while he waited for Valerio to get on with it.

"Finn, I know the last time we talked it was *emotional* for you. I'm hoping we can get through this conversation without any outbursts," Valerio said.

"Maybe you shouldn't have sprung it on me that my father didn't leave me shit nearly six months after his death. Next time, tell me right away," he said, shrugging. "Are there any more surprises like that today?"

This time it was Luna shaking her head. "No. There aren't. You're also right about that. We should have told you right away, but you were gone and on the run. We spent that whole time looking for you and when you came back, you were in such a weird state. Figuring out whether you even wanted this was the first step."

He pursed his lips. She wasn't wrong. Him running would have made it difficult for him to take on any news like that. But he had been home for weeks, they could have told him at any point. He deserved the truth regardless of what he was going through.

It didn't matter now though. He knew it now and it still didn't change anything.

"Well, I want it now. What steps do I need to take or whatever?"

"So professional. Unfortunately, it's not that simple. The Vitali empire saved the Kingsley one from collapsing. They're interwoven just like they should have been at the beginning," Allister said. His tone was sharp, and Finn ignored the digs to focus on what was actually being said.

"So there's no way for me to take over the Kingsley side?" he asked. Immediately, the same fury was returning. At every turn, it felt like he was being betrayed, just one thing after another.

"That's not what we're saying. Instead, there is no Kingsley empire independent of the Vitali one. They rely on each other," Valerio said.

"You'd be partners, dumbass," Dante said.

"Partners? Are you fucking kidding me?"

"Finn," Luna said, shaking her head. "You have to remember that for six months we were trying to stop all these companies and estates from closing. The only way to do that was by merging them together."

"You'll still own them, be the head of the Kingsley empire, and be able to navigate that the way you want, but with the existing businesses, we'll be partners. Anything you open or do outside of them can be independently owned if you open them separately and use your own money, which will take some time," Valerio said.

Finn clenched his jaw, trying to think everything through. Back then, when they were planning on taking down their fathers, Luna and Valerio had brought up the idea of them being partners and running the empires side by side. He hated the idea and was even revolted by it. Mainly because he never wanted to tarnish the Kingsley name with the Vitali's.

Things had changed though, hadn't they? The name didn't mean much at the moment and his father had nearly burnt it to the ground along with him. His sister was married to the Vitalis, and they had offered him a home when he had nowhere to go.

Most important of all, he was in love with a Moretti, the cousin of a Vitali. So really, change wasn't something he could fight much against. Not anymore, it seemed.

"How do I know you mean all of this? How do I know that I'll still have some say in the Kingsley name and that I'll get to run it?" Finn asked.

"Are you kidding me?" Allister asked.

"Let's just say I've been burned before by liars promising me titles like this."

"I'm not looking to take your name," Valerio said. "I said once before that I wasn't going to be my father, and I hope you won't be yours, which is why I have no issue giving it to you."

Luna grabbed his hand, looking at him with soft eyes. For the first time in so long, Finn felt what they all had been feeling. The sense of belonging and of family amongst each other. The partnership, whether it was temporary or not, was a way for them to connect and create the new life for themselves that they needed. Each and every single one of them.

He couldn't believe that it was happening. He had always dreamed about a life like this. Where he was the Don and he had a loyal family around him, and he would have the love of his life standing next to him through it all. Now, that life was at his fingertips. Waiting for him to grab it.

Finn nodded his head. "Okay. Let's sign or do whatever we need to make this happen."

"Why do you assume there's something to sign?" Dante asked.

He shrugged. "With you guys, there usually is."

Allister pulled the papers from his bag. "Well, you're right. Valerio's signature is all here. You can read through it before you sign if you want, but I hope you know there's nothing in here that would harm you."

Finn snorted. "I find that hard to believe."

"Well, don't. You're dating Gianna now. If that goes any further and you're supposed to take care of her, you're going to need the money and success," he said, handing over the papers. "Besides, she's my sister. I would never harm her."

"And harming me harms her?"

"Unfortunately."

"Well, at least we know you'll be financially stable," Luna said, a beaming smile on her face. "The ring Gianna's had picked out for years costs more than you'd ever imagine."

"Of course it does," Finn said, signing the papers.

"Oh, and the wedding, don't forget about how much that'll

cost," Valerio said, a grin on his face. "Especially the dress, and with her taste, forget about it."

This time Allister let out a loud chuckle. "Oh God, you'll never retire."

Finn shrugged, handing the papers back. "If it means giving my princess whatever she wants, I'll do what I have to."

"Whipped man, everyone is whipped." Dante shook his head.

Finn couldn't even fight him on that. Not one bit.

FORTY

GIANNA

GIANNA WIPED the sweat from her brow, taking in deep breaths of air. Practice was over for the day, and she had never been more thankful for it. They were only two weeks out from the show at this point and every practice was grueling and time-consuming.

Everything in her life was beyond amazing. She nailed the dance, she had Finn, she had her best friends, she had her brother, and she had her cousins. This was the life she had always dreamed of. The life that she had manifested for herself before she would go to bed. Back when she was more naive about the world and what she was allowed to expect from it. Now, however, she was allowed to expect it all, and she could get it all.

But there was always a price.

The price came in the form of her mother's visit being tomorrow. As in tomorrow morning, her and Allister would be leaving to go back home to deal with the whole mess. The thought nauseated her beyond belief, and it was also why she pushed herself for the past week in rehearsal like a madman. She wasn't prepared to see her mother, nor was she ever.

Something about this visit felt more terrible. Maybe it had to do with the fact that finally Gianna had fought the demons that had been running rampant in her life for so long and now she deserved her break. Or maybe it was because she knew what it was like to be loved and knew her mother would never return it.

Either way, she was dreading tomorrow.

That was why Finn was picking her up from practice and taking her out for the night. The last thing she needed was to stay bundled up in the house and watch the minutes tick by on the clock until the sun came up.

Gianna made her way into the locker room, changing out of the leotard and leggings into a matching pink sweatsuit set. Her fashion decisions had taken a backseat for the past week, but she still managed to keep the pink no matter what.

She undid the bun, shaking out her hair and feeling the tension in her scalp from where it sat. Finn would have watched her rehearsal like he had been doing at home, but since he signed everything with Valerio, his days kept him busy with actually going into the office to learn the business side of things. When he first brought it all up to her, she was shocked that they would be partnering up. Now, she loved it. He had the support and community he needed and that was what mattered the most to her.

She left her hair down, quickly packing everything up into her bag and checking her phone. As soon as she lifted it, Finn's contact popped up.

FINN <3

I'm outside whenever you're ready. I have a little surprise for you, princess.

An immediate smile drifted onto her face. She made her way out of the building and sure enough he stood there, looking handsome as ever in his leather jacket and black jeans, leaning against his bike. Finn met her halfway, wrapping his arms around her and pulling her in for a much-needed kiss.

"I missed you," he muttered.

"I missed you too," she said, giving him one more peck. "You didn't tell me you were bringing FiFi."

"I thought we could both use a ride." He grabbed her bag, guiding her towards the bike.

"So, where's my surprise?"

"My, my. What happened to manners?" He lifted his eyebrow, placing the bag under the seat.

"They went to hell. Now, give me the surprise," she said, holding her hands out in front of her. "You can't promise a surprise and then not give me anything. That would be a cruel and unusual punishment."

Finn shook his head, a small smile on his face. "Forgive me for ever using that word."

She didn't know what she was expecting him to pull out, but when he grabbed the helmet out of the silky bag, she was stunned. He handed it to her, letting her see all the details on it fully. Whereas Finn's signature one that she usually wore was black, this one was white with light pink hearts on either side by the ears. On the back of it, in pink cursive lettering, it spelt out 'princess' giving her the official title on the bike. Of course it had the safety features that were important too, like the visor for her eyes and padding, but she paid attention to the details that made her heart jump out of her chest.

"So, do you like it?" he asked hesitantly. "If you don't, we can get it customized more."

"I love it," she said immediately. "This is perfect."

The grin on his face had to have matched hers. "Good. I'm glad you love it. I figured you needed one for yourself since the other one didn't fit right and we'll be riding on FiFi a lot. And who knows, maybe you'll get your own bike one day."

She couldn't stop herself from jumping into his arms again,

forcing him to catch her at the last second, but he did. Gianna covered him in kisses. "Thank you for this."

"Anything for you, princess."

When she finally managed to try it on, it was the perfect fit. Much more comfortable than the other one she wore. He handed her one of his leather jackets too, promising to get her a customized one as well if she wanted. For some reason, she preferred to wear his instead. Of course, it had to do with being surrounded in his scent every time she put it on, but he didn't need to know that. Finn got on the bike, and she got on behind him. She wrapped her arms around his waist, holding onto him with everything she had when he finally took off.

No amount of time on the bike could make her get used to the feeling of pure adrenaline rushing through her body. Just the feeling of rushing through the streets, putting all her trust in Finn, it made her feel free. She was able to let go of control, let go of everything if even for a moment.

When they got to the lake, her legs were wobbly. It always took her a moment to steady herself when she got off, but luckily Finn was there to provide a helping hand. She took off the helmet and handed it over to him, letting him place them on the bike before they walked down to the little dock.

The sun was close to setting, but in the golden light she could see just how much everything was starting to come to life. More bugs lingered beside the water, flowers began to blossom around the tree trunks, and she swore that she saw a fish or two though there were probably so many more swimming around.

Finn took a seat beside her, wrapping his arm around her shoulder and pulling her closer to him. "Tell me about your day."

"Well, let's see. I woke up, had breakfast, went to class, and then danced for most of the day with some lunch in between and now I'm here with you." She turned to him, leaning her head against his shoulder. "It was a busy day."

"And why was it so busy, princess?"

"The dancing. It's a lot right now to keep up with and my body hurts and everything hurts and I'm tired."

He was silent for a moment. "It's just the dancing?"

"Yep. Just the dancing."

She knew what he was doing, but she wasn't ready to go there yet. Not when they were in their perfect little place and she had just stepped into his arms. She didn't want the good to always be tarnished by the thoughts of her mother. So much of her life already was and she didn't deserve any more of it.

"Okay."

"Tell me about your day. How was it with Valerio?" she asked, quickly changing the topic.

Finn shook his head. "Well, Valerio is a fucking psycho, but I'm sure you already knew that. He's so specific about the way he wants everything done. I truly don't understand how Luna manages to be around him."

"She loves him, that's how."

"Good for her then because I don't see it. Today though we worked on getting some investors, so I was able to sit in on those meetings. They're so fucking boring."

Gianna couldn't help the laugh that left her lips. "Really? Who would have guessed?"

"No kidding. All they do is talk numbers and profits and blah blah blah. I managed to sell them on it, though. Can you believe I'm good at getting people to do what I want?" Finn asked, his voice holding pride.

She looked up at him, her eyes shining. Just seeing how much he was changing and taking on the new challenges, but finding so much excitement in them made her so happy for him. There were so many things he thought he couldn't do just because he had a parent that didn't believe in him, but now he was doing them all.

"You are good at getting people to do what you want," Gianna said, clearing her throat. "You're great at everything."

He leaned down until their faces were inches apart. "And you're great at trying to deflect. Talk to me, Gianna."

His inquisitive side was just as annoying. She frowned, trying to pull away but he just held onto her tighter. "There's not much to talk about."

"I know you're going to see your mother tomorrow."

"Great, you're all caught up then."

She could tell he was fighting the urge to roll his eyes, but still he kept his tone gentle. "You can talk to me about it. I know it's not easy for you. I know you don't want to do it."

Gianna bit the inside of her cheek. Wasn't that the truth?

"Any time I have to go see her, it makes me feel powerless. I know how it ends, so the visit is always pointless."

It ended with her leaving every single time. No surprise. No change. Nothing. It was expected, but it still hurt every single time. It left Gianna feeling raw, angry, even numb for days on end afterwards. Then she recovered, moved on from her life and forgot about it until the reminder came from Allister a year later that it was time to do it all over again.

"Then don't go," Finn said. "If she makes you feel powerless, take back the power. Don't let her control you."

She shook her head. "I can't do that. It disappoints my father, and I can't leave Allister to do it alone. He doesn't deserve it either."

"So then what? You just keep going with the pain until she decides that she's over the visits?" He was asking a genuine question, but the question still stung because of how truthful it was. Is that what her future looked like? Being led by a leash on these visits year after year, even when she was married, had kids, was fifty years old, sixty?

Maybe it was.

Because it was her mother.

The thought hit her so hard, she swore she felt the pain come from her chest. It was brutal how much she continued holding onto something that was never there, something she had idealized her entire life and become envious of, only to never receive.

"I don't know," she whispered.

"Do you want to go tomorrow?" Finn asked, his voice so quiet.

Gianna took in a deep breath, leaning her head into the crook of his neck. "Yes and no. Part of me wishes she was dead, just so I could mourn her and move on from it. Or maybe not dead. Maybe just that she could leave and never return again. Then I wouldn't have to anticipate it. I could live my life without the reminder. The other part of me holds onto the visits. It's the only way I know where she is, that she is alive, that she actually exists. For a moment, when we're sitting there talking, I imagine that she'll say she's staying and then she'll apologize for everything. That she'll say she was young and confused, but that she loves us more than anything. And I'll forgive her right away because it makes sense to. But it never happens and the visit ends. She gets into the car and drives away and then I hate her all over again. I hate myself for ever wishing she would come back."

"You should never hate yourself for that. Your ability to dream and to try to see the best in other people is what makes you so incomparable to other people. The fact that you would forgive her in a heartbeat says everything about you. The fact that she leaves and comes back yearly says everything about her. When you feel it, whenever you're ready and you decide that you don't want to do the visits anymore, just tell me. I'll be there every step of the way. You're never alone, princess. Not in this lifetime. Not as long as you're mine." His voice carried out into the lake around them almost as if he was giving a speech to the masses, but the words were reserved for her alone. She didn't need to look at his face to know that he was staring down at her. She felt the goosebumps on her skin. He didn't push and he didn't force her. Instead, he put it into her hands. He gave her the control.

She didn't know if the day would ever come. Hell, she didn't know if tomorrow would even come. Life was unpredictable in that way.

What she did know was that with Finn, right there, that was her safety. As long as she had him by her side, she could get through it.

FORTY-ONE

GIANNA

GIANNA DIDN'T KNOW how long they sat on the dock for, but they were able to switch the topic back to more lighthearted matters to get her mind off everything. She didn't know how, but Finn had managed to get laughs out of her, which usually didn't happen on the nights before she went to visit her mother.

But he was telling some story about going fishing and accidentally catching the hook on Augustus's pants, causing them to rip right at the ass. Gianna couldn't help but cackle at the fighting it must have led to between them.

"I really can't believe you even went fishing," she said, shaking her head.

"What does that mean?" he asked, his brow raised.

"You are so not the type."

"Like I said, it was a one-time experience. I don't think I would ever do it again," he said. He looked around, his eyes widening slightly. "Damn, I didn't notice how dark it already got."

She did the same, shrugging. "I didn't either. I do want to say thank you for taking me out tonight and getting my mind off everything. I would have been losing my mind at home."

"You're my princess. I'll do anything for you."

Gianna grinned, feeling a little cheeky. "Now, don't start throwing around phrases like that."

His face scrunched in confusion. "Which one?"

"Saying you would do anything for me."

"I said it because I meant it." He leaned in, brushing his nose against hers. "Why? You have some crazy request?"

She shrugged. "No, nothing like that."

Gianna looked down at the ground, absentmindedly kicking her feet to draw his attention in further. She knew he was hooked the moment he moved in impossibly close, pulling her onto his lap.

"There's something going on in that pretty little mind of yours and I want to know what it is," he said. His eyes were already darker in anticipation, while his hands held her hips.

Sure, he had done a great job providing a distraction, but she could use more of one. One that she had thought about and considered but never knew if he would actually be interested in or not. But in the dark, all alone like they were, there was truly no better chance than now.

Gianna wrapped her arms around his neck, playing with the hairs there. She gave him a small grin, tilting her head to the side.

"I want you to fuck me," she said, pausing for effect, "against your bike."

His eyes got wide for a second before the words actually hit him. He had a devastatingly handsome grin as he said, "Fuck yes."

He lifted them from the dock, carrying her over to where the bike stood. Immediately, the warmth she always felt in her core returned at the anticipation. Gianna pressed her lips to his neck, letting him pay attention to walking so she could tease him. He took his leather jacket off, throwing it on the floor and setting their helmets on it, all while still managing to hold her. His strength was always such a turn on for her and it continued to be the case.

He finally pushed their lips together, devouring her with every movement. Gianna could feel the passion in the kiss with every swipe of his tongue, with every movement of his lips, and she loved every single second of it. His hands returned to her ass, grabbing it the best he could through the sweatpants she wore.

He growled against her lips. "I wish you were wearing that fucking ballerina outfit of yours instead."

"It wouldn't have been comfortable on the bike," she said, pulling away slightly.

"Yeah, but I would have been able to get to your pussy a lot easier."

Finn set her down on the seat of the bike, giving her a moment to pull the leather jacket she was wearing off. She threw it on the floor, looking at him as he stared back down at her. "What?" she asked.

"Just admiring my princess."

The blush on her cheeks was immediate, but it didn't matter because he was lifting her in a moment's notice once more, setting her on the ground and bending her over the bike's seat. She stood with her ass in the air and her back slightly arched.

Finn walked up closer behind her, bending over so his lips were grazing the lobe of her ear. "Is this what you had in mind, princess? Me bending you over my bike and fucking you out in the open like this?"

Goosebumps rose on her skin immediately. He hadn't even touched her anywhere and she could feel the moisture between her legs growing by the second. "Yes," she whispered. "Exactly like this."

He bit her lobe before moving back. She couldn't see him from the angle she was in, which made the anticipation worse. Time seemed to move forever, or maybe it was just her lack of patience that made it seem so. But when he finally pulled down her sweatpants, exposing her pussy to the night air, she couldn't tell if she was relieved or a little bit mortified.

Finn pushed her legs open further, stretching and exposing her for his eyes. Her body was burning like an inferno, ready to turn him into ash if he didn't do something to put out the fire.

"Finn," she groaned, moving her hips to get some kind of friction but there was none.

"So impatient." She could feel his body heat on her thighs, so he was right behind her now. His hand touched the back of her leg, trailing up her thigh and stopping under her ass. "And here I thought you had stopped being a brat."

She wanted to snap at him so badly, and she almost did, but then his hand moved to her pussy. Slowly he trailed his fingers up her slit, going to the spot that was begging for some kind of attention.

"You're not a brat, are you, princess?" he asked. He was taunting her, knowing that it pissed her off and got her off all at the same time.

Gianna clenched her jaw. "No, I'm not."

His fingers met her clit, moving in slow circles around it. Her eyes dropped closed, a low moan escaping her mouth. "What was that? I couldn't hear you."

"I'm not a brat," she muttered, pushing herself against his hand. She needed more pressure, or for him to go faster, or something. He just kept the agonizingly slow pace the entire time.

"Now that is my princess," he said. He pulled his hand away, eliciting a cry from her.

She nearly stood up in anger, but then he finally pushed his dick inside, letting a gasp escape her lips. The fullness was perfect just like it was every single time with him. He didn't move at first, just kept it there, letting out a groan.

"You're so fucking perfect, princess," Finn said, grabbing a handful of her ass again. "And all mine."

With one swift slap to her ass cheek, he began thrusting in and out of her, moving his hips in a way that was driving her wild. She held onto the bike, desperately trying to keep the strength in her legs so she wouldn't fall over. Between the slaps on her behind, the thrusts, and the entire situation, her body felt like there was a wire of electricity running through it.

The driving force seemed to be Finn's need to play with her

clit as he fucked her. There was no silencing her at that point. Hell, he didn't even silence himself. They unleashed every single part of themselves at that moment.

And when Gianna finally came, it hit her so harshly she actually fell against the bike. Finn held her up by the waist, finishing inside of her like he always did now. Tingles rushed through her body, feeling like she had gotten hit by lightning. When Finn pulled her up, he pressed his lips to hers once more.

"Are you okay?" he asked, a slight smirk on his lips.

"Perfect," she managed to say with an actual smile on her face.

"And you know I love you?"

Gianna nodded. "I do. And I love you."

"And you know I would do anything for you?"

"Yes."

"And you know that tomorrow if you need anything at all, you call me. I will be there in a moment's notice. I'm not joking."

Like an avalanche, the stark reminder of what was happening tomorrow hit her all over again. Finn's thumbs brushed her cheeks, bringing her back down to reality. All she could do was nod, and say, "I know."

And when they finally got redressed and everything, Gianna held onto Finn the entire drive home. He continued to hold her in the shower, in bed, and all night. She knew because she didn't sleep and neither did he.

In the morning, he gave her a million kisses and said comforting words that she didn't manage to hear because her ears were ringing from dread. When he closed the car door and stepped back to allow her and Allister to drive away, Gianna looked at him until he disappeared behind the bushes and then the gates.

All she could think about was that maybe he was right. Maybe she was ready to end the visits with her mother.

FORTY-TWO

GIANNA

GIANNA'S HANDS were ice cold, and she felt like she could throw up at any minute. Breakfast that morning had been off the table, so she stuck to small sips of water the entire drive. They were almost there and neither she nor Allister had said much to each other.

There never was much to say.

The neighborhoods they drove through now didn't bring up any comforting nostalgia like it used to. Still, Gianna could appreciate seeing kids playing outside and people taking walks. A stark difference to the city life, this was so much slower moving, which was perfect for their father. He still did some business for the Vitali family, but after Cesare's untimely demise, he took a step back. It wasn't a retirement per say, but he spent a lot more time playing tennis and hanging out with friends at country clubs now than he used to.

Seriously, Gianna loved that life for him. Her father had always been a good man and a constant in her life. He tried his best with having a daughter, but through the years there were things that he just didn't know how to handle. She didn't fault him for it, but he never remarried or dated—that she knew of—so she never really had another motherly figure to go to about things.

When she got her first period or was experimenting with makeup, she had to rely on the girls and their moms—Blair's and Cecilia's to be exact.

Federico Moretti was much closer to Allister and naturally so —that was his heir. Still, it left Gianna feeling a little bit empty when she saw that they were able to bond closer than she could with her father. When they talked about business and law, she couldn't relate to it no matter how much they tried to include her in it.

She leaned her head against the window. Today was never-ending.

The familiar trees and landscape told her they were there before anything else did. Her father had always been so particular about having his bushes perfectly trimmed and the grass mowed all the same length.

They passed the gate and immediately her anxiety only got worse. She hadn't had a breakdown since that night after the club when Finn luckily stopped it, but it seemed like one might have been on the horizon. She took deep breaths, reminding herself that Finn was a call away. She could always leave; she didn't have to stay. She had the power.

There was no other car there, meaning that it was just her dad inside. That managed to relax her nerves slightly. They got out of the car and walked to the front door. It was thrown open by her father before they could even knock. He had a large smile on his face despite everything.

Gianna couldn't remember the last time she had seen him. It had to have been a couple of months at least, but it had been a busy time. Federico had gray hair now and more wrinkles than she could remember. He was a tall man with a lean build, similar to Allister's. However, his bright blue eyes were nearly identical to Gianna's. A lot of times she got told that she looked like her father, which in retrospect she never really took lightly, but he wasn't an ugly man, so maybe it could have been a compliment.

"There you are," he said, throwing his arms open. He

embraced Allister first, giving him a long hug before moving to Gianna and doing the same. "I have some snacks and drinks set up. I wasn't sure how hungry you guys were going to be from the drive."

"I could definitely eat," Allister said.

"Wish I felt the same," she muttered, entering the house.

It was the same as it had been her entire life. A two-story colonial revival home with light blue walls and marble flooring. There were pictures of them from childhood hung up throughout the house and it did bring up good memories. The living room, where they would be for the day, had two big navy couches and then two cream-colored armchairs all set up in a rectangular fashion with a coffee table in the center. It gave enough space for seating, so no one was forced beside anyone they didn't want to be next to.

The table, like every year, was covered in an assortment of foods and drinks: sandwiches, cheeses, crackers, veggies, fruits, dips, juices, teas. It was overwhelming how much food was prepared for such a short visit, but this was how her father seemed to cope with it. Besides, they never had anyone else at the house during the visits, meaning the cooks and staff always had the day off. It was exclusively between the four of them.

Gianna took a seat on the couch, immediately reaching for one of the pitchers of tea and pouring some for herself. Hopefully there were calming elements in it and not caffeine. The last thing she needed was any sort of buzz.

Allister sat on the couch beside her, and her father took one of the cream armchairs, staring at the two of them with a big smile. "So, how has the semester been? It's almost over, right?"

Allister nodded. "It's been good. Finals are next week. I'm top of my class so I'm not worried."

Of course he was. He was a genius. A poster child for all parents.

"What about you, Gianna?"

She shrugged. "I've already finished some of my classes, but

I'm not worried about finals. I'm mostly worried about the recital I have in a couple weeks."

"What is there to be worried about? You're an amazing dancer," her father said, grabbing some grapes off the table.

"There was one move I kept messing up, but I think I finally got it down. You're still coming to the recital, right?"

"Of course I'll be there. I hope you're saving me a spot in the front row."

Her heart swelled at his words. He had never been one to miss any of their events throughout the years and it mattered.

Allister snorted. "Maybe she can save you a spot next to her boyfriend instead."

Gianna's eyes flew open. She looked at Allister and then at her father, who stared at her with an eerily calm look on his face. He didn't say anything for a moment, just blinked and stared. God, she was going to kill Allister.

"What boyfriend?" her father finally said.

She cleared her throat, wiping her now sweaty hands on her dress. "His name is Finn. We just started dating recently."

"Finn? Why does that name sound so familiar?"

"Probably because you're thinking of Finn Kingsley, which is exactly who it is," Allister said. "She has fallen in love with a Kingsley."

Her father ran a hand down his face, muttering something under his breath. He looked at Gianna with a desperate look. "A Kingsley? Gianna, there are so many men in this world, and you choose Finn Kingsley?"

She frowned. "He's a really great person and he treats me amazingly. He actually wanted to be here today to support me, but I didn't let him because it's a family thing."

Her father turned back to Allister. "You know this boy?"

"Somewhat. I'm getting to know him better. I did all the standard threatening the other night to keep him in his place," Allister said.

Gianna fought the urge to roll her eyes. That threat didn't

really do anything, but she didn't mention that. If this would get them off her ass about it for now, she would let them think whatever they wanted.

"Good. I still want to meet him outside of the recital. Once we handle all this here, we'll set up a date for you two to come down," he said.

She nodded her head. "Perfect. Just keep an open mind."

As long as he was willing to meet Finn, she could work with it. It was going to be awkward no doubt when they did run into each other, but her father would learn to love him just like she did.

The knock on the front door stopped all conversations in the living room. Immediately, Gianna could feel the goosebumps coating her skin, the internal dread settling inside of her all over again.

Federico stood up, moving in a haste to open the door. She attempted to take deep breaths to calm her rapidly beating heart, but there was no use. She turned to Allister, who seemed to have the same look on his face. He had always been much better about hiding it, but not now. Not when the moment was here and there was nowhere to go.

The sound of high heels followed her father's footsteps into the living room. She had red lipstick painted on, her blonde hair pulled into an updo, and she wore a black dress that looked more suitable for a funeral than it did for anything else.

But that was her mother.

That was Giulia Moretti. The last name she kept despite not keeping the family associated with it, but it gave her access to things that she wasn't ready to let go of.

She smiled wide, holding her arms out as if she wanted a hug from them. "Wow, look at you both."

Gianna didn't move a muscle, and she was happy to see that Allister didn't either. Giulia dropped her arms awkwardly, clearing her throat. Her father returned to his seat from before, forcing her into the other armchair. Unfortunately, it happened to be directly across from Gianna.

"How have you both been? You look so much older," Giulia said, attempting to keep the conversation going.

Allister spoke up. "We're fine. Still in school; still doing everything we've done before."

That was how they kept it. Generic and vague. Never giving details about where they went to school, lived, or anything really —but then again, she never asked. She was just as fine with the answers as they were giving them.

She turned to Gianna. "You seem to get much more beautiful every time I see you."

"Thanks." It wasn't a compliment she wanted to accept. Not in the slightest, but she tried her best to keep it pleasant. The entire situation made her skin crawl still, no matter how much she tried to not let it.

In the past, the conversation used to be livelier, but they were also children who were desperate to fill their mother in on every single detail she had missed in an attempt to get her home. Over the years, the visits got shorter and shorter. They had nothing to share with the woman who wanted nothing to do with them. Those memories were sacred and reserved for the people in their lives who loved them and wanted to be there for them.

"You're here earlier than usual," her father said, crossing his legs. "Usually, you make your visits in the winter."

Giulia shifted in her seat. "Well, truthfully, I felt a calling to come see you guys again. I was in this beautiful little town in Croatia when this family walked by me. It looked just like us and I thought about the good times we had. Immediately, I called you up and made plans to come down. I want us to be a family again, like we were once before."

Gianna was sure her heart stopped. This was exactly what she had always dreamed about. This moment right here. Her mother wanted to come back and be a family. She should have been overjoyed; she should have been jumping on the couch screaming with glee.

But instead, all she felt was doubt and suspicion. It was difficult to believe a single word that left her lips when it seemed too convenient. How many families had she seen on her travels? Suddenly, this one family rang true to her?

Maybe if Gianna had been in a different place, she would have believed it, but something in her gut didn't allow her to.

She looked over at Allister who did that thing where he narrowed his eyes and tried to figure out what Giulia's intentions were. Judging by the way his hands were clenched at his sides, she was willing to say that he didn't believe it either.

Federico finally spoke up when no one else did. "Respectfully, that's not my decision to make. We are not married, and I will never be married to you again. A relationship between us will never exist. As for the relationship between you and them, that is going to be up to Gianna and Allister."

There was a slight twitch in Giulia's eye. "I wasn't expecting you to marry me again. I just want my family."

"You walked out on that years ago," Allister said. "That family doesn't exist."

"We can create it again."

"No, we can't," Gianna said, finally finding her voice. "You can't pop in and want a family when you feel like you want one. You had one and you left it. You never apologized or took accountability, and even now you haven't done either of those things. You left me and Allister without a mother when we needed one the most."

"I saw you every year."

"Honestly, I almost wish you hadn't."

Giulia's face fell. "I left because I had to. I couldn't be a mother or a wife. I wasn't in any condition to do either at the time."

Allister shook his head. "That's fine, no one faults you for that. But you kept us on a string our entire lives wondering if we would ever get our mother again. If we would get our family. We need to move on completely, and so do you."

"What are you saying?" she asked, looking between Gianna and Allister.

Gianna took a deep breath. It seemed like it was finally the time. She felt the courage rushing through her body, but still she was terrified. Of what? She wasn't sure. Maybe it was the fact that she was finally making a decision about this entire situation—one that was ultimately going to be the best for her but would hurt. Of course it would.

"I think we're done with these visits, or at least I am. I don't want to do them anymore. I don't want to hurt anymore. I want to grow and move on and live without thinking about the way my life could have been."

"I'm done with it too," Allister said. "The future is always unexpected, but we'll leave it at that for now."

"Then that settles everything," her father said, staring at Giulia.

Her face was cold. It was almost like staring at a stranger, but then again, that was exactly who she was. A stranger. Gianna didn't know her any better than she would have known a random relative showing up to a family reunion.

Their relationship wasn't supposed to be that way, but it was. That was the harsh truth. The one that Gianna had to face, accept, and move on with.

"I guess there's nothing more to say then," Giulia said.

With that, she stood and walked away without ever looking back. Not at her kids, or the husband she once had, or the house she once lived in.

She walked away and Gianna knew she would never see her again.

FORTY-THREE

FINN

FINN HADN'T HEARD anything from Gianna since she'd left that morning, so he had no idea whether everything was going well or not. Seeing how broken and distraught she had been about the whole situation was making him consider just driving down there himself, but he knew she needed her space to do this. She was stronger than she looked and stronger than she knew.

Still, he would have loved to have a chat with her mother. Maybe introduce her to his favorite crowbar. If Gianna said the words, he would. Until then, he had to sit still and fantasize about getting his revenge on the woman who continued to hurt his princess.

The day was boring otherwise. It was the weekend, so he didn't have any work and everyone had their plans. His previous plans were obvious, but also unavailable because she was occupied, so he accepted when Luna invited him over once again for lunch. Seeing Valerio outside of work was fucking annoying, though.

These days, he was accepted by the security of the house, not patted down and questioned like he was before. He walked to the front door and was greeted by the same workers that were always kind and welcoming when he stopped by. They pointed him to the living room and that was where he went, but he stopped dead in his tracks when he saw who sat beside Luna on the couch.

It was his mother. Eleanora Kingsley.

She looked refreshed, maybe even younger since she had been out of the country. Her brown hair was cut short to her chin and her eyes held a sparkle that she didn't have in them before. He hadn't spoken to her since he helped her out of the country when she murdered their father. Seeing her hit him so hard, he nearly fell over.

"Finn? Oh my God, look at you," she gushed, standing from the couch.

He didn't say anything. Hell, what was he supposed to say? It was like seeing a ghost. This wasn't his day to be visiting with his mother; it was Gianna's. Why the hell hadn't Luna said anything when she invited him over?

"What are you doing here?" he asked.

"What do you mean?" she asked, confused. "I'm here visiting."

Finn turned to Luna. "I didn't realize that you both were close."

How could he have known when their mother had never defended them the entire time their father abused them? If anything, it seemed like Luna would have never wanted anything to do with her either because of that. However, judging by how close Luna sat beside their mother, she didn't look even a little bit uncomfortable. How did Valerio even let her into this home? He would have hated her too for everything she did to Luna. What was Finn missing?

"Please, just sit down and I'll explain everything to you," Luna said, keeping her voice gentle.

He moved to the seat furthest away from them, which happened to be the couch beside theirs. He sat at the left end, making sure he had space to run just in case.

"I'm sitting, now talk."

Luna nodded. "Well, that day—"

"The day she killed Reece Kingsley," he jumped in.

She could only give him a dirty look. "Yes, the day that Reece Kingsley died, we talked. Then, you sent her out of the country, and we spoke on the phone to work on our relationship. I managed to forgive her for everything that happened in our lives."

Finn let out a sarcastic laugh. "That's great that she's now mother of the year for you, but while he was beating the shit out of me my entire childhood, she never did anything."

"You can talk to me directly, Finn," Eleanora said. "Are you angry at me for killing your father?"

He clenched his jaw. Looking at her brought up memories for him that he didn't like to think about. He was finally moving on from everything in his life, but now another demon stared him in the face. One that should have protected him and didn't. She was almost so insignificant in his life throughout the years that it was hard to even consider her much of a mother figure at all. She was there, but she wasn't. More like a ghost than anything else.

"I'm moving on from his death. My issues with that have nothing to do with you. My issues with you are exactly what I said. You never stood up for me or Luna. You stood by his side," he said.

"I should have been there for you and my biggest regret in life will be not defending you both. I should have taken you out of that home when I had a chance. I should have been a better mother, and I'm so sorry I haven't been," she said. Tears welled up in her eyes and it almost startled him how much emotion she was showing.

Throughout their lives, she never was one for emotion. She kept everything locked away, including her smiles. She wasn't the type of mother they could go to either with problems or good days at school. No, it was better to go to the nannies who cared more than their mother did.

But her apology did something to him he hadn't expected. It hit him so deep in his chest he could feel an ache. Was it an ache for some kind of parental love? He wasn't sure.

"Why didn't you defend us?" he asked, feeling so small. He almost felt like that little boy again, trying to understand his parents to make sense of why they did the things that they did. His father was scorned, but maybe his mother still had some redemption left in her.

"Your father was a horrible man. Everything was a game to him. He always wanted to win and have the upper hand no matter what. He controlled every aspect of my life and kept tabs on what I loved to leverage his control over me. I learned that earlier on in our relationship, and I played the game back. I was never going to let him use you guys to control me, but he still hurt you in such horrible ways." Eleanora wiped the tears from under her eyes, taking a deep breath to steady herself.

Luna grabbed her hand for comfort and suddenly he could see why they had bonded. Reece Kingsley had that same exact control over Luna's life when he tried to set up an arranged marriage for her, and he did the same to their mother. They bonded over their trauma.

"It's a good thing he's dead now," Finn said, clearing his throat. He was shocked by how much emotion swelled in his chest.

"I guess so," his mother said, cracking a small smile.

"I'm sorry I didn't tell you about her visit. It was last minute, and I wanted to get you over here, but something tells me you wouldn't have wanted to otherwise," Luna said.

"You're right about that. I wasn't prepared for this at all," he said.

"I'm not expecting you to forgive me or to understand anything. Seeing you though, that is amazing. You've grown up so much since I last saw you."

"I've changed a lot since you've last seen me."

"Luna told me about some of it."

"She sure loves to talk," Finn said, rolling his eyes.

"Come on, I have to fill her in. You're her son," Luna said, throwing her hands up.

That he was. And being her son left him feeling so fucking unsure of where to go with their relationship. He wished there was a perfect way to approach these types of situations, but there wasn't. It was up to him to make these decisions for himself, and it drove him wild.

He exhaled a long breath. "Listen, I can't decide right now what is going to happen with our relationship, but I'm open to reconnecting. Slowly. Over time. It's been a really long couple of weeks, and I need some time to clear my mind and think about everything before I can make any serious decisions."

Eleanora nodded. "I understand completely. Whenever you feel comfortable, I'm here for you."

Finn nodded his head, standing from the couch. "I'm going to head out. I'll let you guys continue your lunch."

"I'll call you later, Finn," Luna called out as he walked back to the front door.

He just waved his hand and walked out of the house, taking a long and deep breath. The walk back was necessary. He was exhausted, probably more than he had ever been in his life. First the shit with his father, and then his mother entering back into his life. These were the relationships in his life that weren't supposed to be so complicated and yet they were.

He needed Gianna. She always knew what to say and how to handle these situations. He pulled out his phone, noticing there still wasn't anything from her.

By the time he was in front of the home, he saw that Allister's car was parked out front instead of the garage like he usually did. It was also done so haphazardly, as if he'd just pulled in and parked the car before he left it. In fact, the keys were still in the ignition, which was completely unlike Allister.

Immediate alarm filled his body. With hurried steps, he made his way to the front door that was also just thrown open. Finn looked everywhere, trying to find Gianna or Allister. The living room, kitchen, bathrooms, everything on the main level was empty. He ran up the stairs, finally hearing some life in the house coming from the room furthest down the hall: her room.

Finn ran in, looking around frantically to find that Gianna's room was trashed. Mirrors were smashed, pictures were shattered, and Gianna sat on the floor crying her eyes out, nearly suffocating while Allister desperately tried to get her to breathe.

Finn immediately fell into action, pushing Allister out of the way as he looked at Gianna. She looked completely broken. More importantly, her face was red, and she was gasping for air.

"Gianna, princess, look at me, breathe," he said, grabbing her shoulders and trying to shake her out of it.

It didn't work. Fuck.

"Gianna. Fucking breathe," Allister screamed from beside him.

Finn grabbed her cheeks, pushing her hair out from her face and started blowing air into her mouth. He traded off from her nose to her mouth, desperately trying to get her to suck in some air before she fucking harmed herself.

His heart beat frantically in his chest. The panic only grew when it didn't work like it did before.

He rubbed at her throat, trying to do anything he could to just get her to breathe. "Come on, princess. Breathe for me. You can do it. I know you can."

Finn blew air into her mouth once again, rubbing her throat and her back at the same time. Like some kind of miracle, she finally inhaled, coughing as she sucked in breaths of air. Her chest heaved and she looked stunned, but she was breathing.

What had only been less than a minute felt like a lifetime to Finn as he continued rubbing her back. He tried to regulate his own heartbeat, but that would take an eternity after what he just went through.

"You're okay, princess," he murmured into her ear. "Just keep breathing."

"Finn," she whispered, letting tears escape her eyes once more.

"Don't work yourself up. Take it easy. Just breathe for now and then you can tell me what happened."

She nodded, leaning her head against his chest. Finn sat there, holding her tighter than he had ever held her in his life. He looked over at Allister who looked completely drained. Physically and emotionally.

"Are you okay?" Finn asked.

He lifted his head, looking beaten. "I will be."

"She's okay now. I'll be here with her. Go take time for yourself."

He nodded, standing. Allister began walking but stopped directly in front of them. "Thank you," he said, offering out a hand.

Finn took it, shaking his hand and creating an understanding between them. Allister shut the door behind him, leaving the two alone in the room.

"Princess?" he asked, pulling away slightly. "Do you feel alright? Do you need a doctor?"

She shook her head, looking up at him. Her eyes were red and her makeup was smeared, but she still looked every bit as beautiful as she always did. "No, I only really stopped breathing once you walked in. I should be okay."

He shook his head. "What happened? What triggered it?" When Gianna's lip started to tremble again, he almost wished he hadn't asked at all. "Take a deep breath," he said, immediately getting her to breathe when he could tell she was closing herself off again.

She did just that, taking a few deep inhales before she started talking. "She said she wanted to be a family again. I couldn't believe it, and just sitting there hearing that, it solidified that I couldn't do those visits anymore. I don't want to be called upon when she's ready for a family and then be put back on the shelf when she decides she doesn't want one anymore. Allister said the same. Then she just left. Just like that. No sorry, nothing about how much she loves us, nothing."

"I'm so sorry, Gianna."

And he truly was. He couldn't begin to imagine how she was feeling: the shock, the grief, the heartbreak. She had lost her mother. Not to death, but to life.

"I was fine until we almost got here and then it started. The panic, the suffocation, the anguish. She just left and it's done. And I'll never have that mother figure like I wanted, like I needed, and I just have to live with that now. And it hurts so bad, Finn. It hurts so much worse than the stupid visits and I don't want it to hurt," she cried out, holding onto him like he was a lifebuoy ring, and she was out in the middle of the ocean.

"It hurts bad now, but it will hurt less and less. I promise you, Gianna, this pain will fade until one day you wake up, and you don't feel it like you used to. You did what you had to for yourself, and I am so proud of you. You are so strong and courageous," he said.

"No, I'm not."

"Yes, you are. You don't have to see it right now, but you are."

"Just don't go anywhere, please," she said, looking up at him.

He pushed back her hair and wiped the tears under her eyes. "There's no way in hell I'm leaving your side. I'm with you for the rest of our lives, princess. I love you."

"I love you too."

And eventually she stopped crying. When she did, he took them to his room. He helped her shower and wipe the makeup off her face. He did her skincare for her after having memorized it from watching her get ready all those times. He brushed her hair and found her favorite pair of pajamas. He helped her into bed and then ordered her favorite pasta from a place in the city. He watched the stupid vampire romance movies she was obsessed with and rubbed her back until she fell asleep.

And he would do it for her again and again and again.

FORTY-FOUR

GIANNA

A BUSY SCHEDULE was inconvenient when Gianna was barely holding on as it was. She managed to scrape by on her finals, which was a miracle, but with the show a week away, she was now thrown into full-day practices.

It was grueling and exhausting, but while she pirouetted around the dance floor on the tips of her toes, she managed to ease her aching heart. There were so many times that she wondered if she'd made the right decision. She knew deep down that she did, but the pain she kept feeling made her keep rethinking it. She just thought back to what Finn had said. That the pain would hurt now, but it would fade. And the pain was terrible. But so was every visit when she had to see Giulia leave again and again. The permanency of it was what hurt the most, but it was fading.

Very, very, very slowly.

The first day she woke up after it, she felt like a zombie. The girls came in and tried to cheer her up, which she appreciated, but just wasn't in the mood for. Finn stayed by her side and fed her all her favorite foods and let her watch her favorite movies and reality shows while rotting in bed. He got someone to clean up her room too. Without Finn, she didn't think she would have been able to get through any of it. He was her anchor the entire time, being understanding of the entire process even if it wasn't linear and didn't make the most sense.

She managed to get over hating looking at herself in the mirror, which was a relief. It always lingered after her breakdowns when she felt disgusting for letting herself get to that point. But getting over it meant that some things were at least getting a little bit better.

The rest of the week, she went to her classes and to practice, then immediately threw herself into bed once it was all over. She even managed to get ice cream with the girls the other day. Slowly, Gianna was getting back to herself. It was definitely taking time, but she was getting there.

She hadn't seen much of Allister since that day. He had been avoiding pretty much everyone. Luckily, she had gotten him to agree to a hangout with everyone tonight at the house with takeout and drinks to celebrate classes officially being over. There was no doubt that he wasn't in the partying mood, but she was worried about him.

Gianna managed to put on an outfit that was more put together than the sweatpants and T-shirts she had been wearing all week. Finn was leaving the office late, so she got ready in her room alone. She managed to turn on some music, shower, do her makeup and hair, and then put on blue mom jeans with a tight pink shirt on top. There was something cathartic about doing her makeup and getting ready like that.

She made her way out of the room, going straight to Allister's. There was a warm hue coming from under his door, meaning he was still in there. She knocked, waiting for him to welcome her in. It was muffled, but once she heard it, she opened the door slowly, peeking in to see him sitting at his desk with his glasses perched on his nose.

"Hey. Are you almost ready?" she asked, walking in and taking a seat on the bed.

He looked up, nodding slowly. "What? Yeah, I'm basically ready. I might change my shirt."

Gianna frowned. "What are you working on? Classes are over."

"Just some stuff for Valerio."

"I thought he was giving you some time off."

"I don't want any time off," he said, huffing and turning back to the papers on his desk.

"Allister, please talk to me," she begged. "I know what you're going through, literally. I know it hurts, but I'm here for you. We will get through this together."

He closed his eyes and took a deep breath before finally looking at her again. "I just don't fucking get it. How could she just walk out like that? Just leave us? It doesn't make any sense. Usually I can figure things out, I can put together why someone would do what they did or understand their motivations, but I just can't understand this. I don't get it and it's driving me fucking insane."

Gianna gave him a weak smile. She knew exactly how he felt. They were the same things she had been asking herself her entire life. "I don't think there is logic to everything. Sometimes we don't get the apology, or we don't get the closure we deserve, and we just have to make peace with it. I don't know how exactly to do that, but if I figure it out, I'll let you know."

Allister let out a small, breathless chuckle. "Please do. I would appreciate it."

"Of course," she said. "We'll get through this and I'm sure your logical mind can find a way to figure out how true that is."

"I know we will. You don't have to be worried about me. I just needed some space."

"I know you did, but I didn't want you to isolate yourself."

It was a bad habit of his that he did more so as a child, but it looked like it still followed him into his adulthood. He would close himself off to everyone and everything, basically disappearing without a trace whenever he was seriously upset. It used to scare the hell out of them when it happened and then he would show up a day later perfectly fine. Luckily, as he grew older, he stopped doing it. She really just did not want him dropping back into that habit again. He needed to be surrounded by the people that loved him, not isolating himself.

"I'm not going to," he said, giving her a reassuring smile. "What about you? Are you feeling better since that breakdown in your room? I've never seen anything like that, Gianna."

She sighed. "I'm sorry that happened around you."

"I'm not. Could you imagine if you were alone?"

"It was a buildup of a lot, as you could imagine, and it was overwhelming. I couldn't control it, which I know isn't good. It doesn't happen that often, either."

"Finn knew exactly what to do," he said.

"He's seen me have one before. Might have been the thing that actually got me to start crushing on him," she said, grinning.

"Either way, I'm glad he was there to help you and I'm glad you're okay. I don't want anything like that happening to you again."

Gianna nodded. "I know. Now, get ready so we can try to have some fun tonight."

"I told you, I am ready," Allister said, furrowing his brows as he motioned to his body.

"Not in that outfit," she snorted, standing.

She left the room, giving him a chance to actually get ready this time. She was just about to reach the steps to head downstairs when Finn's frantic eyes met hers, but they immediately relaxed when he saw her.

"What's wrong?" she asked, panic swirling through her.

He shook his head, wrapping his arms around her. "Nothing. I couldn't find you and it freaked me out."

"I was talking to Allister in his room."

"I was going there now, but I saw you standing here. You weren't in either of the rooms or bathrooms."

Gianna pulled away from him, frowning. "What did you think happened to me?"

Finn swallowed harshly. "I was afraid that you might have had another breakdown, and that I would have been too late."

Her heart ripped apart at his words. Had she done this to him? Made him fear that badly for her life that he was paranoid he would find her unconscious or worse somewhere in the house. It was devastating, horrifying even.

"I'm so sorry," she whispered.

"No, no, no. What are you sorry for? You did nothing wrong. That was just me being in my head," he said, shaking his head.

"I did this to you," she said. "If I hadn't gotten to that point."

"Gianna, stop. You can't blame yourself for that."

"Then what can I do?"

Finn placed his hands on her face, tracing his thumbs on her cheeks where a few tears had managed to slip out. "You can work on never letting yourself get to that point again. That is it."

"I promise I won't get to that point again," Gianna said. She hoped that he could hear the conviction in her voice, the promise, the genuineness.

And she really would work on it. She wouldn't wait until the pain consumed her past the point of no return. She would be more open and honest, she would let it out, and she would move on. She would talk or scream or do whatever she needed to before she kept it bottled up ever again like that.

He kissed her, accepting the promise that she made for the both of them. Her head swirled from it, but she could feel his fear and his relief. In return, she let him feel her love and apology. When they finally pulled away, she managed to feel lighter than she had in a week.

When he grabbed her hand, all his warmth seeped back into her body. At this point, it was her life force. They made their way downstairs where Luna and Valerio were sitting on the couches with Dante, meaning everyone else was still upstairs getting ready.

Immediately, she ran over and hugged Gianna, holding onto her tightly.

"How are you feeling?" Luna asked, her green eyes wide in worry.

Gianna gave her a smile. "I'm feeling better. Thank you for everything, by the way."

"That's what best friends are for."

Augustus walked in, nodding his head at everyone. "What's up?"

"How did you get in?" Dante asked, narrowing his eyes.

"I have a key."

Finn squeezed her hand, drawing her attention back over to him. He gave her a small smile, leaning in closer. "I have to show Augustus something on my bike. It'll take one second, do you mind?" Finn asked her.

Gianna shook her head. "No, go ahead. I have to catch up with Luna anyway."

He nodded, giving her a kiss. "I promise I'll be quick."

With that the two boys walked in the direction of the garage. When Gianna turned back to Luna and saw the huge smile she wore, her cheeks immediately turned red. "What?"

"I'm still so shocked by all of this. I mean, seeing you guys so lovey-dovey is wild," Luna said, shaking her head. "I'm so happy for both of you though. My mom was actually asking about the two of you when I told her that Finn was dating you. I didn't tell her too much, but I'm sure she would love to see you guys as a couple next time she visits."

"Next time? Was she here for a visit recently?" Gianna asked. She didn't realize just how much she had been out of the loop, but it had been hard to really connect with life. She needed to disconnect to just let herself move past everything that had happened. It didn't help that it left her feeling like an awful friend though. She wanted to be there for her best friends, especially when they had done so much to be there for her.

"Yeah, she was here just last week, the day everything

happened," she said, her voice dropping slightly. "Finn managed to see her for a little bit too, but it wasn't the best visit. I know he needs time, though. I needed it at first too."

Her eyes widened in shock. Finn had met with his mother? Gianna had no idea that she visited let alone that he had seen her. He spoke about his mother rarely, but she knew it had to have been tough on him to go through that.

And yet, he hadn't brought it up at all.

"I agree, he needs time." Her answer was half-assed, but she couldn't focus on the conversation anymore. She needed to find Finn and talk to him about what had happened. Why hadn't he mentioned anything to her? "I'm going to go grab something to drink. Do you want anything?"

"No, I'm okay."

She hardly waited for Luna's answer before she was walking to the garage. Inside, Augustus and Finn stood huddled by his bike, pointing at some piece of machinery. They turned to look at her as soon as the door opened.

"Augustus, go inside," Gianna said curtly.

"That's my cue," he said, immediately dropping everything and walking out. She moved out of the way so he could walk out of the garage. She appreciated that he didn't put up a fight, but then again, he was probably using the intrusion as an excuse to go searching for a particular someone.

Finn stood, his brows pinched together in confusion and concern. "What happened now?"

"Why didn't you tell me that your mother visited and you saw her?"

His face fell. "Luna brought it up?"

"Yes, and you didn't," she said, walking towards him. "Why wouldn't you tell me about that?"

He set the part down and grabbed a rag to wipe off his hands. "It was wrong for me to tell you that my mother had just walked back into my life when yours had just walked out. I wasn't going to put that on you, not when I wasn't even sure if I was going to keep a relationship going with her."

His words hurt despite her knowing that he hadn't meant any harm by them. It was the truth. "Despite what I was going through, you should have been able to talk to me about it."

"I didn't want to, though. I wanted to focus on you."

Finn walked closer to her, throwing the rag over his shoulder like he was some sort of mechanic. He wrapped his hands around her waist, pulling her closer while he leaned on the car behind him.

Gianna shook her head. "I understand that, and I appreciate you being there for me. I seriously do. I want to be there for you as well, though. When were you planning on telling me?"

He shrugged. "Whenever it felt right. I don't know. I didn't know it was going to hurt you keeping it from you. That really wasn't my intention. Everything going on this week just kind of made it slip from my mind anyway, princess."

She nodded her head, finally accepting his answer. She wrapped her arms around his neck and immediately he grinned, pulling her closer. It seemed like he knew he was forgiven. "What did you decide?"

"I told her I need it to be slow. I'll call her when I'm ready and we'll go from there. I'm not sure when that'll be though."

Gianna nodded her head. "You're really lucky that she's wanting to work things out with you."

"If you don't want me to, just say the word." The dead seriousness in his voice made her stop. Was he being serious? He would cut out his mother just because Gianna asked him to? She would never. His mother returning and wanting to fix things was amazing for him. He deserved to have a good parent in his life if that was what he wanted, and she would always support it.

She shook her head immediately. "I would never do that to you, are you kidding me? If you want a relationship with her, I support you one hundred percent."

He dropped his forehead against hers. "I know you will. And I absolutely love that about you, princess."

"What else do you love about me?" she asked.

Finn laughed. "I love your big heart."

"What else?"

"Your selflessness. Your intelligence. Your sense of humor. Your smile. Your ability to be the best person I've ever met in my life. Your strength. Your courage—"

She cut him off with a kiss. It was the only way she could express the emotion that was swarming through her chest. Words didn't seem like they would do what she was feeling complete justice, but the kiss did.

"I love you," she said.

Actually, maybe there were some words that could.

FORTY-FIVE

GIANNA

BACKSTAGE AT SHOWS were always busy, but something about it gave Gianna the rush of her life. It was finally the night of the showcase, the night that everything she had been working towards had been leading up to.

Her costume consisted of a light pink tutu and bodice covered in embroidered flowers of all colors. Green vines and leaves swirled around the flowers, creating the perfect spring look for her. She had her light pink tights on and her pointe shoes. Her hair was in a tight bun and the headpiece she wore had flowers sewn into it, creating a flower crown piece.

The show wasn't a cohesive play, but rather multiple performances from the students to demonstrate their skills from the semester. Some were in groups, some were in pairs, and some, like Gianna, were solo. Everyone, however, was extremely nervous because of the possibility of being scouted for things like professional acting and dance careers. It happened to a handful of students from their program throughout the years. Honestly, Gianna didn't know if she wanted to do it full time or not. She hadn't thought much about her future in that way. She did know that she wanted to continue dancing for as long as she could and maybe teach it someday.

The first couple of performances had already gone. Gianna stood backstage watching them all in awe. They were a talented group of students. It made her feel weirdly intimidated but also motivated to get out there and show everyone what she could do.

She stretched out her muscles, making sure they were nice and warmed up all day. She flexed her ankles and applied rosin to the tops of her shoes to make sure she could grip the stage good.

"Gianna, you're on next," the stage manager told her.

She nodded, standing up and taking a couple of deep breaths. Once the curtain closed and the duo on stage scurried off, Gianna made her way to the center. She got into position, raising her arms above her head and keeping her feet in third position. She took a deep breath and counted down the moments until it began.

The curtains opened, exposing her to the crowd. Her music began.

The melody took off slowly, as did she. She turned on pointe, moving across the stage before she bent over, letting her arms extend down her leg. She lifted her left leg up swiftly, stretching it straight behind her. Just as the music began reaching the crescendo, she let it fall effortlessly.

This was the tough part, where everything began moving quicker and more dramatically. As the violin and the cello in the song got played with quick strokes of the bow, Gianna met every change with a jump, crisscrossing her legs every time. Her arms were held at fifth *en avant* and then they moved to *à la seconde*.

Her legs were already burning, her feet were aching, but she was in the final stretch. The part that had been so hard for her to get time and time again, until Finn had come to watch her that one rehearsal and then so many times after. She used him as her guiding force to nail it.

Gianna looked for him out in the audience, and it wasn't hard to find him. Even with the bright light on her, she could see him sitting directly in the center of the third row; the best seat in the house as she had told him. His eyes were locked on hers and goosebumps trailed down her spine.

She did her series of quick spins, using him as her spot for every turn. She stopped in fifth position. She did the *pas de chat* and then moved into a *glissade* as she got to the center of the stage. The music was loud, and it was finally the moment.

Gianna leapt into the air, pushing off with everything she had and keeping her arms extended eloquently beside her. She had both legs completely straight in the air, practically doing the splits, keeping her feet arched and her head held high. As she ascended back on the ground, she landed on the front leg, immediately doing a series of turns without ever letting the other leg touch the ground.

Her eyes found Finn's as the music slowed. The orchestral sound turned softer, slowly slipping away. With one last *glissade*, she fell to the floor, letting the music finish out. She stayed there for a moment before the clapping and cheering began.

Gianna stood up, sucking in deep breaths of air as she looked out into the crowd. Finn stood clapping and hollering loudly. She couldn't help the grin on her face. She saw Allister beside him, and her father there too. She saw Luna and Cecilia and Blair. She saw Valerio and Dante. Hell, even Augustus was there. She saw everyone she loved in the crowd, clapping and cheering with smiles that made her realize that she was going to be perfectly fine.

She took a bow, blowing out kisses to everyone.

The curtain closed, ending her performance.

———

She changed into one of the dresses she bought for the night and redid her makeup before she decided to go out and meet everyone in the lobby. Immediately, Gianna was picked up and smothered with kisses from Finn. She laughed, wrapping her arms around him.

He set her on the floor, holding her face in his hands. "You were absolutely stunning. Wonderful. Amazing. Magnificent.

Fuck. You were the best thing I have ever seen in my life. I swear, princess. I wish I could watch it all over again for the first time."

She knew she was blushing uncontrollably, but his endless compliments only made it worse. "You really mean all of that?"

"One hundred percent," he said, pressing another kiss to her lips. "Fucking perfection."

"Thank you," she said.

"I almost forgot to give you these," he said, pulling away suddenly. He moved quickly to the huge bouquet of red roses that were being held by Augustus for the time being, grabbing them from him. Finn handed them to her, and she couldn't even wrap her arms around them.

"This is insane," she said, laughing.

"Only the best for you."

"Okay, stop hogging her," Blair said, pushing through. Finally, the hugs with everyone else were able to happen. She got other bouquets as well, but none as big as Finn's.

When she saw her father, she pulled him into a huge hug. He had been calling almost every day to check up on both Allister and her, but she hadn't managed to see him since. Having him in the audience made her heart explode. Something akin to pride knowing her father had been with her through it all, and he was still showing up for everything.

"You were amazing," he said, pulling out of the hug. "The best dancer of the night."

"Oh, come on, Dad," she said, waving him off.

"I'm being serious. My daughter is the best," he said. "I also managed to meet your boyfriend."

She nodded her head, looking over at Finn who stood with Luna. "And? What do you think?"

"He cares about you. A lot. To the point where he was the first person in those seats and his eyes didn't leave you once, not while you were on that stage dancing," he said. "I still want to get together so I can get to know him better, but I'm not opposed."

Gianna was beaming. She knew that her father would love

Finn if he just gave it a chance. "Of course. We have the whole summer now, so we can make it happen."

Allister came over, wrapping an arm around his father's shoulders. "Let's go to dinner. I'm starving."

"We have a lot to celebrate," Federico said.

Gianna could only nod as Finn came over, grabbing the flowers from her and holding her hand. They did have a lot to celebrate. A lot to heal from too. Yet, despite everything that happened, she wouldn't have changed it for anything.

Not a single moment.

FORTY-SIX

FINN

TWO MONTHS LATER

FINN WAS STILL GETTING USED to the new route he drove with his bike, FiFi, but to be fair he had only moved into the apartment two weeks ago. It was still close to everything—everything being the Grand Willow campus, the house he used to live in, and Luna's house, but it was still a different ride.

The summer nights were warm enough to the point where he drove without a jacket. Gianna would complain about the wind on his skin and how damaging it could be, but he liked when she fussed over him. It was refreshing.

He pulled into the apartment's garage, which really was an undeserving name for such a space. Sure, most of the people that lived there just parked their cars there, but he managed to get a private room where he could also work on his bikes and cars during the evenings when he got home from the office. He turned the bike off and dismounted, hanging the helmet up on the wall beside Gianna's pristine white one.

Finn closed the garage behind him and entered the private elevator, pressing the button for the top floor. Within seconds he was there, entering the apartment to see the sun setting through the huge floor to ceiling windows that covered the living room.

Light cream couches sat in front of them, but so did a huge flat screen TV—they had managed to compromise.

He climbed up the stairs by the kitchen to the room where he heard music coming from. Gianna sat in her pink robe in front of her vanity, singing loudly to whatever song was playing. When he first brought up them moving in together all those months ago, she was hesitant about leaving the mansion for less space. It was shocking that had been her only complaint about moving in with him. However, once he found this place, he showed her the room he wanted to make into her closet and vanity area, and she jumped on the idea immediately. Now she had most of her clothes, shoes, and purses, and space to do her hair and makeup all in one place.

He stood by the door frame, watching as she applied the blush to her cheeks. Her eyes found him through the mirror, and she screamed, holding a hand to her chest.

"Fuck, Finn! You could have knocked. You scared me," she said, turning around to face him.

He grinned, walking into the room. "You were having a performance; I didn't want to interrupt."

"I sounded good, didn't I?" she asked, raising a brow.

"Next popstar level." He leaned down, pressing a kiss to her lips. "Are you almost ready to go?"

"Just about. I have to get dressed. What about you? You can't go to a fight like that," she said, looking at him up and down.

Finn shrugged. He was still wearing the slacks and button up from earlier, but it wasn't appropriate attire for a fight. Especially not when he was the one doing the fighting. It wasn't a serious fight or anything, but it had been a long time, and he wanted to let loose a little bit.

"I'll change in two seconds," he said. "You take much longer than I do, princess."

"Well, you can't rush perfection," she said, standing.

She dropped her robe, revealing that she was completely naked underneath. No, perfection couldn't be rushed. Gianna was a goddess, and he was helplessly devoted to worshipping her no matter what.

He eyed every inch of her body, from her nipples that stood rigid from the cold air conditioning to the perfectly trimmed pussy that sat between her legs. Finally, he managed to drag his eyes back up to her face where she wore an innocent grin.

"Have I ever told you you're the most magnificent person I have ever met, princess?" he asked, approaching her.

"You have, but it never hurts to hear," she said. "Now, I should probably get dressed."

He nodded, extending his hand to trail it up her thigh. He found her pussy, slipping his fingers through her slick slit before he found her clit. She closed her eyes, letting out a breathy moan. "Yeah, you should probably get dressed."

Gianna reached down, palming his hardening dick through his slacks. "But also, we could probably spare a few minutes."

He grinned. "I think so."

It didn't take long for him to lift her up on the vanity, kissing her hurriedly while undoing the button on his slacks. He managed to slip them down his legs while she ran her fingers through his hair, pulling and tugging on the strands. Finn wasted no time entering her, letting himself feel her warm cunt while he thrusted into her. Gianna threw her head back, meeting every thrust with her own hip movements.

He attached his mouth to her nipple, biting and sucking while simultaneously reaching down and playing with her clit. She gripped onto his shoulders with her nails, tightening around him.

"Come for me, princess," he muttered. He pushed his lips back onto hers, swallowing every single moan that escaped from them. He came soon after, milking out every single drop of cum for her.

She pulled away, letting out a small laugh. "Well, now my makeup is all messed up."

"You still look perfect," he said, giving her one more kiss.

They did manage to wash up and get dressed, before heading out for the fight. Gianna wore black leather pants and a sparkly pink shirt instead of a dress so they could take the bike instead of a car, which Finn was perfectly okay with. She put on her helmet like a champ, throwing on one of his leather jackets as well once they got to the garage.

Finn's heart swelled uncontrollably seeing how natural she looked with it all. When he looked back on his life only months before, he couldn't believe how far he'd come. He had been so lost, running from his own demons alone on this very bike and now he was helping the love of his life on, leaving their new apartment, while he settled into his role as the heir of the Kingsley empire.

For so many years, he thought that he was undeserving of the life he had now. In fact, he was so sure it would never happen to him. But there he was, living it every day. He had a family, he had his girl, and he had love.

Gianna noticed him looking at her, so she crinkled her nose and took off the helmet. "What? Did I put it on wrong?"

Finn shook his head with the biggest grin on his face. The most genuine one he had ever had. "I'm so fucking in love with you, princess."

She returned the smile, giving him a peck on the lips. "I love you too, Finn."

And just like that, they rode off into the sunset covered in yellows and oranges and reds. With their demons extinguished, they could finally attempt a new life unscathed.

ACKNOWLEDGMENTS

Finn's and Gianna's story was a whirlwind to write. In only a couple of months, I wrote the first draft, did my own edits, had my editor do copyedits, went over those edits, had my editor do the proofread, did those last minute checks, and sent it off to the first batch of readers. When I first saw these characters in my head, I knew they were going to be electric, but I never expected them to completely consume me the way they did. There was a lot of realness and a lot of vulnerability that I could relate to in both Finn and Gianna, and I know many people could relate to them as well.

But as much as this story is a figment of my mind (and contributed to my intense back and wrist pains) there were so many people who helped this book come to life. The first being all of my family who support me endlessly every single time I embark on a new book. Thank you all for accepting my long days, the moments where I cry, the days where I cancel plans, and the conversations where I talk your ear off because I need advice on what the characters are doing. Seriously, your support means the world to me.

This book also could not have been possible without the support of the wonderful Gabby D'Aloia. You are the most incredible editor and support I have been fortunate enough to find in my book writing journey. Sharing early drafts of a novel is so nerve-racking, but every single time my books are in your hands, I know they are being well taken care of. I am so happy to have worked with you on two books now, and I can't wait to work with you on future projects.

I am also beyond thankful for my amazing cover designer Georgia Stove, who has made the most beautiful covers for the past two novels. I can't wait to see what you come up with for future novels.

Finally, thank you to Ellie from LoveNotesPr for helping me through the ARC sign ups and releases for the past two novels. You are an absolute joy to work with and make the entire process seamless.

And to everyone who has read this book and Heir of Darkness, thank you. From the bottom of my heart, thank you for making my dreams come true. Writing books and sharing them with the world has always been my dream, and in a world where there are millions of books, thank you for picking mine up.

Like always, this is not the end. More is coming in this series! Stay tuned to find out what is coming in Book 3!

ABOUT THE AUTHOR

Lejla Muric spent most of her life reading about fictional characters falling in love before she finally decided to put her daydreams onto paper. She hopes you'll fall in love with her characters the same way she has time and time again!

Follow her on all of her social media platforms to keep up with updates and news regarding future books!

ALSO BY LEJLA MURIC

Heir of Darkness

Heir of Fire

Book 3 - Coming Soon!